A grotesque spectacle of ι

— Matthew Baker, autho

Somewhere between Bradbury and Ligotti, Rice folds centuries of Americana into a space unstuck from time, where everything is an anachronism. Here, he explores the blurry divisions between adulthood and childhood, the seeming impossibility of atonement, the madness of certainty.

— B.R. Yeager, author of *Negative Space*

I'm trying to remember the last time a collection of stories so captured my attention by the strength of its voices and sense of presence in each of its living moments. Think Brian Evenson's *Fugue State*, or Susan Steinberg's early collections. There's such life here, such clarity of vision. It's exhilarating to watch a writer like Rice engage his ambitions so immediately and with a seemingly inexhaustible well of ideas. This is a magnificent book.

— Grant Maierhofer, author of *Works* and *Peripatet*

The horror in *Drifter's* meticulous and exquisitely bleak stories does not impose itself from without, but is instead woven into the very inscrutable necessity to exist, so that even with the more abstract or extramundane tales there's this same intimidating sense of compulsive human duty – out of nowhere and for nothing. The details, however familiar, are always in devious service to some shadowing alterity, some arcane yet immersive otherness, enacting a kind of doubling, a superpositioning of identity, that through its overdetermination makes David Leo Rice's creations seem both eerily dense and unreal. Gloriously inventive, sober and freakish, this is a collection to relish.

— Gary J. Shipley, author of *Dreams of Amputation* and *Stratagem of the Corpse*

Grotesque and tender, irreal and grounded, nostalgic, forward-looking, and of the moment, David Leo Rice's *Drifter*, as its title suggests, isn't easily sited. Imagine going to a video store ca. 1998 and renting tapes at random from the "Cult Movies" section, but every tape you pick makes you want to tell all of your friends, "You *have* to see this." You *have* to read *Drifter*.

— Gabriel Blackwell, author of *Babel* and *Correction*

Dylan sang, "Something is happening here, but you don't know what it is." The stories of David Leo Rice's *Drifter* slip between reality and surrealism continuously, showing us how thin the fabric of reality really is. No matter which side you find yourself on, you can just make out the shapes on the other side. These stories stack up, brick by brick, creating a literary Tower of Babel, where language and image obscure, muddying the waters of perception. You catch glimpses of clarity as the current pulls you downstream. The stories, while complete in themselves, create a larger dialogue when combined. In "Housesitter," a character's fall down a flight of stairs is described, "And it wasn't just the impact of the concrete bottom that broke her up... It was each individual stair, one after another after another. Relentless." These stories hit you like those stairs, one after another after another, truly relentless until you hit the bottom. Looking up at those stairs you can see just how far you have fallen, just how far Rice has pushed you. These stories are packed with meaning, reality and unreality shoved inside "with no way out and no reason to leave." Though you look around at unfamiliar surroundings, you're not lost; you live in motion now. And it's all in flux. You're moved, constantly shuffled, until you get "a sense that standing still was no longer a good idea, if it ever had been." Rice writes, "they made her feel like she was in both places at once and thus, sickeningly, in neither." These stories exist in the in-between. Intangibility hangs like a veil, but whether a bride's or a widow's is hard to determine.

— A.S. Coomer, author of *Birth of a Monster* and *Memorabilia*

Like peering through a slit at some brilliant, brutal new world, *Drifter* is unnerving and audaciously intelligent, full of wild possibility, dark humor, and lurking doom. With all the visceral detail and haunting logic of a beautiful, disturbing dream, Rice stylishly explores the grim, the hidden, the unhinged.

— Kimberly King Parsons, author of *Black Light*

David Leo Rice's *Drifter* is a wonderful, new form of entertainment devised for the growing ranks of the Poison-Ivy League educated precariat. Text-based stories — short enough to be enjoyed in those lulls between low-paying jobs — concerning people slightly worse off than oneself. A salutary break from the grinding spectacles of moving pictures and comics. As advised on page 109: you can read the text, then close your eyes and enjoy your own self-generated images in a style and texture of your choice. Highly recommended!

— Ben Katchor, Guggenheim and MacArthur-winning author of *Julius Knipl: Real Estate Photographer*, *The Cardboard Valise,* and many other classic American comics.

DAVID LEO RICE

DRIFTER

STORIES

Cover Art & Typeset by Mike Corrao

Summer: 978-1-948687-29-4
Winter: 978-1-948687-30-0

Library of Congress Number: 2021908902

Printed in the United States of America

FIRST AMERICAN EDITION

9 8 7 6 5 4 3 2 1

DRIFTER

STORIES

WITH AN INTRODUCTION BY
MATTHEW SPELLBERG

By
DAVID LEO RICE

11:11 PRESS MINNEAPOLIS

For Vasco Banchi, who stood beside me on a rooftop in Brazil while fireworks rained down on the new millennium.

TABLE OF CONTENTS

Introduction

Three Towns and a Video Store:

On the Fiction of David Leo Rice

by Matthew Spellberg

When David Leo Rice was a little boy his parents would not let him watch R-rated movies. I happen to know his parents quite well, and they are unbelievably kind, gentle, generous, artistic, liberal-minded people. It's always been hard for me to believe that they could have really done this—I can barely match the fact to their faces. But if it's true, then it's proof of their wisdom and foresight: the ban proved an inestimable gift to their son. Because he couldn't watch R-rated movies, David was forced to imagine them instead. He'd go to the video store and grab the forbidden videos and hold them in his hands and try with almost physical exertion to picture what was imprinted on those locked up spools of VHS tape. From the meager clues on the slip-cover—the banner image, the thumbnail stills, the promotional copy and the critics' blurbs—he conjured as best as he could the orgies of violence and sex that he would never see, at least not until he was deemed to have crossed over some threshold into a maturity that seemed to him at the time arbitrary, distant, and unjust.

This prohibition on graven images is, I am quite convinced, what made David Leo Rice a writer, and it is what gave him his absolutely singular style. His novels and stories are R-rated movies re-created in the mind of a seven-year-old child who does not yet know the straitjacket of commercial narrative, whose sense of pacing and probability still owes more to dreams than to stories, who renews the genre of horror with the first-person intensity of actual nightmares. His is a world on fire with thwarted wanting and parched by that seriousness that only children possess. A key theme in Rice's work is the way imagining the unseen perversion of others becomes the ultimate perversion. The desire for the forbidden becomes an end in and of itself; the thing originally wanted is murdered by the image conjured to represent it.

The video store is the navel of the Ricean world. People of his and my generation will remember what the local independent video store was to the 90s and early Aughts. The dingy carpeting and the smell of vinyl and dust. The older kids who had shifts at the counter and looked dismissively at you for coming in with your parents. The Borgesian organizational system, intuitive but arbitrary, marked out by homemade signs stenciled in colored pen: NEW RELEASES, COMEDY, ROMANTIC, FOREIGN, MONTY PYTHON, HORROR, SCI-FI, QUIRKY, CULT, OFFBEAT, STAR TREK, GANGSTER. The beaded curtain in back which no one was ever seen entering or exiting, but through which you could, if you were quick about it, catch a glimpse of the dirty pictures.

People of a certain temperament in our generation will remember, too, the long Passion Play that was the video store's decline at the hands of media capitalism. First, the mass sell-off of VHS tapes during the switch to DVD (which guiltily we took advantage of to expand our own film libraries). Then the early demise of some stores when they unwisely bet on LaserDisc or BluRay. And then, after a steady decline, the final blow, the last fire sale, after which both movies and porn ceased to exist as physical things altogether, and became streaming pictures rentable in perpetuity for $12.99 a month.

In its brief Golden Age the independent video store was a reservoir in the desert, the promise of a cosmopolitan world delivered to the world-less suburbs. It was a mingling of high art, schlock, and sex, of cultural drivers and cultural symptoms. The video store occasionally appears as itself in Rice's fiction, for instance in the story "Circus Sickness." But its sensibility suffuses the atmosphere of everything he writes. The fiction smacks of a mash-up, a bleary-eyed all-night sleepover movie binge, a conflation of slasher and art-house and sexploitation, a true democracy of taste. The highest goal in his art is to achieve, like the Friday night rental once did, a cosmic rupture in the everyday space-time of little towns. In his novel *Angel House* Rice calls this phenomenon "The Town's City": the dream of a boring quiet little town which somehow contains within its limits the overwhelming megapolis of the movies. This is the mission of the video store glorified into phantasm. In real life this seedy utopia was fragile and fleeting, and became one of the first casualties in the relentless war digital capitalism has waged on our habits and habitats.

The stories collected in this volume ostensibly take place in many different locations, with many different characters. But they all inhabit the same world, a world as distinctive and local as the Macondo of Gabriel Garcia Márquez or the Yoknapatawpha of William Faulkner. The geography looks something like this: at the center of the universe is the Video Store, and there are three towns that surround it in concentric circles, so that when you're in the Video Store, you're at the heart of each.

The first town is the most concrete, though in the fiction it's never actually called by its true name. It is Northampton, Massachusetts, where David Leo Rice grew up. The video store is the now defunct Pleasant Street Video, so important that Rice dedicated *Angel House* to its memory. It is impossible to understand Rice's stories without knowing something about Northampton, a small town that is somehow also a city. It sits in a sleepy and distant part of western Massachusetts, but it's famous for its music scene, for the radicalism of Smith College and other nearby campuses, and for welcoming a diaspora of New York and Boston intellectuals who wanted to raise their kids in utopia.

Like with so many New England towns, Northampton's cheerful progressivism and recent urban renewal are an unconvincing lacquer over the grain of history. Just out of view is the collapse of the industrial economy, and also the unresolved hatreds of class and race endemic to the rust-belt. But the haunting goes back much farther than that. It was in Northampton in 1733 that Jonathan Edwards unleashed his Great Awakening in a frenzy of preaching so convincing that at least two of his congregants killed themselves in despair at the thought of their own damnation. It was also in Northampton that the townsfolk eventually turned on their own prophet and banned Edwards from preaching after it was felt he had offended propriety and hurt local business. Deep in the town's history, then, are two crimes against authenticity: to have fallen prey to fanaticism, and to have abandoned it for mere respectability. Outrage at both is present in Rice's fiction. Lingering behind these crimes, even more repressed, is another horror, dating to the founding of the town in 1654: the land was freed up for English settlement by a smallpox epidemic that ravaged the Pocumtuc who had lived there. This last nightmare has its analogue in the history of every town, city and county on the American continent.

Nevertheless—and this cannot be emphasized enough—Rice's Northampton is an idyllic, beloved place, full of wonder, redolent of childhood fantasy, suffused with genuine happiness. Everything lurking beneath the surface does not cancel out the pleasures to be had above-ground. Hence the unsettling mismatch between tone and content in Rice's stories. These are gruesome parades of horror written with sweetness and charm, in a state of almost exquisite innocence, as if a boy on a bicycle were dreamily riding toward the community pool at the height of summer over a road made from the bones and charnel of his own family. Characters like this dreamy death-boy abound in Rice's unholy stories, little creatures enjoying a sheltered, privileged life full of atrocity but without care. His work makes visible something usually well-hidden: the placidity of the suburbs and the bloodbath of history are part of the same phenomenon, and in fact they live side-by-side in conditions of mutual aid.

If Northampton is the womb of Rice's imagination, then its adolescence unfolds in the godforsaken boomtowns of the West: in shorthand, we can call this second zone in Rice's world *Dodge City*, after the title of his first novel. Dodge City is every dusty, eviscerated, violent, meth-addled town up and down the interstate, founded in a goldrush or an oil boom, now pitted with Walmarts and cheap tourist attractions, swarming with grifters of every kind. Dodge City is severed from childhood and ancestry by greed and cynical hustle. There are no romantic anti-heroes here like in the classical Westerns, just scoundrels and victims, sometimes both at once. The first story you will read in this collection is "The Brothers Squimbop." It begins in a futuristic Dodge City that has metastasized over the entire continent:

> The Brothers Squimbop, Jim and Joe, plied their trade in the dusty American interior of the 2070s, which, following the logic that Y2K was the Zero Hour and it was all linear reversion from there, mapped almost perfectly onto the 1930s. They rambled through the Dust Bowl in a beat-up Chevy, taking semester-long postings at forgotten, often nameless community colleges, teach-

> ing the students, such as they were, about what the nation used to be. "Addle-brained giants used to walk this land," they would say, "picking up cities and putting them down thousands of miles to the west, once confusion slowed their progress to a standstill," or, "Overnight, all land and water in this nation traded places, such that America was once nothing but a constellation of small islands, the largest of which eventually became the Great Lakes."

The passage describes a school lesson; but it is also a lesson in reading the stories of David Leo Rice. Squimbop—sometimes appearing as one character, sometimes, like here, split in two—is an essential figure in Rice's imaginarium. He is the mad professor, the false prophet whose falseness doesn't make him any less touched by the divine, or at least by the demiurge. The Squimbops are guides to the intellectual framework of these stories. They are like venal and stupid Virgils carrying us through the layers of a Hell they are making up as they go along. What the Squimbops do is only a more distilled version of what all the characters living in these Dodge Cities are trying to get away with. History is turned on its head. The future is the past. Everything is present at once. The characters have no real orientation in this world; they are completely adrift. And so they try to fabricate a past and a purpose off the top of their heads. What they come up with is both complete bullshit and also uncannily accurate. This is key to the terror of Dodge City. You think you can go West and make yourself anew, forge a future bent to your own will. But each act of creation just resurrects all the horrors lying dormant in the past. For this reason, Rice's grifters are terrified of being caught telling the truth, for then they must accept they've been its prisoners all the time: "The horror of being taken seriously, of a student actually listening to what he'd said and acting as though it meant something, swarmed him"—so runs a typical line. The American Dream is an attempt to make bad fiction: fiction that no one believes and that therefore makes everything permissible. But the American Reality is a counterbalance, always revealing where it comes from in every despicable detail. Therefore it is a prison-house.

In much American art, a trek through the delusions of the West would eventually lead to California. Think of Hitchcock's *Vertigo*: once you've made it to San Francisco, the only options are destroy your past, or fall to your death. But though the Pacific does crop up from time to time in Rice's fiction, his endgame lies somewhere else. Beyond Dodge City, the road points not farther West but rather back East. The last zone in his universe is made from the ancient villages, the places of tradition and unbroken suffering, what we might collectively call *The Old Town*. The Old Town has many avatars: the unconvincing cheer and genocidal underbelly of German *Dörfer*; the fly-blown colonial cruelty of Caribbean outposts; the fascistic hedonism of Fellini's *Amarcord*; the heretical, cabbalistic dangers of the Litvak Shtetl and Bruno Schulz's Drohobycz. The Old Town, as its name suggests, is as old as old can be. In it there is no denying history or myth, no imagining you can make something new. It's all there already, what you were, what you will be, what will be inflicted on us again and again. But in Rice's fiction this does not always result in resignation or listlessness. In fact, paradoxically, The Old Town is the site of the greatest transformations. That's because the whole past is present like in a pregnancy, awaiting ritual rebirth (occasionally, as in "Living Boy," the birth is quite literal). Some of Rice's finest stories take place in The Old Town, which might be located in Austria ("Gmunden"), Switzerland ("The Painless Euthanasia Rollercoaster"), or on a remote island in Japan (the magnificent "Hate Room").

The horror that was greeted with childlike acceptance in Northampton and with adolescent denial in Dodge City unfolds in The Old Town with hard-won self-awareness: Rice's characters cross into a knowledge of their own destruction that prevents nothing and helps no one, but is superb all the same. It represents the only maturity possible at the end of a history that has been gradually regressing human beings into emotional babies with ever more powerful technological tools to amplify their tantrums. A late story in this volume, sequel to the very first one, is "The Brothers Squimbop in Europe." On that continent of Old Towns, the professors' fabrications are no match for reality: or rather, their outrageous Hollywood lies immediately *become* reality, and send the Americans running home from the truths they have uttered. In "The Hate Room," the doomed boyfriends Johannes and Rodrigo travel the world until they finally reach their portal into The Old Town—to them it appears as a Japanese inn on a tiny island one of them has won as a prize competing on a sick reality TV show. That's where they finally come face to face with everything they had earlier fled rather than try to name. What's more, their inn with its Hate Room becomes a huge success over in the U.S. It turns out the citizens of Dodge City and Northampton are desperate to pay good money to spend the night in a place that finally allows them to call their own deep hate by its real name.

This volume is called *Drifter: Stories*. Rice's Drifters are the ones who can move freely through the whole range of his universe—from Northampton to Dodge City to The Old Town and back—who can rent any movie in the video store without fear of parental intervention. They are able to do so because they have given up on restriction and taboo, though also therefore on the desire and vitality that restriction and taboo make possible. The others—children, mothers, fathers, filmmakers, editors of the Homeowners' Association E-Newsletter—are fastened in place to their native zones, incapable of transformation or understanding, censored by themselves or others, trapped eternally between wanting and the self-denial that makes wanting possible. This imprisonment in self-denial for the purpose of stoking desire holds true for almost the full range of Rice's characters: the spoiled would-be artists who cling to adolescent fantasies of their own genius; the kids living in communes whose religion consists of denouncing the unseen perversions of adults; the attendants and tour operators listlessly selling tickets to various local monstrosities, like the giant whale beached along the Eastern Seaboard in "Out on the Coast." The Drifter is the only one who escapes this fate. He experiences the dreamworld as the dream that it is, yet has no illusions about there being somewhere else to wake up into. His cogitations sprawl across the surface of the page in the many passages where you can't tell if something is being imagined by a character, or actually happening in the story ("he pictured wolves coming up from their dens to eat what she'd thrown their way and wait for more, until there was none left and they were fighting over the bones and she was long gone, deeper into the woods, to haunt the island forever"). The Drifter accepts the dream as both dream *and* reality, and therefore transcends the infantile idea that imagination is merely wish-fulfillment. In an age where every image has become a tool for monetizing desire, this may well prove to be the starting point for a radical political philosophy.

According to Kafka there is hope, but not for us. According to Rice there is hope, but only for Drifters. Anyone—child, mother, father, spoiled artist, attendant or tour operator—can become a Drifter. It is almost an act of Providence, an election by lightning-strike, touching some characters and inexplicably not others. Some of the most beautiful passages in these stories are about the transformation of a person into a Drifter, as for instance at the end of "Jell-O." But—and this is a big *but*—to become a Drifter means you are no longer yourself, certainly not one of us. So there is hope for us, but not for us *as us*. What it takes to become a Drifter is initiation into a very simple, but very painful, secret: you must learn that you are already dead. This knowledge is the only antidote to horror, for horror is that which the living inflict on one another in their attempts to deny this truth.

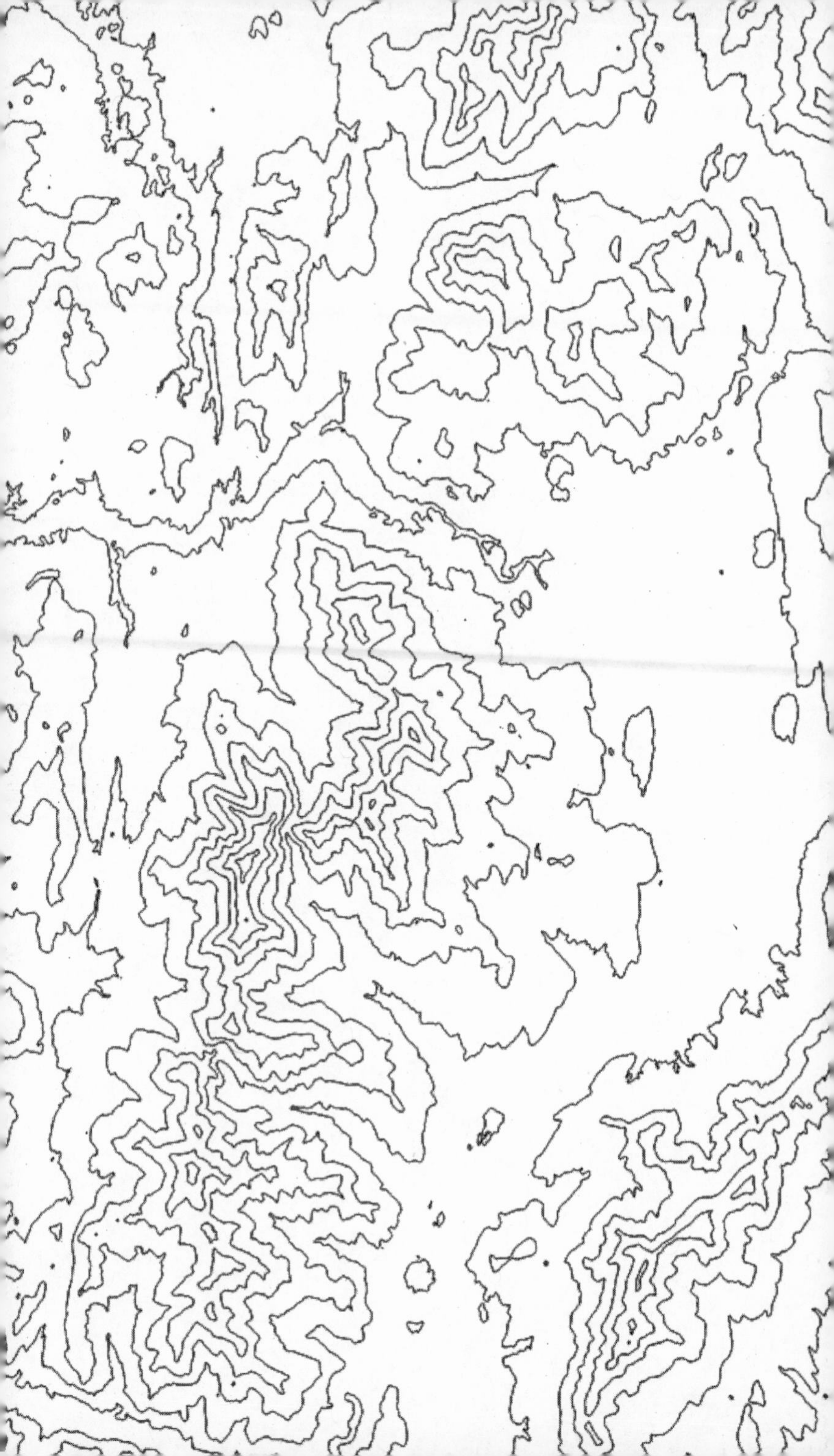

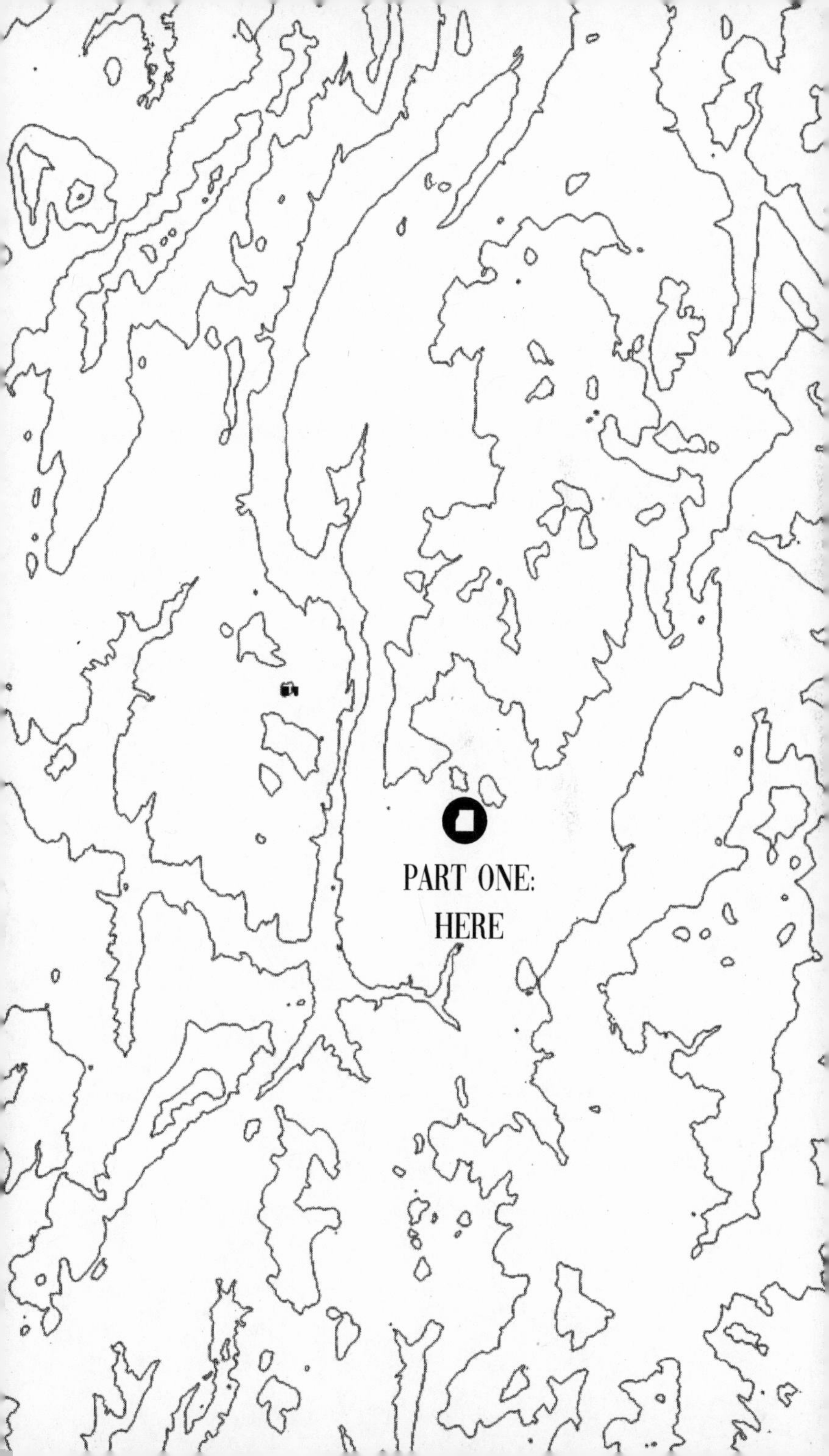

PART ONE: HERE

THE BROTHERS SQUIMBOP

The Brothers Squimbop, Jim and Joe, plied their trade in the dusty American interior of the 2070s, which, following the logic that Y2K was the Zero Hour and it was all linear reversion from there, mapped almost perfectly onto the 1930s. They rambled through the Dust Bowl in a beat-up Chevy, taking semester-long postings at forgotten, often nameless community colleges, teaching the students, such as they were, about what the nation used to be. "Addle-brained giants used to walk this land," they would say, "picking up cities and putting them down thousands of miles to the west, once confusion slowed their progress to a standstill," or, "Overnight, all land and water in this nation traded places, such that America was once nothing but a constellation of small islands, the largest of which eventually became the Great Lakes." The students would yawn and stare at their crackling yellow notepads, dragging their pens along the lines and then off the edges of the paper and onto their desks. Others would pull cold hocks of meat from paper bags and hold them in the air, sometimes remembering to gnaw them, other times not.

It was a dying art, that of walking into cavernous lecture halls and holding forth with the presumption of authority, despite the water damage, despite the mildew, despite the boxes of smudged documents floating in puddles, but the Brothers Squimbop were determined to keep it alive as long as they could. They sensed that its death would coincide with their own, so they took turns standing behind the podium in Tulsa, Aberdeen, and Eau Claire, careful never to be seen together so as to maintain the illusion of being one slightly inconsistent man, though no one ever pointed this inconsistency out.

Still, the idea that someone might was the source of no small degree of hilarity. Modest pleasures, the Brothers Squimbop had determined long ago, were the only pleasures within mortal reach. The confusion caused by their alternation, even if only theoretical, was a good example of this. *We are, in this sense, a sort of comedy duo*, they liked to tell themselves, *a pair of entertainers plying our trade in the vast interior of a nation that long ago lost any claim to psychic or even geographical coherence. A nation that is now nothing but a tattered platform upon which anyone passing through can mount whatever road show accords with his*—the Brothers knew no women well enough to joke about—*sense of humor, and, with luck, extract a few nickels before shuffling on.*

They might go for whiskey and pork at a Beale Street barbeque joint on their way out of Memphis, if they'd already been fired from whatever institution they'd been teaching at, and ruminate on the nature of their journey, forcing their minds away from any speculation as to its unremembered beginning and unimaginable end.

Hovering, as they were obliged to, in the temporal and spatial middle of all things, they ribbed one another constantly and mercilessly, each claiming, as often as possible and in the lewdest possible terms, to be the other's father. The things they claimed to have done with their ostensibly mutual mother, whom neither had ever met, nor even ever heard from, made each Brother blush so heavily that it was nearly impossible to complete the boast without devolving into gusts of nervous laughter, like boys watching pigs rut on a farm, had they been farm boys, which perhaps they had been, since no images from before the age of forty existed in either of their minds.

Aside from the one-upmanship inherent in these tales of the circumstances surrounding the other's conception, their greatest game involved devising new and increasingly salacious means of getting themselves fired from their already-tenuous teaching posts. Each delighted in returning to the Ramada Inn or the EconoLodge where the other was sprawled on the bedspread with the blackout curtains drawn at three in the afternoon, and announcing, "They've run us off campus again! This time I suggested that the moon was in fact the locus of all legitimate human activity, while the earth was a sort of penal colony for those too dimwitted or depraved to take part in the larger social project, and I had a whole lecture prepared on this premise"—the Brothers always prepared their lectures separately, to ensure maximal disjunct as they traded off teaching duties—"but then I found myself laughing so hard I was, in short order, choking on great spicy wads of phlegm, and I had the impression that the moon itself had heard my blasphemous claim and was punishing me for it, in the manner of actual lunatics, and, anyway, I was…."

But by this point in the story the other Squimbop Brother would already be packing his bags, stealing a few Douwe Egberts coffee packets if they were in a motel that provided them, and preparing to peel out of the parking lot in their '27 Chevy, tearing onto the abandoned highway like a couple of bank robbers, Dillinger 1 and Dillinger 2, burning rubber in high dudgeon as they put another failed venture behind them, *Me and the Devil Blues* wailing over the transistor radio.

♦

These were the times when the Brothers fancied themselves the only mobile entities left in the nation, elected to that position by forces residing either deep within themselves or else far off in the surrounding murk. The highways were abandoned save for the occasional unlabeled truck or caravan of gypsies, and the motels and gas stations seemed to be the only anachronisms, pointing to the existence, in the past or the future, of an era other than the 1930s. Everything else, as far as they could tell, had reverted and was perhaps reverting still, toward the medieval or even the prehistoric, not that either Brother had a stable notion of what this meant. Memory and imagination, they found, had grown so intermingled that it was no longer possible even to claim a distinction between the two words, let alone to find out what it might be.

As they lurked in a strip club in New Orleans, watching men and women covered in sores circle sweaty poles in a daze, slamming into one another when the music stuttered, they considered how a smothering, smoke-smelling curtain of forgetfulness had been drawn over the country, so that now history was nothing more than whatever they said it was.

Because the saddest thing, or one of the saddest things, they thought, each Brother keeping it to himself, *is that we are never, in actuality, run out of the colleges we teach at, because no claim we make ever gets enough traction to become taboo. As there is nothing for us to clash with*—each Brother imagined himself lecturing to an empty room now, laying this all out in great detail—*we are only run out in the sense of wanting to leave, of seeking, once again, the romance of the open road, knowing full well that any exit off the highway, chosen either at random or after painstaking deliberation, will produce the exact same result, like a die whose every face displays the same black dot.*

To avoid the grim prospect of giving voice to this fact, each Brother kept his die well hidden, insisting to the other that his transgressions were real, and that the consequences, if they stayed in town, would be swift and decisive. Each was thus, in the eyes of the other, a genuine outlaw, or so he told himself.

"Want to walk through the French Quarter and see if any murders are going on?" Joe Squimbop asked, unfurling a few bills to pay for the beer and chicken they'd consumed, and stuffing another few under the bandage of a stripper who'd cantilevered out over their table to receive them.

Jim nodded, eager to lighten the mood, so they walked off their dinner in the French Quarter where, indeed, three people were murdered in quick succession, a knifing and two shots to the head. Though the Brothers weren't unmoved, they seemed to stand apart from it, bullets whizzing inches from their noses without grazing them, nor even seeming liable to. *It's as though we are both here and not here*, they found themselves thinking in the relative private of their respective heads, *present in name only*.

Before the evening wilted the rest of the way into bathos, they returned to their Red Roof Inn in Metairie, cutting through alleys where ambiguously human shapes bedded down in piles of trash, their eyes shining yellow in the humid night. Others clung to doorways, backlit, their fingers merging with the soft wood surrounding them until it looked like they'd grown there.

As the Brothers slipped naked into the motel hot tub, they coined a new term—*mushroom-people*—for these entities, though of course neither mentioned it to the other. Outwardly, it was just the two of them in a chlorine-smelling annex, laughing about the lecture series they would deliver in Arkansas as soon as they found a suitably decrepit college to decamp at until their next scandal uprooted them yet again.

♦

Two days later, the Brothers Squimbop had secured themselves a post—if one allows the word 'post' to mean 'empty lecture hall'—at a taxidermy school in Mountain Home, and a room in another Red Roof Inn, where they joked that the day's journey had, in the end, consisted of no more than moving a few doors down a single ashy hallway. They seemed to be the only guests, and were most certainly the only professors in the American History Department.

At the start of a new post, the Brothers drew straws to determine who would teach first. After this, they would alternate daily. This time it was Jim, so, the following morning, he showered and shaved, put on the sweaty tweed suit the two of them shared, neither quite fitting into it, and walked to campus with his empty briefcase under his arm. Standing behind the podium, facing two young women and a young man with cauliflower ears, he began by summarizing what had gone wrong with America in the last century. "Americans evolved from mushrooms," he began, "and would have been much better off remaining such. But, around the year 1995, a torrential downpour saturated our ancestors' systems and, unable to absorb the excess moisture, our fungal crevices became capillaries, which in turn became veins, which in turn became arteries, and, within the span of a generation, we turned into what we now are, hopelessly trying to inhabit an environment we were never built for.

"And yet those who fared the worst," he added, picturing the entities sprouting from doorways in New Orleans, "are those who stayed inside during the downpour and thus remained mushrooms, or mushroom-adjacent. A collective species-consciousness now compels them to attempt to leave their domiciles and join the larger human family, but they are stuck too tightly to the walls—indeed, they are *part* of those walls—to ever do so. Imagine, if you would, being left behind in such a state."

At this point in the lecture, a wolf sauntered into the

room. It stood in the middle ground between the podium and the students, swiveling its head from one side to the other. Then it yawned and sauntered out. When Jim looked back at his students, his eyes locked onto those of one of the young women, who had an animate keenness about her that unnerved him.

After class, he retired to his office, which in this case was an electrical closet on the third floor. He took his shoes off, leaned against the wall, and shocked himself on a loose wire. Jolting forward, he kicked open the door just as the young woman was standing outside, peering in.

"Professor Squimbop?"

She appeared certain that it was him, so he didn't respond.

"Are you having office hours in here?"

There were few things in the objective world that he hated more than office hours, but he nodded and watched as she pulled a crate from a pile stacked against one wall, and sat down on it, as far away from him as the cramped space would allow.

Clearing her throat, she leaned forward and said, "I was interested in what you were saying in class. I've seen the mushroom-people too, up in Minneapolis where I'm from, and also… well, I was wondering, how do you know where they came from? How is it that you remember what America used to be, while no one else does?"

Jim licked the backs of his teeth, anxious to see how long he could get away with not responding.

Time ticked on, until, quivering slightly, she repeated her question verbatim.

I can tell she isn't sure if she asked it already, Jim thought. He had half a mind to try his not-answering act a second time, but feared it would escalate the situation, and, being at heart a coward, he knew that any escalation would eventually turn out poorly for him. "How is it that I remember? I might ask the same, er, rather, the opposite, of you: how is it that you don't?"

Another silence. He could feel the tables turning, though he wasn't yet sure how. The horror of being taken seriously, of a student actually listening to what he'd said and acting as though it meant something, swarmed him. He started to fear that the air in this closet would soon run out.

"Are you seriously asking me that?" she asked. "Because I live in the same country as everybody else. The exact same thing that happened to them, whatever it was, happened to me. You, on the other hand...."

Her eyes flickered with a kind of intensity he'd never seen before. The gaping stares of the zombies he'd addressed from all the podiums he'd ever lectured from now seemed benign compared to the attention she was leveraging against him.

Either she's not really here, Jim found himself thinking, *or I'm not. We can't both be.* He knew that all it would take on his part was the presence of mind to insist that he was the real one and she the interloper. But, just now, he couldn't tell if he had it in him. He shivered as she leaned in, expecting an answer.

Isn't this what I've always wanted? He wondered. *A genuine conflict, a real reason to flee town?* Faced with it just then, he couldn't be sure. If he had to guess, he would guess that the answer was *No.*

"Why should we believe this is what happened?" she asked, making it clear she wasn't going to simply vanish because he wished she would.

Jim shivered and wanted to cry. *Why, indeed? Perhaps nothing at all happened, and this is simply how it's always been. All my Brother and I ever wanted,* he wanted to tell her, *was to comfort ourselves with the possibility that the truth is knowable. That something, rather than nothing, resides at the very bottom. Is that so shameful a thing to want?*

Yes, he imagined her saying.

He opened his mouth, hoping that some of what he'd just thought would come out, but nothing did. He left it open until he'd forgotten what he'd wanted to confess. Then he licked his palm and grabbed the exposed wire, praying it would shock him violently enough that she'd run away, or at the very least yawn and saunter off, just as the wolf had.

One way or another, he woke up alone in the closet what felt like many hours later. His first thought was that he was dead. Then he considered that perhaps it was the other way around, that he'd been dead all this time, and now he'd shocked himself alive.

He got to his feet, falteringly, and made his way out of the building, past the damp classrooms, so empty they seemed as though they'd never been occupied, past the grim gallery of taxidermy equipment on the first floor, past piles of armadillo shells under a dripping spigot, past the wolf from earlier sitting so still it looked stuffed, across the campus, up HWY-62, past a Shoney's where a crowd was fighting in the parking lot, and back to the Red Roof Inn where, he prayed, his Brother would be drunk enough to refrain from asking how the day had gone.

Bursting into the room, which smelled of chicken skin and hot sauce, he yelped, "The day went great!" Then he stripped down to his boxers, removed his journal from the nightstand, and got into bed with it. Aware that his Brother's eyes were on him, he undid the novelty lock, opened to the first blank page, and wrote:

Unutterable abyss of loneliness, deeper than the deepest, darkest depths of the ocean, wider than the widest breadth of space in the asteroid-choked nothingness beyond the orbit of any planet, habitable or otherwise: this is what I, in my heart of hearts, believe with absolute certainty lies at the bottom of everything that ever was, and ever will be. Student today wanted to know why I was spared the forgetting while no one else was. The answer I should've given: I was spared nothing at all. I remember nothing save for what I've made up.

I'm simply less gullible than you are.

So thank God (ha-ha!) that my Brother is an imbecile and thus incapable of perceiving what I perceive. Thank God my Brother lives in childlike ignorance, thereby allowing me to tag along with him for the comedy of errors that makes up our blessedly circumscribed life. This is the sole mercy that allows me to persevere.

"What're you writing?" Joe asked, as he finished his own writing and prepared to turn out the bedside lamp, to which Jim replied, without hesitation, "How I raw-dogged your mother in an alley behind a Denny's in Fresno with the busboy watching, and then how you popped out two months early, so freak-looking the doc said you were a rare hybrid of rat-lady and actual rat!"

Closing and locking his journal after pretending to read these words from it, Jim nodded off with a mixture of fear and envy at the prospect of his Brother waking up to face the young woman tomorrow, while he would spend the day drinking alone in this room, fending off Housekeeping if it tried to ferret him out. Like a sow pregnant with many piglets at once, his mixed feelings went all the way to his center.

Joe Squimbop, meanwhile, smiled as he too turned off his bedside lamp. His final thoughts before sleep were: *thank God my Brother's too dumb to understand what our situation here actually is, how precarious it has become, and perhaps has always been. Let him joke his life away. It spares me having to commune with someone who sees the truth as clearly as I do.*

Then he pulled the sweaty pillow over his head, determined to get a few hours of real sleep before it was his turn to wake up, put on the tweed suit, and head to campus in the morning.

EGON'S PARENTS

Ed was in his pickup truck driving the gravel out back of his shitty town in Idaho one Friday night in spring when he hit and killed Egon, until then a freshman at the town's college, where, it was said, East Coast fuck-ups went to die.

Before it happened, Ed had been hauling out to Jeff's house for a late-stage high school free-for-all of the sort that had only been getting more frequent and vivid since the start of senior year's semester two, and would peak, he assumed, sometime in midsummer, just before it all came crashing down and a critical mass went their separate ways in August.

He, Ed, for what it was worth, had lately been thinking he might head out to California, try to see what that meant. He'd learned, from a war vet he knew in town, that San Francisco and San Diego were two different places, and that one shouldn't be averse to kicking around awhile in both or either. And what's more, this vet had added, there was Mexico.

All decent places to kill time in until he'd made it somehow into his twenties, as Ed saw it, by which point there'd probably be something he'd have to get around to.

He hadn't spoken to his parents in over a year. He rented a room above a hardware store on the section of Main Street that started to become the Strip, which led all the way up past Walmart to the westernmost highway entrance, which he planned to take onto the highway to California when the time came, handing in his keys and name tag at the hardware store where he worked a few dead-boring evening shifts a week in exchange for the room and a little something on top.

Jeff lived way out, probably the farthest of anyone Ed knew. He was still driving, getting closer.

His thing lately was he liked to tell people he was still a virgin though it wasn't technically true. He couldn't have said quite what the appeal was, but it had become something he could be relied on to say at parties, an entertainment, almost a routine, even though it was only a single sentence, and once he'd said it, it was done.

He pictured a California, as he drove, that would shear off the virginity that Idaho had failed to touch, offering one pale Caitlin and Jennifer after another in lieu of the real thing. *Only out there*, he thought, *is real, lasting change possible.*

He enjoyed ideas like this. They kept him awake and made him feel like a more with-it guy than he necessarily always was.

He drove fast, though not as fast as he could have. Probably everyone who was already at the party had driven much faster. It only mattered that he didn't drive so slow that the freaky road-feel of being this far shy of downtown hit him all at once.

The back center of the pickup was weighted down with three plastic gallon vodkas and two thirty-racks of Keystone Ice, under packing blankets that covered scrap metal from the hardware store he was supposed to have taken to the dump.

It was his night to haul. Until he got there, the party was BYOB, no one's idea of a good time.

Everyone had their own way of buying it. For Ed, it was that war vet he knew, a reliable bastard though a bad piece of work, so they said. Two for you, one for me was the vet's deal these days, whether it was bottles or cans.

So here he was hauling $100-worth of booze that had cost him $150, running lists and numbers, cost-benefit analyses, a little manic, around 11PM, when Egon's SUV came rattling up the road toward him, scraping the shoulder of the opposite lane, not that there was any drawn median to speak of.

It was not only the first other vehicle Ed had seen tonight, it was the first he'd ever seen on this road any time after dark since he'd gotten his license over a year ago.

The first thing he saw was the New Jersey license plate. Ed wasn't a plate-reader by nature, but the unlikelihood of coming across any car at all out here was enough to beg the questions of who and from where?

That plate was where his eyes started out. If they'd stayed down there, Egon would be alive today or dead by another means, and Ed would probably be a middle-aged man hanging around the same liquor store he'd just loaded up at. The physics were such that it would not have been hard to glide past.

But Ed's eyes slipped up, off the plate and over the hood and clear through the windshield, coming to rest on Egon himself, alone in the universe behind his steering wheel on this shitty town road far enough from his fuck-up college to be fully unknown to it, cruising almost certainly without a destination.

The path that Ed's eyes traveled into Egon's kept him going in that direction, wrenching him out of his lane and across the gravel, almost off the ground, through the air.

In brute response to what he saw in Egon or felt in himself, a pity or a fear, Ed seized and firmed up in his system, got thick and sure very fast, felt time getting wet and slimy, gripped the steering wheel so hard his hands went numb as gloves, and shoved himself head-on into the SUV, ducking to one side so the airbag didn't maim him.

He barely heard the impact, only heard Egon give way.

Or didn't so much hear it as feel it like an armored insect being crushed by a rock.

There passed a spell with Egon dying and Ed huddled beneath and beside the airbag, waiting, doing nothing.

Then he leapt onto the gravel, running head-down to avoid glimpsing the carnage, though he smelled it burning, around to the pickup's bed, which he climbed into and hurled off the blankets and pried open and tore with engorged and sharpened fingers into the beer cases, looting out fistfuls of cans and squeezing open the gigantic plastic bottles, spraying it all up his nose and into his eyes and around his collar, making a bath of his neck and head.

He chugged hard and fast, scarcely breathing, pouring beer and liquor down his throat at the same time, with some splashing into his ears, feeling his chest and belly swell to hold it, burning the gassy liquid straight up his system.

He figured he had at best fifteen minutes to get convincingly drunk enough for there to be no question in anyone's mind, ideally not even his own, about what'd happened here, and he was starting from scratch.

By the time the cops and ambulance arrived, racing each other—the road was not so remote that the crash hadn't been heard in at least one home, or, if no one heard it, then someone saw the flames—Ed was more than drunk enough, almost so drunk that it seemed implausible he'd been driving at all.

Hands were on him, muttering voices, flashing lights.

He was locked up, told he'd be dealt with in due time and to sit tight till then.

He knew everyone locked up around him, and all the guards, but no one would engage. It wasn't hatred; it was just that no one wanted any part of it.

He could tell his life would be different from here on out, and that that difference had already begun.

Egon's body had been towed and scraped and cleared away, and the rest of Ed's senior year fed into a blur. His friends paid their respects and then dissipated, and he came and went from his arraignment, uncertain whether there'd be a future, much less what it could hold.

After his last visitor had come and gone, he spent a few days in silent reflection, trying to get clear on what he'd done and wanted to do now. Then he requested writing materials and wrote a letter.

He tried to make his apology profound without implicating the truth. He stuck with the folktale of being seventeen and drunk, a little too happy for anyone's good. He said he really meant it, that he was sorry, that he was far into shame and guilt and might or might never come out. That he had done something he hadn't intended and would give anything he had to undo.

He asked his captors to post it to Egon's Parents, wherever in New Jersey they might be.

The letter was taken and Ed was again told to sit tight.

He did, for a month by his count.

He did push-ups like a chump in a prison movie and slept a great many hours and did some more thinking, until his thoughts began to loop and echo.

Then a letter came for him. It had been opened and probably scrutinized, but there was no redaction:

Dear Ed,

It took us a month to open your letter. We had to let it sit that long, on the radiator. We talked about tossing it. You killed our son. Our only.

We came close to tossing it.

But at last we read it. It was the right thing. Then we prayed, and waited, and went on grieving, and pondered your admission, the pain it was clear that you felt, and we came to the consensus, hard as it is even for us to accept, that we forgive you.

Well and truly.

We do not understand, and never will, but we forgive you.

You are forgiven.

Sincerely,
Egon's Parents.

Ed took his time drafting a response.

He felt the matter was not concluded, though he could see good reasons why it should have been, and would in retrospect wonder whether perhaps a simple failure to reply, on his part, at this point, would have been enough to keep things close to normal.

Instead, he requested the same writing materials he'd used the first time, and wrote:

Dear Egon's Parents….

It seemed he'd written only this when they showed up, talked to the people who were holding him, and brought Ed out, into the only café in his shitty town in Idaho that he never went to because his parents were always there.

They weren't there now.

The fact of it being a café he never went to had the effect of making him feel like the whole town had been transformed, everything he could see, taste, and otherwise grasp made new, washed in the arrival of Egon's Parents.

They sat behind blueberry muffins and paper cups of coffee, their names written in Sharpie on the cardboard sleeves. No one ate or drank.

There was a rack of Christian sympathy cards on one side of the café, books and pamphlets on the other, and the shell of a theater across the street, haunted by teenagers who formed a segment of the circle that Ed used to belong to.

Egon's Parents watched him. He couldn't tell if they were waiting for him to make a move or freezing him in place.

Finally they said, *"The horrible thing was not set in stone in the future, before it happened, but it is now set in stone where it resides in the past, and, all platitudes and pleasantries aside, we are here to help you accept and understand the truth of this, since you are both the perpetrator and now the only living victim of the horrible thing. We have accepted what you must now accept."*

He wasn't sure if they'd said all they were going to or if there was a second part slipped in while he was stuck on the first, but very soon it was decided.

He would come back to New Jersey to live with them, to cope.

"The body has been adequately disposed of," Egon's Parents said, getting into their Audi, sporting the same NJ plates as Egon's SUV.

"So there is nothing to keep us here."

They handed him an envelope, sealed with the insignia of his high school. He looked for some confirmation that he should open it, and found what he was looking for.

Inside was an official diploma in his name, claiming that he'd completed all credits and graduated with a 3.2 GPA, despite having missed more than a month of the end of senior year and made nothing up, taken no exams.

"You are free of this place," said Egon's Parents, getting onto the highway at the entrance at the end of the Strip that he, Ed, had for so long envisioned as the start of the road to California, in a future that had back then seemed likely.

It took a very long time to drive to New Jersey, far longer than he would have guessed. His idea of how far it was hadn't been realistic. He'd seen plenty of maps in his time, but had never internalized their scale.

He slipped down on the back seat, restrained from going edgewise by the seatbelt, which Egon's Parents had insisted he wear.

As they sped across the States, even apparently dipping up into Canada, the seatbelt cut off his circulation. He slumped over and felt like he couldn't breathe. What was passing by the windows started to look soupy and secondary, like a scum between him and the real thing.

He blinked, as if by wiping his eyes he could also wipe the windows, and came to in a smell of fried chicken. He accepted the container Egon's Parents offered. After a few bites, shifting the bones to one corner, Egon's Parents summoned it back.

"For later," they said, returning to the highway that led through what the signs said was Ohio, patrolled by unmarked aircraft.

When they got off at their exit, it was so late that even the all-night gas station convenience mart was closed, so it meant no milk or OJ. Egon's Parents griped about how, since a new family had taken over the all-night mart, it was hardly ever all-night anymore, though they'd declined to remove or amend the sign.

"Even the gas is worse," they added.

Their opinion seemed perfunctory, part of a well-established homecoming ritual. Ed nodded, happy to agree.

They stepped inside their house and toppled a pile of mail. Seeing and hearing it fall, he was reminded of the letter he'd sent them, which had sat unopened for a month on the radiator but had then led to this.

"Your room is upstairs on the right."

It was only upon entering his room, which seemed not only dark but darkened, as if some preparation had gone into the effect, that he remembered he'd brought nothing with him. He had no clothes, books, materials of any kind. He felt like an undocumented immigrant, save for his diploma.

He stripped to his boxers and peeled back the bedspread, lying down on sheets that smelled clean but felt pre-touched. His eyes found the ceiling, which began to drip with memories of the killing-crash, long wet strands like pumpkin innards, dripping down onto his chin and Adam's apple.

He was starting to imagine that he didn't like it here, enough to decide that it might be best not to fall asleep. So, he prepared to lay awake all night with the question of whether, given the chance to kill Egon again, he would.

He expected this question to grip him through to a miserable dawn, flopping back and forth inside him like something beached, but, instead, he got his answer right away, just as he had the first time, out on the road.

"Yes," was the answer. *"I'd crush his skull with a brick if I had one and he was here."*

Having burned through the thoughts he'd summoned to keep him awake, he fell asleep. He went way down into Egon's bed, all the way to the root.

In the morning, he put on Egon's flannel robe, sweatpants, and leather slippers.

He had not yet put on Egon's underwear, but, as he pissed and washed his face before taking the stairs, he could see this would soon become necessary. The boxers he wore now, old and rank from Idaho, would be lost in the wash, and he knew he'd never see them again.

Egon's Parents were sitting at the breakfast table, a newspaper fanned out between them. Looking through the glass doors behind the breakfast chamber, he couldn't firmly tell what season it was. He feared he'd be unable to remember the four options just now, so he didn't try.

He tried, instead, to peer over at the newspaper, but Egon's Parents crinkled it away, subtly but not so subtly that it wasn't clear they were hiding it.

Even the name of this town in New Jersey was hidden. It seemed fair to expect the paper to reveal this much—*The Somewhere Herald* or *Something Gazette*—but it looked to be a mere *New York Times.*

He saw a pile of older papers in the dry sink beside the breakfast table, and pictured the current one lost among them soon enough.

He poured a bowl of Frosted Mini-Wheats and sat down, farting a little as he did, looking forward to a shower. There was still no milk, so he ate his Mini-Wheats dry like pretzels, and drank black coffee and water.

Egon's Parents sat there, having apparently awoken much earlier—their food was long gone, coffee cold and sedimented—but they were in no visible hurry. They didn't even seem eager to clear their places and move from early to mid-morning within their own home.

The light outside looked pale and mild. Ed didn't imagine it'd give him any trouble if he went out into it, but he didn't plan to try just yet.

Not today.

He went up to Egon's room after breakfast and waited till lunch. Then till dinner. The light stayed pale for a long time, trying hard to give him a chance.

Then it went black.

He held his position in the bed, making it very clear where he was and where he was not, like a needle was planning to fall from the ceiling and would miss him if it could.

He could smell that he still hadn't showered, but knew he couldn't manage it right now. Later tonight maybe, or tomorrow at the latest.

There were mobiles and dreamcatchers hanging from Egon's ceiling, none close enough to clank together, but they kept trying.

The surfaces in Egon's room were undisturbed. The main desk, the night table, and the top of the dresser were covered with papers and notes, business cards, coins, safety pins and buttons, ticket stubs from concerts and sporting events, and the bookcases were stuffed with books, folders, binders, CDs, and DVDs.

His eyes roved from the bed over all this material.

A few days passed.

There were still meals downstairs, but they made little impression. He sat quietly at the dinner table until he was told to go up to bed. The meals were chicken potpies and beef stews, defrosted in the oven. There was never takeout or anything cooked from scratch. They never got milk, to the point where he stopped pouring his cereal into a bowl, eating little piles of it off of paper towels and napkins instead.

He spent so much time in his room that he couldn't tell if Egon's Parents left during the day to work and shop and run errands in town, only returning at dinnertime, or were still spending their days downstairs, quietly drinking coffee from some diminishing supply in the basement.

There was no explicit prohibition against his coming downstairs except for meals, but he never tried it.

He finally reached the point where his crotch and armpits were so rank he had to wash them. In the shower, free of Egon's Parents, he began to cull the strength to empty the bedroom, purge the detritus that was turning more minatory the longer he spent amidst it, like a bed of grass and reeds turning cold and wet as the water table beneath underwent some climatic shift.

These things are stifling me, he thought, emptying a bottle of conditioner over his head and neck. *I will never be able to live here until I cleanse my room of the stranger's trace.*

Getting out of the shower, he dried off and stepped into Egon's boxers, elastic busted so they hung like a diaper, clearly one of the pairs he'd left behind when he packed for college.

Over a few more days, he formulated a plan to steal a trash bag from the kitchen after dessert, in the minutes when Egon's Parents were puttering around with the recycling by the garage.

Throughout the hours in bed, the plan came to seem immensely detailed and complex, but when the time came to execute it, there was almost nothing to be done. He simply pulled the trash bag from the roll under the sink and walked upstairs, just before the parents returned from the garage.

Then it began. He stuffed everything he could inside, all the scraps of paper that Egon had left behind, covered with scribblings that, apparently, amounted to the miscellany of his mental life during the years he'd lived in this room, before somehow ending up alone in outermost Idaho.

All the journals, sketchpads, card collections, rolled-up dollar comics and a few valuable ones in plastic sheets, baby teeth and stale unused condoms and back issues of *GamePro* and some *FHM*s with the body pages ripped out, the ads and articles hanging ragged from distressed bindings.

Once the bottom of the bag was lined with loose material, he went further, tearing down posters and postcards strapped to the walls and all those mobiles and dreamcatchers from the ceiling, crushing and stuffing them into the bag like badly-killed birds, their wiry extremities tearing holes in the plastic.

It was his bid for survival.

This came as an obvious but long-delayed revelation. That's why the plan had seemed so elaborate. He hadn't seen it this way a moment ago, but now it was clear. He would pack the bag as tight as possible, despite the holes, and fling it from the house. If he could get Egon out of this room, he could go on living in it, possibly forever.

Building toward mania, he tore down the wallpaper and peeled up the floorboards, all of it coming off as easily as the skin from a piece of overripe fruit. The room got see-through as he peeled it, its walls turning membranous, subtly veined, gray and shrimp-like, encasing it from the night outside.

He took a break, huffing, the air cold and fresh now.

Looking down through the floor, he could see that Egon's Parents had left the kitchen. He had to hurry; he shouldn't have rested.

Dragging the trash bag, too heavy to lift now, he heard their knock and had to open the door.

"Empty it," said Egon's Parents.

He tried to picture what would happen if he disobeyed, but couldn't.

So he did as he was told, pouring the contents into a pile on the floor that grew so tall and sharp it choked the room, the soft membrane sagging and groaning, resisting puncture.

Then he handed over the empty wrinkled plastic bag and Egon's Parents bore it away.

When they had gone, he tiptoed around the pile, trying to keep his balance like a kid in a blow-up bouncy house.

The bed had been completely obscured, so he crawled into a nest of paper and metal and closed his eyes. Spikes rested on his back, just heavy enough to tickle, and the night outside settled in to watch.

At breakfast the next day, Egon's Parents read their *Times* as usual, expressions glum and fixed. The incident was not mentioned except that he was informed he would receive his meals in his room from now on. A tray would be set out twice a day, the first of which would contain enough to save some for lunch if he so desired. It would be the same tray both times, so if he desired dinner he was advised to set the empty tray outside his door no later than 4PM.

He lay huddled beneath the pile he'd reduced the room to, his face pressed into the transparent floor, and, deep in the night—insomnia had arrived at last—he could see Egon's Parents sitting at the table, facing one another.

At first, he couldn't tell if they were talking. They were very still, like they were sitting there posed, perhaps in positions they'd sleepwalked into or fallen asleep in, but, despite the lack of evidence, he became convinced they were discussing his future, deciding what to do with him or, having decided long ago, when to do it.

It took him back to the beginning of his life, when he'd lived with his parents and made his requests for pets and special privileges just before bed, and was always told they'd discuss it while he was asleep and tell him their verdict in the morning.

Each morning he'd come down and ask them what they'd decided, and they'd ask him what he was talking about.

Eventually, the suspense became too much.

He'd known since the beginning that his time in this house might take a turn or come to an end, and had even, to a degree, known it before sending the letter, and was prepared to accept whatever it proved to be, no matter how dark, but watching Egon's Parents through the floor, as they sat at that table and talked about him, became more than he could bear.

Exhausted, eyes hot and dry, mouth sour and salty, he stood up under the pile of rubble, balancing on the gummy membrane of the floor, and began to piece the room back together.

He grabbed handfuls of material, which had decomposed into a paste since he'd torn everything down, slicked by its own juices, and spread it over the floor and the walls, standing on his tiptoes to minimize footprints.

When this was done, he threw up handfuls at the ceiling, closing his eyes as it rained back down.

It smelled like mulch and wallpaper glue, caustic and dizzying.

When the floors and walls were fully covered, returned to opacity, he lay down, feeling streaks of paste hardening in his hair.

It was a tremendous relief to be spared the sight of Egon's Parents at the table downstairs. Whatever they were discussing, whatever they had in store for him, they could come up and knock on his door when the time came.

He would open it when they did and insist he was Egon,

safe in his room, where he'd been all this time, brooding on the possibility of life after death.

THE MEADOWS

Casey showered and put on her black Sunday dress and her black buckle shoes and strolled out of the big house she lived in alone. She didn't bother to lock the door because all the children had houses and plenty of food and no need for money or stolen things from other children.

She walked up her street eating a bag of fruit snacks, falling in with the others when the nearest cross-street dead-ended on the Children's Church lawn, in the shadow of the Sick Sequoia. She kept her head down as she filed in through the narrow door, taking her seat on a pew that had long cracks down the center, as most of them did, having last been repaired… she had no idea when. It was impossible to imagine who had built the Church, same as it was with her house and all the houses on her street. They were just there, like the rocks on the ground, like the clouds in the sky. *Like me and everyone else*, she thought. *All of us just happen to be here.*

When everyone was seated, Sullivan, the children's de facto leader because he'd had a growth spurt and smelled like sweat and no one would challenge him, walked up to the altar and pressed PLAY on the tape recorder that slept all week under a dirty white cloth. Then he sat down on a chair beside it with his hands in his lap and his eyes squeezed shut, mimicking the listening pose that all the children were expected to assume.

The children live in the Neighborhoods; the grown-ups live in the Meadows, the tape began. The children, having assumed the listening pose, recited along with it. Casey moved her mouth in case anyone was watching, but didn't speak. *The children are sacred and the grown-ups are evil*, it continued, as did they. *The children live in peace and harmony in the Neighborhoods, while the grown-ups live in sin and degradation in the Meadows. They grope blindly through an endless fog, belching, farting, and waggling their dirty pee-pees behind rotting bushes, or sticking their long filthy fingers up their gaping hoo-haws and laughing like donkeys, knee-deep in swamp water and slimy rotting leaves.*

The children grew antsy in their seats as the tape reached its final and most crucial point. *The children cannot hurt one another, for they are all equally sacred. They cannot die because they were not born. They simply are, God's Creations one and all, safe here in the Neighborhoods, on the holy side of the line that separates them from the Meadows, the line that must never be crossed.*

Here the tape sputtered to an end and began to rewind.

With a great whooping, the children rose to their feet and streamed out of the Children's Church toward the Park, following Sullivan, their pace a little slower than his. Casey lagged behind, still strolling while the others skipped. She watched them hurry toward the rusty Tin Locomotive in the center of the Park with a sort of glee she could sometimes mimic but never feel. As she often did after Church, she found herself lost in daydreams of the Meadows, unable to shake the image of those rotting grown-ups wandering in the fog.

Sullivan and a few other boys were now scrambling up the side of the Tin Locomotive. Sometimes, when a heavy wind had blown all night or a few days had passed without much foot traffic, large piles of locusts would appear under the trees, and the braver children would climb the Tin Locomotive's steam spout—the highest point in the Park—and hurl themselves into the pile, squishing the locusts like chocolate-covered caramels.

It sometimes delighted Casey to watch, when she was in one of her lighter moods, but she never joined in and many days, like today, watching the others sickened her with a sense of all-pervasive and inescapable idiocy. So she sat on a bench, one foot on the other knee, and stared at the houses of the Neighborhoods, most of them identical, one of them hers, and couldn't shake the feeling that there must be more to life than this.

She shivered and, because two boys were coming her way and she knew they were about to tease her for sitting alone, and maybe also call her a creepy old witch and ask where her cat was, she got up and hurried away.

As she slowed to a walking pace a few blocks from the Park, she kept imagining herself getting lost and winding up in the Meadows. She pictured the sweaty and shivering grown-ups she'd meet there, coughing, oozing secrets, and she got so turned around she ended up in ULTRA MAX, which was abandoned at this time of the afternoon. To avoid feeling like she'd come here for no reason, she took a jar of peanuts and a box of sweet cereal off the Dry Goods Shelf and brought them to the Self-Service Kiosk. When the icon that read ARE YOU SURE YOU NEED THESE? appeared onscreen, she clicked YES, though it wasn't quite true. She blushed and swallowed and felt the lie land like a wad of gum in her stomach as she walked across the parking lot, unsure what she'd do if a child-cop came running after her.

When she got home, she sat at her kitchen table and ate cereal from the box and tried to keep her eyes open, because every time she closed them she saw herself pushing Sullivan off the

Tin Locomotive and smashing his face on the concrete, pulping his skull like a pumpkin. *Then we'll all find out*, she thought, one hand gathering cereal, *whether it really is possible for children to die.*

She got in the shower. Under the water, she couldn't help imagining herself waist deep in the Meadows, kicking her feet in the blue-gray marsh grass. The water turned cold and oily and she turned it off, wiping away the soap and shampoo with a towel, her skin red and covered in goosebumps.

Then she got in bed and closed her eyes and pictured the Park as it was now, the children departing, walking hand-in-hand back to the Neighborhoods, sticking together until they had to separate for the night. They'd part ways saying, "Sweet dreams, everyone," as they did every night, as soon as Sullivan gave the signal to disperse. She wondered what they could possibly dream of if not the Meadows. *They probably just dream of the Neighborhoods*, she thought, *their nights no different from their days.*

Idiots.

Pulling the sheets over her head, she tried to force her way asleep, but could already tell it wouldn't work. There were times when you could force it and times when you couldn't. So she got back on her feet and dressed and grabbed a handful of peanuts and walked back up her street in the pitch black, making her way to the Park by instinct. She sat on the same bench she'd been sitting on earlier in the day, and listened to the locusts swarm overhead, imagining what the grown-ups were doing now, cast out and cold in the endless Meadows.

In the morning, as the first children made their way back to the Park, Casey was still there. The long, cold hours had left her slightly crazed, her skin wet with dew. She'd been listening to the locusts swarm, intent on seeing them die, but she must've drifted off because now here they were, dead as usual, and she couldn't say how or when it'd happened.

"Bonzai!" shouted Sullivan, leaping from the top of the Tin Locomotive into the fresh pile of locust bodies. Then he got up, wiped himself off, and started a play-fight with a boy named Jack, the biggest kid after him.

"Go, go, hit him!" children shouted from both sides. It didn't seem to matter who got hit as long as someone did.

Casey watched them feint at each other, their fists swinging through air and stopping an inch from bone and skin, like a force field had repelled them. *One child may not kill another….* She mulled the line over while Jack and Sullivan went on play-fighting and the crowd cheered for real blood.

They sound hungry, she thought. *Starving*. She was on her feet now, amped up, heart pounding, eyes trembling, and now she was climbing the Tin Locomotive, which she'd never done before, and now she was on top, shouting, "Sullivan! Hey Sullivan!"

He turned from his play-fight after the third time she shouted his name, as did the crowd. Even Jack, panting and spitting, looked up at her. She wavered there, unsure of her purpose, though deep down she knew.

"Sullivan!" she heard herself shout again. "Why don't you get up here and fight me like a man?"

He stared, looking from her to Jack and back again, as if seeking an approval he hoped wouldn't come. But Jack didn't respond, so eventually Sullivan backed away, head hung low.

As he neared the Tin Locomotive and began to climb, he puffed back up, his old swagger returning to his legs and arms and, once he made it to the top, to his face, as well. He flexed and posed for those below. They cheered. Then he turned to Casey and said, "So. You wanna fight me? The old witch wants some of this?" He grabbed his crotch and cackled.

As he reared back on his hind leg, Casey watched herself ram into him with everything she had. His feet left the Tin Locomotive's surface and he went flying through the air, eyes bugged open and fixed on her until his head smacked against the concrete and its top came off.

Casey leapt down, landing with her knees on his chest. She peeled off the flap of scalp and started stuffing his skull full of locusts. She jammed in as many as she could, filling what seemed like his whole brainless body, using up all the locusts within reach. Then she rose to her full size and, wiping her hands on her pants, said, "So I guess children *can* kill children after all," and hurried away.

She broke into a run as soon as she'd crossed from the Park back into the Neighborhoods, and didn't slow down until she was inside her house, gathering fruit snacks and granola bars and filling two plastic bottles with water, putting it all in her backpack along with a change of clothes.

She washed her face with hot water and her favorite washcloth and soap one last time, and used the toilet. Then she ran out the door, blood pooling in her neck and burning her lungs.

This time she turned left, toward the Strip, away from the Park and the Tin Locomotive and the other children, who were still pursuing her in a stunned, locust-thick mass, crying, "Kill her! Kill her! Kill the witch!"

She ran past ULTRA MAX and further up the Strip, in the direction of the highway onramp, where, it was said, in earlier eras, travelers had come and gone. She ran under the underpass and across the cracked lot of the abandoned motel with its MO--L sign, VA---CY written underneath, and through the bushes, across a wasteland of culverts and tall grass and the skeletons of ancient dogs, then through a moat of puddles and finally through the mist and into the Meadows, to which she had surely earned admittance by killing Sullivan.

The shrieking of the children behind her ceased as soon as she crossed over, and now she could hear nothing but a *shhhhhhh* sound, like the whispering of spirits.

She pressed her hands into her thighs and leaned forward to breathe, trying to slow the pounding in her neck. The air was clammy and it smelled like flowers left too long in a vase. She gagged as a shadow passed through her line of sight and she looked up, into the withered face of a man in loose jeans and a Champion sweatshirt. He pinched a long droopy cigarette between yellow fingers, and Casey was sure his teeth, if he had any, were yellow too. He smoked slowly, coughing between drags, watching her.

When his cigarette was done, he ground it under his heel and said, "Mornin'," and retreated into the fog. *So that's who lives here*, she thought, scanning the fog for others like him. But there was nothing to see aside from a slight movement in the distance, perhaps that of the same man disappearing.

Cold and discomfited and thus eager to keep moving, she wandered through heavy cloud cover, past corner stores and bars and movie theaters that all looked like half-developed photographs, faded to bluish gray in the background, far-off-seeming even though they were probably close enough to touch.

A few more grown-ups lurked as she passed, smoking or clutching coffee cups, some of them leafing through newspapers whose pages fell to the ground and sopped through as soon as they landed.

♦

Nothing else happened until she got hungry. She'd quickly finished her fruit snacks and granola bars and realized she'd have to find something more. She had the feeling that ULTRA MAX, even if she could find it, would no longer operate on the honor system, and she had no access to money. She had to pee as well, so, after vainly searching for something to crouch behind, she dipped into the fog and took her pants down and squatted, feeling steam rise between her legs, a momentary reprieve from the cold.

As she stood back up and adjusted her pants, she began to hurry, hunger merging with cold now, and fear, not of anything specific, perhaps, but fear nonetheless, a rushing in her guts, a sense that standing still was no longer a good idea, if it ever had been.

In time, she made her way back to what appeared to be the cluster of buildings she'd passed earlier, and went in through the ringing door of a diner, where she found an empty table. The fog penetrated in here as well, the grayness, the somber cold, and she remembered that she had no money, no plan for when the bill came, but she ordered nonetheless, a burger and fries and a chocolate shake.

The bun was soggy and the meat crumbly and partly frozen, as were the fries, and the milk in the shake tasted off, but Casey gulped it down. As she did, she tried to keep her eyes on her fingers clutching the bun. But she couldn't help looking up, across the diner, through the fog and into the eyes of… Sullivan?

She looked down, at the mess of runny ketchup on her plate, but she felt his eyes on her, burning. She had to look up again. Back into Sullivan's eyes, sitting at a table with a crumpled newspaper covered in napkins. It wasn't exactly him, she thought—he looked old, and worn out, and unwell, like he'd begun to molt but stopped partway—but it *was* him, too. Somehow. It was too much like him to be anyone else.

She tried again to focus on her fingers clutching the slowly shrinking bun, but when she next looked up, Sullivan was looking down at her. He cleared his throat and nodded at the seat across the table, either asking if he could sit there or telling her he was about to. He settled in, put his elbows on the table, a few inches from her plate, and looked without shyness into her eyes.

"I know you," he said.

Yeah, I killed you when we were kids, Casey thought, but said nothing. The idea felt old, like something she'd heard too many times to still ring true. An old Church legend that only idiots believed.

He reached into her plate and took a fry, watching her watch him eat it.

She pushed the plate in his direction, done with it, and wondered what to say. Shrugging, she finally said, "I don't have any cash. Can you spot me?" Her voice sounded strange, twisted somehow, raspy. She swallowed, determined not to speak again.

Sullivan mashed a handful of fries into his mouth with one hand and leaned forward to peel a limp twenty from his pocket with the other. "Good seeing you, I guess," he said.

As he stood up, he scratched the line where his hair gave way to his bald spot, and Casey could've sworn she saw a locust crawl out of a slit in his scalp. She blinked. By the time she looked back, Sullivan was pulling his knit winter cap over his ears.

She got up as soon as he was gone, placing the twenty under her water glass without waiting for change and pulling her shirt tight around her sides as she prepared to face the fog. The bell on the door dinged as she pushed through it.

As she looked back at the diner, she shivered with déjà

vu, a sense of familiarity attaching itself to the place in a way she wanted to dismiss but couldn't. The feeling that she'd spent years and years here, eating at this diner because it was the only one in town, was both too vivid to ignore and too vague to comprehend. She tried to walk away and soon found herself running.

After she'd run herself into exhaustion, another period of slow wandering commenced, with only the dim, flickering bulbs of streetlights to orient her. The ground underfoot was soupy and uneven, and there was no difference between street and sidewalk. Occasionally the neon of a Shell sign came visible, always distant, always dim. No matter how hard Casey tried to walk in a straight line, she couldn't shake the sense that she was walking in circles. The Neighborhoods—if they were now her destination, if she was already homesick enough to return in defeat—seemed equally likely to lie in any direction. The Meadows felt all-pervasive, effortlessly occupying the entirety of what was now the world.

She knew she'd get hungry again before long, and would thus need to find her way back to the diner, where she'd have to find someone else to lend her money if she didn't see Sullivan again, which she hoped she wouldn't.

Then the Tin Locomotive emerged from the fog, inches from where she stood. Its cold metal stopped her outstretched hands, and she leaned against it until she had to look up, into the fog, deafened by the sound of locusts pouring from the sky.

She staggered away, shielding her face, until a bench cracked the backs of her knees and she had to sit down. She looked over and saw an old woman beside her, balling up a loaf of bread and throwing the balls on the ground. "I know they're not pigeons," the old woman said, with a chuckle, "but I like to feed them anyway."

Casey stared at the whitish pellets accreting among the brownish locust bodies, and remembered Sullivan as a boy with his head cracked open and stuffed with wings, and again as a man with a single locust peeking through his bald spot, and she wondered which world these images belonged to. *Whichever it is*, she thought, *I guess it's the one I'm in too.*

She looked over at the old woman, feeling herself to be equally old now, and said, "Mind if I throw some with you?"

The woman smiled and tore off a hock of bread and handed it to Casey. "Not at all. Not much else to do before Church, is there?"

Balling the bread between her fingers, Casey shook her head. "No. No, I suppose there isn't."

They both sat like that until the dimness got dark and their bread was gone. Then they wandered toward Church together, two old women who'd spent their lives in the town where they were born, dreaming sometimes of other futures and other pasts, but not too often. Only on cold nights when, alone in their big houses with their TVs on in the dark, they found they couldn't get to sleep.

Nights like tonight will be, Casey thought, as she and the woman joined the crowd of grown-ups on the Church lawn, waiting in the shadow of the Sick Sequoia for Sullivan to open the door.

When it was time, they found their way in together and took their places among the cracked pews to wait while Sullivan pulled the dirty white cloth from the tape recorder and pressed PLAY.

The grown-ups live in the Neighborhoods, the children live in the Meadows, the tape began, with all the grown-ups reciting along.

The grown-ups are thoughtful, mature, responsible; the children are stupid, greedy, violent. We have managed to overcome the shameful instincts of childhood in order to arrive on the enlightened plane of the Neighborhoods, where we live as adults in peace and harmony, but we must remain ever on our guard against the incursion of evil, sex-crazed children from the Meadows, where God has banished them to wander in the cold and the damp and the dark, as reminders of what we all once were, and might one day again become, if we ever….

Casey recited along, afraid of being seen with her mouth closed, but her mind was elsewhere, reeling with the hauntedness of the Church, and of the streets, and of the Park, and of the cold kitchen where she'd cook tonight's dinner if she found any food in the cupboard, and the empty crowdedness of all these familiar locations, the only ones she'd ever known, with their unease of spirits superimposed, the way they made her feel like she was in both places at once and thus, sickeningly, in neither.

CIRCUS SICKNESS

Friday

"The circus is in town! The circus is in town!"

Everyone was shouting this on the first day of the summer of 1991, so loudly it took us awhile to realize we were shouting it too.

My friend Corey Inch and I—I don't call him my best friend, as he was my only, and is no longer—were the first children to join the grown-ups streaming in line behind a jester in green tights with bells on his cap. He must've come clanking in along Bridge St. specifically to round us up.

We fell in with the procession, leaving behind the video store where we'd spent all our time since school let out on June 16th, handling movies like dormant rattlesnakes, praying some of their power would rub off without killing us. We were nine now, so we'd seen a lot—it was the summer *The Silence of the Lambs* came out on video—but the jester with our whole town behind him was something else.

The procession kept growing as we crossed the square with the shuttered cinema on one side, the diner with its taped-over windows across from it. Grown-ups emerged from the auto body shop and the payday advance store and the shell of the Dunkin' Donuts that had technically closed more than a year earlier. They streamed out of clinics and offices, parks and restaurants, and now other children were joining in, streaming out of the candy store and the ice cream parlor, making so much noise it sounded like a disaster was underway.

All of us—even Mayor Dodd, even our teachers, even our parents—followed the jester up Bridge St., through the outskirts and the dead zone after the outskirts and under the interstate underpass, past the abandoned motel, toward the swampy meadow where the circus was setting up.

I can still hear the dark, negative sucking as all human warmth and energy left our town. It sounded to me, as we all streamed toward the circus, like our town was popping.

As we emerged onto the soggy land on the other side of the underpass, we saw generators and tents and trucks parked everywhere. Giants, midgets, men with tattooed faces and women with wispy beards were milling around, pounding in stakes, stringing up canopies, leading lions and apes and a tremendous elephant from a series of trailers into a series of cages.

Corey and I hesitated as the procession streamed around us. I looked at him, trying to hear what he was thinking, and was disturbed to find I couldn't. It was like we'd entered a forcefield that was shooting waves of static through the mind we'd shared since we were little.

"Corey," I whispered.

"What?"

He sounded exasperated, so I didn't reply. But as the crowd forced its way past us, I was afraid we'd be trampled if we stayed put.

"C'mon," I finally said.

The mime and the lion-tamers went about their business as we crossed over the rest of the way. They observed our arrival without extending themselves to welcome us or making any effort to hold us back. *As far as they're concerned*, I thought, *the two of us are the same as everyone else.*

We began to wander freely after the jester merged into the general crush of people, his bells inaudible among them. As we inhaled, we grew dizzy on the breath of the animals, the exhaust of the trailers, the sweat and perfume of the men and women and those whose gender we could not determine. It was all bleeding together, clouding our shared mind and making us reel.

We wandered in this state among the people of our town, watching as they scarfed caramel apples and cotton candy, giant slushies and sno-cones and sodas, as we would have too, if we'd had any money. They whooped and skipped along. Some parents held hands with their children, but we could tell they were losing track of their roles, meeting each other on some level where they were all free to do as they pleased.

A woman sang in a foreign language on a stage under the Ferris wheel while a midget cranked a box that produced a scrappy tune, and there were grills covered in steaming meat and tents with big, smelly men in front, their nipples hanging out of their tank tops. We considered everything, soaking in the atmosphere, trying to quiet our longing to return to the video store and our slow, steady process of becoming great directors by handling the tapes and praying.

Now it seemed all that would have to be put on hold. *But the circus too is fodder for movies*, we thought, or I thought and hoped Corey was thinking too. *Here, for now, is where we're meant to be. All we have to do is soak it up. When the time is right, we'll be released, better off than we were before.*

It had become late afternoon, the sky rich and heavy.

"Yeah, we're summering here this year," we heard a man on stilts lean down to tell an elderly couple. They looked deliriously happy to be talking to him. "We winter down in Florida and come up this way once it gets warm. Depending on how things go, we could stay till October. Or take off as soon as August, go as far up as Nova Scotia. It all depends on...."

We left before we learned what it depended on, wandering over to a bench at the edge of the grounds, beside a row of puddles too deep for anything to park in. Sitting down, we closed our eyes and tried to see this meadow as it'd been before today, the cold, dim swamp we'd always heard lay on the edge of town, just before the highway, which led, depending on whom you asked, either to No-Man's-Land or to the Land of Opportunity. But the lights of the games and the rides and the clatter of the singing midgets refused to fade, and we found we could not daydream our way beyond it.

So we got to our feet and fished a tub of fries from a metal trashcan and went to explore the rides—the Viking Ship, the Teacups, the Tower of Terror, Cleopatra's Dream, and the light-studded Ferris wheel.

The crew was still plugging wires into generators, testing seatbelts on straw dummies, and screwing together the pieces that must have been detached during their long trip from Florida, wherever that was. Our image of the outside world was, at best, an inkblot, so all we could picture was the flotilla of trucks drifting off the highway and under the underpass, coming to a stop in the meadow when the puddles got too deep to drive through.

We tossed our fries and sat down on another bench, and would've sunk back into daydreaming had a sweaty man in a tank top not taken a seat beside us. He was the kind of man who looked both fat and strong at the same time, a gold chain around his neck, its pendant lost in chest hair. He belched, yawned, and looked us over.

"You kids from here?"

I froze, but Corey, always the bolder one, nodded definitively. A little defiantly too. Like being from here gave him some class.

The man lit a cigarette and blew smoke in our faces. "Thought so. But you're not like the others." He gestured at the crowd of frolicking, yipping children and their parents. "I can tell. How old are you boys? About eighteen?"

I laughed. Corey nodded, sitting up straight.

"Thought so."

Then he was silent a long time and a quiet terror passed through me at the possibility that he was serious. Like, wherever he was from, this was how eighteen-year-olds looked. Or, scarier, that inside the circus there was a disconnect between how people felt and how they appeared, so we really did look eighteen now, the way our grandparents, before they died, used to say they still felt twenty. Or, scarier still, that time had passed here without us knowing it, and now our whole childhoods and adolescences were gone, and here we were, two guys on the verge of their twenties without having accomplished anything or even having had much fun.

"Since you're not out there dicking off, I take it you two are thoughtful." He finished what he'd been smoking and lit another. "Meant for bigger things."

I looked over at Corey, trying to gauge how he felt so we could present a unified front.

"Here." The man handed us each lit cigarettes, forcing our attention back onto him. We felt the filters burn our lips and gagged a little and fought to keep from gagging more. He didn't laugh this time, just watched us smoke, impersonating eighteen-year-olds as best we could.

"Name's Ghoulardi, after the kids' show. Popular before your time. I'm the king of this little circus. It's not much but, as they say, it's mine." He paused, shifting gears. "You two wanna help out? Bag trash, sweep sawdust, stock condiments? I pay room and board."

I only noticed how dark it'd gotten when I again tried to read Corey's expression and found I could barely see his face.

We stalled.

"Let me tell you the truth about towns," Ghoulardi went on, filling our silence. "They're all the same. You guys don't know that because you've only lived here and you've had a helluva lot of thoughts here, but take it from me. I've seen enough to know." He looked out at the crowd and sighed. "We show up somewhere, draw you out, bring you together, let you feel like more than yourselves for a while. Like you're special. Like the buck stops here. But it doesn't. The buck just keeps moving on. That's the truth about towns."

As he got up to leave, the terror of being stranded here, alone and with no money and nothing to do, chilled us. The other children swarmed in the background, whooping, their mouths full of candy, and our old houses seemed impossibly distant, lost on the far side of a glacier that only grew colder the more we pictured it.

"Okay," we said, almost in unison, despite the static in our shared mind. "We're in."

Ghoulardi smiled, putting a hand on each of our heads. When he took them away, he rubbed his palms together, lit another cigarette, and said, "Great. You start tomorrow. And one other thing… I'm gonna dress you as clowns. Paint your faces. I don't employ civilians here. Kills the mood."

We left the bench a few minutes after he did. Now the circus was lit by paper lanterns on strings hanging across the walkways and a few spotlights on high poles. Everything looked orange, like we were inside a jack-o-lantern, and the faces of the other children and the grown-ups were shadowed and strange.

Unsure whether to rush through the night or draw it out as long as possible, we continued to wander, picking cotton candy from trashcans, visiting the Porta-potties, and watching teenagers kiss behind the generators and scream as the Viking Ship knifed them up and down.

The vendors at the candy apple and the dart-gun and the beer stands stared past us, straining to discern the young women of our town, including Mrs. Redding, the English teacher we both had a crush on.

Eventually, everyone processed into the central pavilion, but we stayed outside. We could already tell that our position here was peripheral; what bound the others to this circus didn't bind us. We could hear the *oohs* and *aahs* behind the canvas flaps, and imagined flying trapezes, rings of fire, the elephant rearing up on its hind legs to juggle with its snout. We knew our parents were in there, along with the parents of all the other children, transfixed, determined to believe that Monday would never come.

We stared so long the barker outside snarled at us and shook his coin pail, so we wandered to the edge of the meadow, where the circus' ring of light ended, and hid behind a pickup truck.

When the show let out, we watched the crowd drift by, laughing, yawning, swigging beer from plastic cups. They passed us and disappeared in the direction of the underpass and the motel beyond it. Since it was too dark to see, I imagined the whole horde of them seeping into the motel like a school of fish into a reef.

When they were gone, we went back toward the center of the circus, where the mime and the strongman and the bearded lady danced while one midget cranked the music box and another bowed a saw. Ghoulardi sat on a stool, smoking and, I'm pretty sure, crying a little.

It got late. It was already normal-late, like 10PM, but soon it was scary-late, like 2AM. A time we'd never seen before, when, we'd always assumed, the teenagers and grown-ups went out on the town, watching the pornography hidden behind the Cult section in the video store basement, and drinking vodka, and doing heroin in the park.

When we couldn't keep our eyes open any longer, we returned to the pickup truck we'd hidden behind earlier and curled up in the back, bedding down amidst a pile of shovels and duct tape.

Saturday

We woke up on cots in a trailer with thick bodies in hammocks above us, dripping sweat into our mouths. Navy blue sheets were hung over the windows, blocking out the sunlight, and a dog looked us over when we stirred.

We got carefully out of our cots, which were marked 'New Clown 1' and 'New Clown 2,' and went to the doorway to look out at the circus in daylight, squinting through something caked around our eyes.

"Morning," said Ghoulardi, appearing from behind a curtain to hand us each paper cups so hot we dropped them, scalding our toes. He laughed and motioned for refills. These we took more carefully, forcing back tears as the skin on our feet puckered. We sipped from the top of the black liquid, richer and sweeter than anything we'd ever tasted, and watched as the lanky mime rehearsed in the shadow of the yawning elephant.

When we were done, Ghoulardi took out a barber's mirror and held it up so we could see the makeup job he must've done on us in our sleep, after moving us to the cots: our faces were bone-white except for red circles on our cheeks and chins.

"Here," he said, handing us each red foam noses.

We put them on while he found us floppy shoes and baggy pants with suspenders. They were far too big, meant as they were for eighteen-year-olds, but it went without saying that they'd make us more endearing until we grew into them. As we practiced walking, our motions turning clownish by default, he took our old clothes and shoes and said he'd put them where they belonged. We understood that this meant he'd throw them away.

Now it was time to work. He showed us how to muck out the elephant's slop bucket and refill the water pail so its trainer could focus on bigger issues. Then he showed us how to make sure the concession stands had enough paper cups and napkins and that the hand-sanitizer in the Porta-potties never ran out and the trashcans didn't overflow. He said we could take a lunch break at noon, then it would be time to refill the ketchup, mustard, and relish before the dinner rush, which could start as early as four.

We worked all day, not talking much, trying not to think much, either. All around us, we saw a mix of people we knew and people we didn't. They were blurring together, growing less and less distinct. By dusk, we barely recognized Mayor Dodd as he passed by nuzzling a large stuffed pony he must've won in a shooting gallery, his face sunburned and streaked with sweat.

Somewhere in all this, we knew, our parents were making the rounds with their friends, taking in the sights, probably looking back on when they were younger and what the world had seemed like then, before they'd had us. Perhaps they were remembering this meadow and the circuses that used to stop here, similar to this one, but, in some way they surely understood better than we did, not the same.

We put ketchup, mustard, and relish bottles on the counters of all the concession stands and emptied the trash into huge bags as the lanterns came on and the familiar lights of the rides started flashing, and everywhere long lines started to form.

After we finished the evening's chores, Ghoulardi filled our hands with tokens and gave us the night off, saying not to get used to it, that for us the circus was real life, not the recess from real life that other people paid to pretend it was.

"Still," he said, "I like to ease people into things. Don't mean to burn you clowns out the first night."

So we took our night off seriously. We rationed our tokens, sharing a burger and a chocolate shake and a caramel apple, its flesh as soft and brown as its coating. We played the darts game twice, winning nothing, and we rode the Teacups and a green, snake-shaped rollercoaster that chugged up its tracks very gently, designed, as it was, for children even younger than we were.

After we got off, we were standing on the damp grass catching our breath, our hands on our thighs, when a jingling startled us. We'd been planning to go back to our trailer, saving the rest of our tokens, but it was impossible to ignore the sound, and then the sight, of the jester dancing by, hopping on one foot and leaning way over to that side, then switching, back and forth like a wind-up toy.

Powerless to resist, Corey and I followed him away from the rides and the food and the game stalls, across a dark, swampy patch of meadowland toward a distant glowing sign that read ADULTS ONLY, same as the sign on the door at the back of the Cult section in the video store basement.

By the time we reached the funhouse, the jester had vanished. Whether he'd gone inside or into the deeper dark beyond we couldn't tell. All we knew was that, having come this far, we couldn't turn back. So we took out the last of our tokens, put them in a bowl outside the door, and shouldered it open. It creaked on its hinges and admitted us, and there was no bouncer or guard to stand in our way.

So there we were, creeping along the slanting floors, through the hall of mirrors. The air got thick, like it was full of grease, and a strobe came on overhead, making us feel like we were spinning. Maybe we were. We closed our eyes until a crowd of people caught up with us, pushing eagerly into the dark.

"This is where the brave show their true faces," I whispered to Corey, as we made our way down a hall of rotating floorboards, toward a doorway painted like a giant, slavering mouth. The jaws opened with a whoosh when we got close, and I pictured us diving down the throat of some ancient beast.

The thing on the other side looked like a giant skin heap, a body with no center, no heart, and no brain. The crowd behind us immediately mixed itself in. It took a while to see what it really was: grown-ups, completely naked except for bull and cow masks over their heads, crawling around on the floor, making wide circles, nudging each other's butts with their horns.

In the center stood Ghoulardi, done up in white and pink face paint. He wore a white wedding dress with a giant foam erection attached to his waist on a harness, and he was making loud grunts, laughs, and groans through a bullhorn, his head tipped way back, his free arm swinging in the air like he was orchestrating the climax of a movie we were years away from being allowed to see.

We were frozen where we stood and I thought, *somewhere in here is Mrs. Redding, naked as we've only ever imagined she could be.* Time sped up, whipping past us like wind in a blizzard, and I was on the verge of passing out when Ghoulardi shrieked, "Now!!!"

The grown-ups squished together, rubbing and squeezing each other's behinds with no space in between, making weird, low noises through their masks. Their horns were locked, their backs arched, their bodies indistinguishable. They seemed like they couldn't stop now, even if they tried.

We made a run for it, tripping over them in our clown shoes as we went. The only thing that mattered was that we got out, back home if possible, out of this circus, which we didn't like anymore.

As we ran, trembling and confused, I panicked and looked back. Trying not to stare at the grown-ups, I locked eyes with Ghoulardi. He looked straight into me, his gaze sad and clear through his makeup. Then he looked abruptly away and I knew he was giving us our last chance to flee.

So we flew through the doorway on the far side, which was painted to resemble an anus. It whooshed open and spit us out into a throbbing, blue-tinted chamber where the air smelled of perfume and more naked grown-ups sat on benches, toweling themselves off and drinking from plastic cups. They glanced at us but didn't say anything.

For a moment, the feeling of danger abated and it seemed we'd made it to safety, but then a moan from the other room electrified us again and we were back on our feet, shoving desperately toward the EXIT sign, forcing it open with all our combined might.

We fell through and landed on our faces in the gas-soaked woodchips outside.

"No time to rest," Corey murmured, so, despite the pain, we got to our hands and knees and then to our feet, facing the dark, assuming our town must be somewhere in that unlit distance.

We hobbled as fast as we could away from the lights and the noise, until, just as we were passing the last row of generators, a pair of hands grabbed the backs of our necks and pulled us off our feet, carrying us like puppies into the back seat of a parked car.

When we were settled, Ghoulardi got in front and turned on the interior lights, staring at us through his melting makeup. He was as out of breath as we were, his foam erection bunched in the seat beside him, the straps of his wedding dress down around his elbows.

"You guys live here now. Get it? There's no point trying to run because there's nowhere to run to." He sighed and took a swig from a flask that hung from a chain around his neck. He didn't offer us any and we couldn't find the courage to ask.

He looked like he was about to cry. "I was hoping to have this talk later. Years later, maybe. But you guys had to go in there, so… I guess that means you're ready." He tipped out the last drops and let the flask fall.

"Do you know what entropy is? It means wearing out. It's what's happening. It happened to your town, and it'll happen to this circus. We're like a giant animal that's returned to its birthplace to die. I'm from here too, you know. This town. Same as you guys. I didn't want to tell you yet. I'm not a well man, but I made it back. I had to. You'll never know how much that took. Remember when I said all towns were the same? Well, it's true and not true. They're all the same except to the people from them. I knew guys like you. I was the same way. Still am, if I'm honest. Only difference is I got out and made something of myself. But so what? One day I'll be gone, and when that day comes, I want my body to end up here. Not out there. I'm not saying that day's coming tomorrow, or even this year, but it's coming. And I need you to be ready. None of the other clowns, not the strongman, not the mime, not the trapeze artists… none of them know what it means to be from here. So I'm leaving the keys to you."

He took out the car keys and jingled them, staring at us to see if we understood. We tried to seem like we did, afraid the night would only get worse if he saw that we didn't. He smiled, clearly relieved, and said, "Now let's get you to your trailer. It's back to work tomorrow. No more nights off for you clowns."

Thereafter

Sunday came and went. When Monday arrived, no one left the circus. Not one child or grown-up. Every morning that week, they streamed forth from the motel across the street, desperate for the abandon of that first weekend to go on and on and on.

And, in a sense, it did. This was the beginning of the long haul, the years that passed in the meadow. Soon, even the idea that the circus could leave—that it was a fundamentally mobile enterprise, with a population made up of visitors rather than citizens—was forgotten.

Our parents were lost among the ranks of wandering grown-ups, many of whom still wore their bull and cow masks, their hair and beards growing long underneath. Whenever the masks came off, they seemed like strangers, gaunt, creepy, skulking around, spending less and less money once they realized they had no way of earning more, except by gambling or stealing from one another.

We'd see our parents and teachers occasionally and they'd mumble, "You okay?" and we'd nod, and they'd pass on.

As we went about our business, endlessly refilling the napkins and the ketchup and the mustard and the relish, we dreamed of the town. We pictured it sighing, in loneliness or relief, now that it was empty. *Surely*, we thought, *it must be turning strange, becoming whatever towns become when they're no longer anyone's home.* Sometimes, as we daubed off our makeup at night, we imagined that a new population had made its way in, settling in the old houses like explorers who'd come across the ruins of a lost civilization.

As time passed on this new scale, the grown-ups began to die. They were buried in the swampiest parts of the meadow, where the trucks couldn't park. We stood on planks, watching as bloated bodies were lowered into pits the strongman had dug in the night, our heads bowed, mumbling along to the liturgy sung by the bearded lady.

Our parents must have been somewhere among them, but they were so changed by then we couldn't tell. This was surely for the best, as no good could have come from seeing them in that state, their faces wracked with guilt at the turn their lives had taken, the ease with which the homes they'd worked so hard to build had slipped away, and the secret relief that letting them slip away must have brought.

And Mayor Dodd—I remember when he died, and was dragged to a place of honor in the center of the marsh, on a wooden pallet that was tipped vertical until he slipped off and bobbed, refusing to sink, even when the strongman weighted him down with a tire. Corey and I left the funeral at Ghoulardi's command, along with the other bystanders, while the strongman kept working, doing whatever it took to make sure the body sank under and stayed.

When all the grown-ups were buried, a new cohort took their places. This included Corey and me and the others who'd been children when the circus arrived. And all along, of course, people had been breeding in the funhouse, so babies came, and were cared for, welcomed into our order, brought up in a world made solely of circus.

We were in our thirties now, and then our forties, doing the same things we'd done for well over twenty years, instead of the other, equally repetitive things we would have done in our thirties and forties had we stayed in the town, or moved to another one, or even to the city. Our clown costumes, once so loose, were tight now, ripping around our bellies and thighs so they hung off us in ribbons.

New shipments of frozen fries and burger patties and candy came in once a month, on a truck that stopped at the edge of the property. Ghoulardi said all we had to do was sign the invoice.

Eventually, it stopped delivering meat. Now it brought only popcorn and Junior Mints and Sour Patch Kids, so we took to calling it *The Candy Truck*.

As the rides and games wore out and eventually shut down, the graveyard became the main attraction. We'd go out there whenever we had a free moment, eating a tub of stale popcorn or sharing a beer if we could find one in the back of a fridge, watching other people do the same. We all fought to keep our balance on the planks over the muck, scanning it for skulls like carp in a fishpond.

Strolling the graveyard in the lengthening periods between chores, Corey and I discussed the town, especially the video store, the dream of making movies. We kept our voices down, unsure if the topic had become taboo.

Now movies, like circuses, seemed superfluous. We felt nothing but longing for our boring, slow life in the town, the grind of school and home and Friday nights and Sunday nights and summers and winters, and on and on, the grind we'd dreamed of escaping, and that we had escaped, and now dreamed only of somehow escaping back into.

One day in what I'd guess was our mid-forties, when Ghoulardi must've been close to eighty—it was amazing he'd made it this long, withering steadily without yet giving out—he lurched over to where we were sitting and pointed toward his car with his cane. We nodded and followed him, getting in the back seat where our meetings were always held.

"Look, guys," he said, wheezing. "You know what I'm about to say."

We looked at each other, then at him. "That you're ready to die and for us to take over?" Corey hadn't lost his boldness over the years.

Ghoulardi nodded, devolving into a coughing fit. Then he reached into his pocket and found the keys and held them out to us. Corey looked away, so I took them, smiling as reassuringly as I could.

"You are Ghoulardi now," was the last thing I heard him say, to both of us or just to me.

As I remember it, he died immediately thereafter. We followed the jester onto the planks and watched as the strongman shoved him under, our heads bowed, the sky gray above us, the mime miming tears.

When the burial was complete, everyone looked at us. Clearly, Ghoulardi had told them the deal. I fingered the keys in my pocket, wondering if there'd be mutiny, violence. "We're going for a drive," Corey announced, before I could reach any decision of my own.

"C'mon," he whispered, nudging me in the ribs.

So we got in Ghoulardi's car. I put the keys in the ignition and drove us, very slowly, across the meadow.

I wasn't sure we'd make it out; part of me feared a forcefield would intercede, or the strongman would appear in front of us, threatening to flip the car. But before long I was driving us under the underpass, past the motel, and up Bridge St. It was my first time behind the wheel of a car, but the road was so straight all I had to do was tap the gas with my clown shoe. And, of course, there was no traffic.

We drove in silence through the dead zone and the outskirts and into downtown, past the video store, the *Silence of the Lambs* poster peeling off the front window, past the ice cream parlor and the shell of the old Dunkin' Donuts and the place that sold secondhand children's clothes, their roofs sagging, covered in guano and black leaves.

It felt like a sunken town, like one of those towns flooded to make a reservoir. Rats and pigeons roamed the streets and trash blew into the old interiors wherever doors were open or missing. I tried to remember how different it had looked before we all left, but found I couldn't focus on this while continuing to drive.

At Corey's direction, I chugged us up the hill we used to live on and parked on the street between our two houses. I wanted to stay in the car and look at them from here, just long enough to refresh our memories, but Corey undid his seatbelt and got out. I watched him go, then got out too, locked the car for some reason, and walked over to where he stood.

Now we were side by side, staring at Corey's old house, our backs to mine. It seemed truly haunted, frigid with inhumanity, a house no longer capable of being a home.

Our shared mind, if there had ever been such a thing, was silent.

"C'mon," I said, when it felt like we were on the cusp of standing there too long. I jingled the keys, at first subtly and then loudly, desperately, like a charm I could only pray would work.

I remembered Ghoulardi telling us about entropy and

shivered with the fear that it was coming for us now. It felt like a reversion was imminent, like we'd lose everything that made us who we were if we stood there any longer.

But Corey wouldn't budge. I could feel myself losing him even before he spoke. "No," he said. "This is where we belong. I don't know how you could forget that. No one's making me leave here ever again."

He patted me on the shoulder, like there was something he knew that would take me years and years to learn. Then he walked off, bending to pry the key from under the Welcome mat, and he let himself in, back into his old house.

In the days since, I've often wondered which I'd prefer: the notion of him losing his mind amidst true, utter aloneness in there, or that of him falling into a fellowship of revenants and outcasts wandering the streets, living a sham version of small town life, or even something close to the real thing, looking back on his years in the circus as a period of youthful indiscretion he was glad to be done with.

I can see neither possibility very clearly. All I can see is him vanishing through that doorway, not turning to regard me, simply letting the dark and the cold swallow him up. In my memory, the door blew shut on its own, sealing him in, though in reality he must have turned to close it.

By then I was back in the car, drifting down the hill in the direction we had always walked to school in the mornings. I drove that way now, past the school, its main hall like a caving-in waxworks, and onward, through the black bowl of the central square. I paid it my respects and moved on, toward the pulsing lights of the circus in the distance, the Ferris wheel looming over everything though it was half-sunk in the mud.

♦

By the time I made it back, the jester, the mime, the midgets, the bearded lady, the strongman—everyone who could—had left, taking the trucks with them. I noticed, too, that the elephant had died. With no one to haul it out and bury it in the muck, it lay in its cage like a beached whale.

Now, everyone who might have called me Ghoulardi was gone. I was alone with the dead-eyed children, weaned entirely on candy and soda, immune to whatever charm the circus had held. Some were already the children of the children born here, conceived on the same sticky funhouse floor as their parents.

They scared me. I didn't like being among them, defenseless against their staring and their hot, sickly breath, their long tongues grained with sugar. So, after a night locked in my trailer, wondering if I had it in me to drive back to town and find Corey, I reached a decision.

In the morning, I rolled out of my cot, put on my clown nose and makeup for the last time, took the key to the elephant cage from Ghoulardi's old office, and traipsed across the grounds. I luxuriated in the walking as I went, stretching my legs as much as I could.

When I got to the cage, I unlocked it, slipped in, reached through the bars to re-lock it, then threw the key, and the car keys with it, as far as I could, watching them land in a puddle by the candy stand.

Then I sat down in the musky woodchips, in front of the carcass, to plan my routine. *I'll do it every night*, I decided. *For whomever shows up.*

At the end, I'll reach my hands out for candy. And if they don't oblige, I'll simply die here, like the elephant, like Ghoulardi before me....

"But the thing you guys don't know," I hear myself say, to the sparse crowd assembled before me at dusk, "is that there was a town. Not that far from here. Just up Bridge St., actually. I'm from there. There was a whole world outside this one. It only sounds like a joke when I say it now."

The children's laughter makes a faint crackle. I watch them slug soda and tip Sour Patch Kids down their throats, choking as they laugh, wiping their eyes and noses on their sleeves.

I have to admit, it sounds pretty funny. I wish Corey could see me now, commanding an audience.

"And in this town," I go on, emboldened, "there was me, and there was Corey, and we went to school, which was a room where they wasted our time, but the great thing was we were free to daydream. They couldn't keep us from that. So Corey and me daydreamed about movies, which were basically daydreams made into black boxes. We had a shared mind in those days, we were completely on the same page, and in our shared mind we shared the dream that, one day, we'd make the greatest movie of all time, so great it'd remove the need for anyone else to ever dream again, because… because…."

I lose my train of thought. I'm dizzy and confused until something hits me in the face. I look down and see a Sour Patch Kid lying in the woodchips, red and oblong. Grinning at the children, I do a pratfall and, lying on the ground, begin to nibble the candy.

More follows, at first just a few pieces, then a steady barrage, raining over me, more than I can get in my mouth. Candy lands in my hair, my ears, my eyes.

I come up to my hands and knees, chewing as fast as I can, and crawl toward the bars, mouth open. Here I begin to nibble straight from the children's hands, laughing as they laugh. I feel their fingers on my tongue, between my teeth, stuffing sugar down my throat. All I want is for this to go on and on and on. For the notion of the town to remain as powerful as it is right now.

And I want to stay crouched like this, flaring my nostrils to breathe, with the source of sweetness inexhaustible and well within reach, the laughter warm and enveloping, the crowd riveted on Corey and me, both of us speaking through my mouth now, united and indivisible and forever young.

A heavy silence pulls me out of myself. I look up. The children have stopped laughing. They're standing on the other side of the bars, licking their lips. Some put their hands to the metal and I can tell that, in a few seconds, if I don't go on entertaining them, they'll start shaking the cage. I picture myself and the dead elephant in a pile, woodchips covering us both, the bars digging into my back.

Carefully, I get to my feet and force myself to focus on dredging up more to say. I close my eyes and try to picture the town, to remember what it looked like, what it actually contained beyond the video store basement.

"And one day," I go on, "one day, our dream came true. Corey and me, well, you see…."

The flood of candy returns. Soon I'm back on my knees, my face at the bars, telling the story of how our dream came true, how we made our movie and how great it was, the greatest ever, how we lived full lives in the world and only came back here at the end to die, and right now, deep inside the laughter, I feel like I have it in me to believe what I'm saying, and there's nothing but joy in the knowledge that everyone who could've said otherwise is gone.

HOUSESITTER

Housesitter left his last family and moved on to his next, a man and woman in the northern part of the state who had engaged him to look after their house with their son Josef in it while they were away in Spain.

When he'd first taken up his profession, almost ten years ago, he'd moved around only in his own city, from one district to another, at first just from one street to another or even from one house to another on the same street, among families he more or less knew. But inevitably he'd started moving among the suburbs, and then reached the point of moving among towns, sometimes crossing wide swaths of open country from one house to the next, traveling a loose but effective web of word-of-mouth. He was now in among people whom other people knew but whom he himself could not until he was already inside their houses with them.

He packed all the things he had stowed in the last family's house, in their closets and cupboards, and the clothes he had hung on their hangers, among their clothes, and brought them onto the highway and across the state to the new house, on the new street where Josef, who was seven, lived with his parents, who were leaving. He had written the address, beneath the word

"Josef," in a monthly planner that he checked again and again as the taxi from the bus station drove him down the street. He was checking it still when the front door of the house opened and the parents said, "Welcome, Housesitter," and ushered him in.

He was so tired he wanted to go right up to bed with his clothes piled on a chair blocking the door. But he knew he'd have to stay downstairs to hear the parents tell him everything first, all the phone numbers to call in case of all the things that could happen, and the nuances of the schedule they'd bound their son to.

He went to the bathroom to shock himself awake with cold water and remember that he could always pretend he was already asleep and dreaming in the guest-room bed he knew was waiting for him at the top of the stairs. He was so tired he couldn't remember whether he'd been this tired on the bus and in the taxi down the street, or if it was only hitting him now, after years in abeyance.

He dried his face and returned, ready to look like he was listening.

The parents showed him the cupboards where the dry goods were kept, and the door to the basement where the brooms hung—"Junior," the one with a plastic handle and yellow bristles, "Senior," the one with a wooden handle and yellow bristles, and "Moe," the dustpan.

"One of our babysitters," said the mother, "name of Vangie DeWardner, fell headlong down these stairs, end over end like a boulder, and was found in a heap at the bottom with two of her ribs broken up into one another so that at first the paramedics thought it was just one rib that'd broken and swollen to the size of two." She made sure he was listening. "And it wasn't just the impact of the concrete bottom that broke her up," she added. "It was each individual stair, one after another after another. Relentless."

She seemed very intent on his understanding that this story had to do with the particular flight of stairs they were now standing at the head of, and not another flight, unseen in another place. Nor was it a story about stairs in general. He wondered what it was about him that made her doubt whether he could grasp this.

The father trailed behind with a pad of paper, making notes. "A pharmaceutical company gave me this pad of paper," he said, barely audible at the back of the procession. "At a conference. But you can ignore the dosage information and the long chemical names that adorn its borders, because all that we need you to know is the information that's written mainly in the center of this pad of paper's sheets."

He had a pharmaceutical pen, too.

They kept going through the house. Housesitter's feet dragged like his shoelaces were caught on something in the previous room. He would not have been surprised to observe himself falling obliquely onto the carpet, his face cushioned from the shock of impact by the slow motion of sleep, his nerves shutting gracefully down before he landed. He could not tell how surprised the parents would be.

"This is where Leon Garment, a film-club friend of my husband's and not the most beloved member of our community, spilled nacho cheese on the carpet, and then tried to wipe it up with his shoe, not understanding that this is actually the sort of thing that makes something worse," said the mother, and stopped to show the shoe-shaped stain. "It made us realize the value of stains," she continued, "of keeping rather than erasing them, so as always to remember what has happened in the places where things have. But now we're not sure. This is one thing we're going to discuss on the veranda in Spain. We are planning to reorient our life, so when we come back it'll be like the first time. It'll be our second chance, but we'll be so far inside it it'll seem like our first, which, really, a second chance must if it's to be a real one and not just a 'second chance.' We will stand before this house upon our return, with our bags in hand, and say, 'What do you think, honey? Shall we settle in this one?' 'Yes.'"

He could feel sweat running down his thighs when he put his hands in his pockets. The inside of his belt was steaming and he knew how it probably smelled. He looked at the mother talking, the father writing: it was easy to tell there was something furtive, guilty about her; with the father, it was harder to tell.

The father put the pad on top of the TV and picked up a plastic crate of travel guides, sighing like the weight hurt him. The mother held these up one by one, explaining how they had auditioned and rejected each possible country before deciding on Spain.

"Malaysia," she said, holding up the Malaysia guide, "upon further research, turned out to be not quite what we had been led to believe. We felt a tiny bit betrayed by this book."

She pressed herself back into her husband and he leaned in around the crate, reflexively kissing the back of her ear.

Housesitter looked away. He'd been in similar moments with other couples on the nights before their departures, though he'd never been this tired. While he was looking away, he tried to regroup. "This is all just par for the course," he whispered. "The part of the job before the good part."

"This is the slot where the mail falls from," the mother interrupted, pointing at the front door. "It can fall very quickly and startle you, so be on the lookout throughout the afternoon and well into the evening."

She paused to let this sink in, then went on. "This is the closet, which we call the 'Front Closet,' where my husband, who used to have a sleepwalking problem, used to pull his pajama pants all the way down and pee on the shoes." She stood now in mimicry of her husband's former problem, perhaps taking a moment to imagine how it might feel to have a penis.

"The shoes are now clean," she said.

Then she said, "Please don't look away. You come very highly vetted, but we need to know for ourselves that you're right. It's not too late to call things off.

"This is the couch, for example," she went on, pointing to a futon under the windows, "where a political canvasser was once invited in, off the doorstep, for a glass of iced tea, but then requested rum, without having been offered rum, and our son, who knew where the rum was kept and was home alone at the time, went to the cabinet and got the rum and, when we came home in the evening, we found that this man had drunk the whole bottle of rum and had spilled his leaflets, here," she scratched at an area of the floor with the toe of her slipper, "and our son was back upstairs, so this political man was drunk all alone on the couch, and could not be roused until morning. And we never found out his name." She looked at Housesitter with concerned eyes, her expression loaded with a kind of objectless empathy.

He realized this was the first time she'd mentioned the son, and was fairly certain that if he asked to meet him now, or asked even what the boy liked to eat and do, he'd be shushed with a tone that would communicate the opposite of *ask us that again in a few minutes.*

She led the way back into the kitchen where they'd begun, showing him the hook by the door that held the car keys, then pulling open the blinds to point to the car they were leaving him to use in the driveway, then opening the drawer under the phone to show him the envelope of spending money.

He tried to picture the room where the boy lived, directly overhead no doubt, as they sat in the kitchen, the mother grasping for words to convey their loathing of rotten lettuce in the crisper drawer and their method for avoiding expired milk at the shop, where some cheaters were employed.

The mother warmed turkey soup on the stove while the father sliced the end of a loaf of rye in three, and put the slices in the toaster oven, and got out butter and a jar of fish in water or brine. Housesitter pushed aside the pharmaceutical pad to make room for his bowl.

He watched the deepening colors settle in around the kitchen windows, spilling out the last of the blue across the hanging plants behind the dishwasher. His eyes wanted to sink down into the center of his skull like two cherries in a bowl of gelatin.

After a few bites, his shoulders and elbows fell slack by his sides, his spoon resting on his knee under the table. The mother said how important the vacation was to her and her husband, and therefore how important it needed to be to him, because he was now part of the family, even if only temporarily. "Things have just reached a point," she said. "And beyond this point, for us, lies Spain, and for you… well, here you are."

She'd changed her voice in such a way that it felt both like she was trying not to wake or disturb someone, and also like she was trying to mask the sound of something she didn't want to be heard.

"We are packing a kit of prophylactics," she continued, "because we want it to feel as though we are at the beginning again. We will go through all the motions that starting a family involves, without this time bearing those motions' consequences."

All Housesitter wanted, as he peered at her talking with his head nearly in his soup, was to call them a taxi for the airport right now and force them to get in it. Again picturing the boy upstairs, he professed to understand what he'd been told and asked if he could please go up to bed.

In the guest room at last, Housesitter thought about tomorrow, when he'd move into the parents' room and begin to sleep in their bed.

The guest room was where he always started, in all the houses. Always the same pastel sheets and blanket half-folded at the foot of the bed and pillowcases with yellow stripes or a border of green ivy or pink hearts.

The room and sheets were cold. After the parents leaned in to whisper goodbye he began to hear low, elongated screams, filtering between his body and the sheets.

The screams filled first his room and then every room, like a gas leak. He closed his eyes and pictured the father's pharmaceutical pad fluttering off across the kitchen floor and away to a place where it would never be found, taking with it all the instructions he'd been given.

He drifted in and out of sleep, staying in bed until the screaming died down. Then he put on a bathrobe and walked downstairs, through the living room like a boy coming down on Christmas morning to find his presents piled up in the dark. His bare feet clenched at the tiles and the grout between them as he filled a glass with water at the kitchen sink.

He heard soft footsteps as soon as he turned off the tap. A girl in a blue nightgown came into the kitchen and stood in the doorway, looking at him.

He looked back at her as she went to the sink, took another glass from where it was drying, and filled it. Then she went back to where she had stood and took a long sip from the surface as the water that had come out white turned clear.

When she finished, she put it next to the sink, again to dry, and sat down at the table. The two sat together very quietly until he got up and asked her what she'd like for breakfast, and then poured two bowls of cereal and milk and sat back down, pushing hers into reach.

As they ate, she said, "I crept into the bathroom and unwrapped a German blade. I was in there for hours, doing it. They thought I did it before. That's why they tried to escape. But I waited until they left. I was very patient."

He looked at her again, preparing to accept the fact of her. When he had, quieting whatever alarm he might have felt, he asked her name. "It's Johanna," she said, like no one had ever asked her until now. "I knew you were here when I heard you snoring in the guest room."

"Hi, Johanna. I heard you last night too. Screaming."

"That wasn't me," she said. "That was Josef. Now he's gone, off to be quiet."

She finished her cereal. "He had to go. What about you?"

He was stuck on an image of the parents high in the air, feeding each other pretzels with the rest of the world and everyone in it five miles below, under a layer of cloud solid as ice. "I just got in, from another town. I'm here with you now," he replied, shaking it off. "In this house. Just the two of us."

Johanna got up from her seat, put her bowl next to the sink, and came back to the table, taking the other seat now, on his left, while he stayed fixed in the middle.

"Do you think we should go up and have a look at that

bathroom?" he asked her. "To see if it's all clean?"

"It is. I stayed in there all the rest of the night, working. I went down to the basement and got the whisk broom and the cleaning bottles and everything."

"But I heard screaming all through the night."

"This house is sticking up from the ground and straight into the world. You can hear almost anything that's going on." She shrugged and looked up, toward where those things were surely going on still.

He looked over at the drawer that held the kitchen knives, guessing how long it'd take to grab one, if it came to that, and if it'd do him any good.

He wanted to ask, *and there's no one in there now? No one buried, or stuffed away?* But he didn't. He asked, "Have you taken a shower yet?"

She looked at him like she knew there was another question behind this one. "You mean as myself? To wash off what I did?" Her voice was almost accusatory, like he was the one who'd done something.

"No," he said. "Just to get ready for the day. Let's go out somewhere, get lunch, walk around in a place you like."

She stayed next to him for a further moment, then nodded and went upstairs.

He went to the parents' room and was in there when he heard her shower start. He stood very still, waiting until the water got warm.

He was aware that she was naked now, and now covered in soap. He picked up the parents' clothes hamper and was about to take it across the hall and into the laundry room, but didn't. He looked down at the dirty clothes, recording the last few days of their lives, and then poured his own underwear—

yesterday's underwear, from the long bus journey—on top, and his socks and undershirt on top of that. Now, also naked, he walked over to the dresser, opened a drawer in the middle and looked at everything in a row, folded and fitted exactly to the rectangular space. He opened the other drawers, feeling their cold polished wood against his thighs, looking at himself from the waist up in the mirror that reached from the dresser to just under the ceiling. Behind him he saw the bed, where, he decided, the child had been conceived.

Just after noon, Sunday, they went out.

It was the last weekend of November, the pane of days that obscured Christmas growing clearer by the minute. They left the windows of the second-floor bathroom open so that clean air could drift in, easing southward from the Arctic and upward from the earth.

Though the day was mild, each wore a winter jacket and enjoyed wearing it. Housesitter had taken a long red scarf from the downstairs closet and wrapped it around his neck, and Johanna had taken a scarf from her room and wrapped it as well, and they each wore a pair of gloves and a hat, to pretend it was already late December, the days dark by three in the afternoon.

He drove them into town with the spare keys he'd taken off the hook. They looked everywhere for a binder of CDs but couldn't find it, so they turned on the radio and it played Johanna's favorite song.

He asked Johanna where to park in town, and she told him. Flyers for bell choir and choral concerts clung to the streetlamps, which were already on, filling the dark afternoon with an especially romantic glow. Two boys rang a Salvation Army bell, and two girls rang another across the street.

This was to be their one day in the open air, out of the

house, browsing in all the stores, the joke stores and the clothes stores and the toy store with a nearly full-sized stuffed horse peeking from a stable, and a model train set called The Santa Fe Howler, which chugged out of sight into a model tunnel and returned a long time later, on the far side of a model mountain.

The bakeries all had fresh cakes and cookies for the new season, filled with almond, ginger, and cinnamon, the smell of baking butter filling the narrow streets.

They drank Mexican hot chocolate in a café, nodding benignly to other children and their parents, and Johanna smiled and said she felt like there were a few days off from school coming up, like Winter Break was here early. He smiled too. There was woodsmoke in the air, new books on the shelves of the bookstores, and tables laid out with shining piles of cards and calendars for the new year.

They held hands and looked at the posters for the new movies that had come to the two-screen theater, and at the posters on the windows of the video store for the movies that'd played there before. They filled a plastic bag with comedies and cartoons from the 99-cent bin, like there really was a long vacation coming up, or an unbroken chain of snow days, and they bought fudge and peanut brittle and butterscotch at a store called The Emporium, where they also bought chamomile tea and cocoa mix and mini-marshmallows.

Cool evening surrendered to cold night. They got back in the car and drove home, picking up Indian food on the way, and went indoors, closing the bathroom window now that fresh air had come in, and ate with all the lights on, even in the rooms they had no reason to enter, and then they watched one of the comedies from the bag. It prolonged the feel of the day, but then it really was night, and there was no way to warm the house, not with dessert or hot chocolate or tea.

So they went upstairs, each to their own room.

Just before this, they had unpacked the sweets, arranging them in the cabinets and cupboards of the kitchen, which already smelled sweet from the dried fruit and boxes of cookies that had been in there before. They also unpacked the other parts of the day, putting moments from it on top of the tins and in between the boxes, so that in the future when they reached for an Oreo or a cluster of caramel popcorn, they'd come away with a piece of this time they'd spent together, hand in hand in the waning afternoon.

He spent the night in the parents' bedroom, having moved his suitcase in there from the guest room. His clothes surrounded theirs in the hamper, and his Right Guard stood next to the mother's Speed Stick and the father's Old Spice on the ledge atop the dresser.

He slept for several hours at a time, among their sheets on the big bed, but the house and the driveway and the front and back yards, and all the trees and hedges, stayed up all night. They started to change, taking on personalities they hadn't had before. The sticky sugar treats in the cupboards lay open, their plastic wrappers peeled back, as a tongue came into the house and reached out to lick them.

Over the course of the first week, during which they stayed in bed as much as possible, only coming downstairs to eat candy and smile at one another in high daylight, Housesitter found the parents' room less and less amenable. He swam in their huge barren bed, staring at the mauve ceiling as he listened to the tongue scuttle and whisper downstairs.

Finally, one night while Johanna slept down the hall, he got up and carried his pillow into an empty bedroom with a bed shaped like a truck, smiling faces painted into the wheels, and a poster of a smiling hammer climbing a pile of trash that stretched up to the moon. He'd passed this room many times before without working up the courage to open the door.

Opening it now, he believed he'd feel the tongue's presence less in here, maybe just because the bed was smaller and he could fill more of it by stretching out, or because it felt like a boy's room, not a weird older couple's. As soon as he closed this new door behind him, he knew he'd never go back into the parents' room, not even to gather his suitcase. He was amazed he'd slept in there at all, or even tried to.

In the morning, relieved, he awoke and came downstairs and had his glass of water, and then Johanna came and had hers, and then they had their cereal, also with water now that the milk was gone.

Thus began a period where they stayed indoors all day and played card games and board games, and rewatched videos they had just seen. Never before had time been spent so freely, nor had there ever been so much of it.

These were the days of socks on thick carpets and smooth wood floors, all-day pajamas and lying on stomachs, heads propped on elbows, moving plastic figures across boards that charted battlefields and lives wound along a pastel path. As they played Monopoly one night, Johanna picked up one of the green plastic houses and asked, "Which one would you live in, if you could?"

Housesitter looked at all the houses, spread across the board, and the others still in their plastic baggie. "They're all the same, aren't they?" he finally said.

Johanna shrugged and smiled, making it clear that she knew he knew they weren't.

Now Housesitter always slept in the truck-shaped bed. Some nights, though less frequently than when he'd slept in the parents' room, the sounds in the house still woke him.

On one such night, exhausted by the effort to sleep, he went into the bathroom and ran the bath. While the tub filled, he went out and stood naked in the hall, by the door to her room, which he'd never entered and never would. He kept very still, the wallpaper sticking to his back. To wake her now would be to catch her before she was ready, when she wasn't quite herself. If they couldn't meet in the morning, with the night behind them and the day ahead, she would become a stranger to him, and he to her. The question of Josef would return and the plank on which they stood together over a long drop would tip and fall away, and then they wouldn't even have each other for company.

As he listened at her door, he heard: *never quite empty… people too, feelers… bed… see and or, discern… grip… came over or called to, and… she… in its fingertips that… because she… and it would… and, in time, him, too.*

He went back into the bathroom where, he'd been told, Josef had left this world. Blind in the steam, he fingered the box of German blades in the medicine cabinet. Then he turned the lights above the sink as low as he could and turned on the fan, dribbled a little Epsom salt into the bath, and heard her voice whispering on, as loud in here as it'd been in the hall, as if the steam were conjuring her.

He sank into the scalding water, peeing and nearly biting his tongue, and lay back, turning on the jets, smelling the steam, closing his eyes. *If it comes for me in here*, he thought, *it will have been in the place of my choosing.*

He slumped down, easing into memories of all the baths in all the houses since he'd taken up his profession, since before he'd heard much in the nights, before he'd unnamed himself, and he wondered where in his journey he was, if not at the very end.

Toweling dry, he dabbed his groin and armpits with talcum powder and walked down the hall and back to the truck-bed room.

He turned on the light on the nightstand, shaped like a miniature streetlight, and took a pile of comics from a drawer. He knew that Johanna was still whispering, but, spreading the comics around his body on the mattress, he resolved not to listen.

He tried to read aloud, but soon lost his voice. It sounded ragged, like he'd been shouting over something, and his ears hurt. Maybe water from the bath had seeped in. He pressed at his earholes, at first gently and then with anxious force, but it only brought him further from equilibrium.

He could feel the tongue again, breathing up from under the bed, panting, as far from sleep as he was. Legs hardening into a tangle, he tried to lie very still and let its breath dry away the last of the bathwater.

It was whispering, or perhaps shouting against his stopped-up ears, echoing Johanna down the hall while adding what she could not know. He could tell that the truth about Josef was there in the room with him.

He could neither grasp it nor tune it out.

He decided to close his eyes but found they were closed already. The effort to close them again wrenched them open.

His spine, pressed deep into the child's mattress, vibrated along with the tongue directly beneath, and he looked up at the dreamcatchers that Josef must have made at school or in an afterschool program. Now nightmares were streaming freely through them.

The effort to sleep became oppressive.

He stood up, shedding comics, and saw the mistake he'd made in assuming he could sleep off the rest of his time in this room.

He made as little contact with the floor as he could manage until he was out of the tongue's range. After catching his breath in the hall, still pressing on his ears, he resolved to force his way back into the parents' room and from there face what was in the house, or was coming, as a man, not a boy.

He lay back in the parents' bed, stretching out as if to convince the sheets he'd never left, drying the parts of himself that the towel and the truck-shaped bed and the comics had missed.

He looked at his suitcase, which he'd left in here all this time, and felt both glad to see it again and suspicious of what its role might have become, now that his traveling days were over.

He thought about Johanna and the time they still had together, in this house, and the fact that, during this time, they were free to indulge in the feeling of living here, truly here and not just provisionally so. He came close to sleep but still couldn't get the rest of the way. He rolled around in the sheets until he grew dizzy, then got up again.

He opened the parents' bedroom door and walked back into the hall. It wasn't hard to hear her shuffling from the other direction, though her toes barely escaped her nightgown.

Each recognized the other, but, for a second, because it was night and dark and they were only half-present, each looked away. Then they looked back, and he offered her his hand, and she took it. She knew where the window was, how to lead him there.

It was a long walk. The wall stayed solid a long time before opening, as if for the first time. When it did, they stood before the window, looking out at the street, where cans and leaves stirred, and sacks of garbage tipped onto their sides. He squeezed her hand tight enough to feel the German blade flat against her palm, clean and ready.

After a while, a delivery van passed by, on its way to the small college a few streets over.

Then more nothing.

Then, as the first blue of dawn was starting up, a black town car appeared, its headlights in full blare. Johanna's hand tensed as they watched it cut through the leaves and garbage, its lights dimming as the morning grew brighter.

Then it was gone. Housesitter fixed his eyes on the blank window, but couldn't keep from imagining the town car in the driveway, the parents spilling out.

He could picture them coming inside, as so many sets of parents had before, leaving their luggage in the trunk for now, or letting their driver, if they had one, unload it for them. They'd take off their shoes and catch their breath in the kitchen before venturing upstairs.

When they found him in the hallway, they'd say their thanks, proffer their money, and then it would be time for him to go. In the life he'd lived until now, this was how it always ended. But today, he could sense, pressing his palm against the German blade, nothing like that could be allowed to happen. There was no next house, and so, if the parents dared to come up here, if it came to that, then he'd release Johanna's hand and close his eyes, waiting a good long time before opening them again.

LIVING BOY

In snow so thick each could barely palp the other, a woman and a boy stood side by side at the property-edge of a cottage neither had seen before, beside a motorcycle that had just finished crashing, waiting for its gashed-open rider to die. This was the one time they would stand together with nothing between. It was 1988, the biggest blizzard to reach this part of Colorado since the 19th Century.

They stood in poses of familiarity, like they knew they'd been meant for one another, this first meeting fraught with the relief of reunion. Mother and son together at last.

They shivered and danced at the knees. She wore a robe and held it tight. This was their middle moment, paused as if in wait for a long-abandoned house in winter to get warm after arriving at midnight and turning on the heat.

The property extended away from where they stood for an unknown or unfixed while. The man beside the motorcycle lay on his face. The gash in his side streamed forth in welcome. The back of his leather jacket spelled ṬARKOV in white thread lost in the falling snow.

Last words in a language they could not grasp escaped his mouth.

Those words finished, the air turned.

Committing to memory the shape, the sized blur of the other, they went in opposite directions, Laura Selwyn into the cottage, Fritz into Tarkov.

Something was almost there, before his eyes, on his back, across the millennium lip in 2008. A blizzard was coming tonight to exceed that which had overflowed the night of his arrival, bridging a twenty-year lull.

Fritz sniffled, sucked down sour, turned over inside his shell so he was facedown, his back to Tarkov's face, his face to Tarkov's spine. He was the size of a boy and also a molecule, Tarkov the size of a man and also a mansion. Fritz could fill almost all the space he'd been given, stretched thick in a stiff sleeping bag, or he could fill almost none, miniaturized in unlit depots, trains rolling in after two in the morning, grease-headed passengers pressed against unshaded windows, looking out at piles of rubble and factories with letters falling from their flanks, street signs in a pile, home to all the scavengers of Kiev.

He yawned, scratching the surfaces around him, agitating the wreckage of the dead mind he inhabited: the summer steppe, Tarkov at nineteen. A farmhouse, a family at ease around a broad unsanded table with benches on two sides, bowls and platters in the center, high seats for the patriarchs at the head and foot, bottles making the rounds.

Tarkov was out in the meadow behind, his place set, his bowl untended and losing steam. He had taken the two-man worksaw from the shed, dragged it on the ground through the wheat.

Sufficiently alone, the wheat cold and sharp at that distance from the family meal, he took it upon himself.

Its teeth ground into his skin, redoubling the noise of insects grinding.

It was clumsy, meant for two, but he worked it. The image lingered inside him of cutting down an unused wooden structure, something built long ago and isolated now in a field whose home had moved away. He would cut it down like an old tree.

He pulled the saw across himself and pushed it back, amazed at how much skin he had. He knew it would take a long time, and that it would not be pleasant work, but grew surprised at how long, how unpleasant.

It came clear that it would not end this way. There was progress only toward adornment, not conclusion. He was tattooing his insides, carving channels with the worksaw, new courses and grooves in his physical self like the surface of a record, but he would not die that night in the Ukraine in 1978.

The cuts instead revealed something that, if not quite fate, was energy, and a map, going in a direction. Something geometric in which he was a corner, to and from whom lines to others would connect, the whole shape carrying such charge that he could not pull away.

So he stole an uncle's motorbike and peeled off to Kiev, never taking his seat at that unsanded table.

The worksaw had, though Tarkov never saw it for what it was, described the shape of the gash in his side that the blizzard would cut in 1988, like a mark on a patient in preparation for surgery.

A decade later, riding alone through the Rocky Mountains, the blizzard coming on all around him, Tarkov closed his eyes and saw himself onstage, as he would be, or would have been, later that night, in the Superdome in Denver, on his first and soon to be last American Tour. He shrugged with a surge of adrenaline, aggression, ambition, TARKOV embroidered in white on his leather jacket, pulled taut with motorcycle speed, doubling the thickness of his hide, smoother than a man's back should be.

He leaned, like he had all along the mountain and desert

roads of Eurasia, all through the Urals and the Caucasus and across the plateau of the Ukraine and up the Bulgarian coast ten summers running, building his name from nothing to something with a shadow, but this time the ground was an inch closer, rising with the snow, and it tongued his shoulder, enough to flip him off and over the wall of the path he'd been cutting, and to skid and tear across planes of ice, as the edge of the sky reached out sideways to slash into him, deep and wide enough for Fritz to fit through.

He came to rest in what, thereafter in history, would serve as winter garden to Laura Selwyn, who would stand nearby and watch him in death, housing the boy she had for a moment stood beside, and with whom it would then be her lot to live.

Laura Selwyn came out at dawn, 2008, to see the snow she'd heard falling from her bed last night.

It had fallen so hard it covered the body. No visitor to the cottage would have begun to perceive that she did not live there alone.

She stood on her porch with the shovel, dusting the snow around her feet, debating whether to uncover the body or leave it under, as if the snow were earth and had been called to bury it forever, as it had the motorcycle, twenty years ago.

She had her big boots on over her socks under her nightgown, and a heavy coat over that, its hem down to her ankles. She was by now well into middle life, beyond the span of anyone she'd known or expected ever to know.

It went on like this another minute. She was not mistress of her own schedule but it—that which she could not renounce, though she wouldn't call it God—would permit her to linger a while longer. She imagined the body swallowed up, leaving her alone from now on. She wanted, tried, to feel gladness at the opened plane before her, the room for breathing, but felt only the tragedy of abandonment, of too much space and too little person.

So she hurried to uncover it, digging faster than on other mornings not only because the snow was thicker but spurred by the fear that her passing wish for its absence had been taken up, and that she would find nothing but densening snow the deeper she dug.

There, eventually, it was. She could feel sweat running down her fingers inside her gloves, making them heavy.

She would turn the body over to avoid bedsores. Smiling under her wool head-covering, she put her foot where the handle was screwed into the shovel's bowl and worked it under the body's belly. It slept—spent its nights—facedown in the humble affairs of its planet of origin. Come sunrise, she'd flip it onto its back, to face what was beaming down from above.

Wills for mercy and torture competed to govern her use of the shovel. She chose the middle path, shoveled without much abrading the skin though not without nicking and, across the forehead, scraping it.

She likened this flipping of the body to the turning of an hourglass, setting the new day adrip.

Now her face and its face had nothing but cold between them. She looked down at Tarkov's scars and beard, his frostbitten neck and broken nose, the teeth that remained jagged in the gums and stuck through the lips, and saw, in the eyes, the animate presence of Fritz within, and knew he could see her.

She went to fetch breakfast, came back carrying a bowl and a cup, both steaming, the bowl more so because it held plain porridge, the cup less so because of the milk in its coffee.

Kneeling, she spooned a few drops of one onto the lips, waited for them to sink in like water on the dirt of a plant, then spooned a few drops of the other.

She pictured Fritz bunched up birdlike near the mouth, sucking down the spoonfuls that would take him through his day. Some of what she spooned in leaked out the gash in Tarkov's side, but not all of it, she was certain.

Now she wanted to speak, to ask Fritz how he had slept and what his plans for the day might be, but she resisted, seeing in such urges signs of a loneliness-madness that she wanted for as many years as possible to keep, at its closest, confined to her outer edges.

Diverting these urges, she looked out at her property through the morning that was turning bright, at the fallow field and the rocks halved by snow. This had all come with the cottage, but, she told herself, had grown over time. Had grown *as* time, time accreting like roughage over a farm gone to seed, roamed over by half-feral animals that humbly bred, died humbly under such cover as they could find.

It was a twenty-year field.

The year, as she knelt there with the shovel, catching her breath and smelling bread that would soon be ready, was 1988.

No, it isn't anymore, twenty years have fallen on top. She scolded herself, like she'd gotten confused again, or like someone else, her daughter or granddaughter, was scolding her in hopes of bringing her back to sanity. Perhaps the time for such confusion, for the blending of times in preparation for when all times would be one, was upon her already, and the time to do the thing that had been hers to do had long since gone sweet with rot.

No, she thought, swatting such worries away. She cleared her throat and got a hold of herself. Then, gathering the bowl and cup, she turned indoors from the body, its mouth steaming with sunlight.

♦

Bread taken from the oven, somewhat burnt, and coffee

cooked—she had always loved that phrase, *to cook coffee*—and poured, she sat scraping black knots off the loaf with a butter knife, piling them on the tablecloth.

Time, for now, was hers; there was no squeezing fist on the day. A faintly perfumed steam filled the air as the snow she'd tracked inside on her boots began to melt onto the rug in front of the fire, where, in the evening, she would lie and stretch her ligaments. This mixed with the bread smoke, seeking the chimney.

There was nothing on, neither television nor radio nor even a dishwasher or digital clock. A space heater was the one exception. There were outlets, but they were free. The cords of several appliances—microwave, iron, toaster—she kept rolled up nearby, their teeth in tiny bags, to be used for brief minutes at a time. It wasn't silence she wanted, but other sounds, buzzings that rose up when the air could accommodate them.

Out her window, she could see the broad, fallow field. 1988. The fact that it'd come to her this morning stayed with her now. She could see that she would have to use part of her day to float back to the convent.

First, though, she would plug in the telephone. Whenever she thought of 1988, she thought of Tarkov—not in death, as she saw him day and night, but in life, the living, singing, crusading man. She had ordered his audiocassettes from a distributer in Iowa, all four of his hit records in their original Soviet-Pop editions, and paid by credit card, but they had yet to arrive. She called, asked when they would come.

"They are coming," she was told.

"When?" she asked.

"They are in the middle," she was told. "In a great middle, coming your way by truck."

She hung up the phone, unplugged and bagged it.

The convent, Summer of '88.

She was there now, lying on her bunk with three other sisters listening to the gasps through the wall, where one of them was Taking Her Turn in That Room.

It had been the same mountains then as now, but she remembered then as always summer, hot and bright and dry and piney in a way she could only call Tuscan. Like that whole part of her life had been summer, and this whole part winter.

Days at the convent were spent on the terraces surrounding the one-story structure where the nights were spent, attending to chores with a marked and encouraged slowness.

There wasn't any leadership that announced itself.

She and her sisters passed the time, singing if they felt like it, or working the grounds and gardens, fruits and vegetables, making honey and citrus liqueurs. She was, as long as she wished to be, in charge of lemonade.

Then one night, for each of them, came Her Turn in That Room. They were virgins until then.

When her turn came, she could order anything she liked for dinner and the other sisters would take the vehicle with tinted windows down the steep private way to the access road to meet the delivery van, and pay from their savings.

She would then unload the paper bag with all of its sub-containers and eat right from them or transfer their contents to a plate, or any number, however many she liked, and she could drink a little, if she liked, and then it would be time for her shower, and the sisters would abate.

They would be gone into their bunks by the time she came out, wearing a bathrobe made ceremonial in light of the way it would soon be opened. Thus clothed, she would enter That Room and find the bedding still warm from the dryer, a dryer sheet balled up amidst it. Even the curtains and rugs would seem fresh and dry.

Laura Selwyn tried to open her eyes in her cottage in 2008, to turn from this next part and elide or creep out of its way, or say to it, "How about a light lunch instead?"

But no. There was a daytime reprieve in the blizzard now, between two nights of it, and there was nothing in this reprieve, for Laura Selwyn, to spare her the reminiscence.

She'd known on that night in the convent, when her turn had come, just as she knew now in her cottage, that something was coming, only didn't know it consciously. She treated her conscious mind like another person, an infirm mother or grandmother, not to be shaken or upset, to be whispered and euphemized around, while the rest of her, the majority, sat long and quiet with the truth of things.

Her takeout meal, Greek, reached the convent, and plastic plates and forks were laid out. The sisters stood in a silent quorum as she ate, forestalling their own dinners until morning, when they would eat and she would not.

She knew they were watching her, as she had so often watched others, one at a time over the years. She tried to eat at the same rate and in the same way as ever, trying not to taste the change on her fork, but she did taste it, it and nothing else.

Then she was in the shower. The hot water was so dizzying it gave her to wonder if something had been laced through her eggplant. She listened to the shampoo dripping and foaming, performing the sounds of her thoughts, which focused on people stuffed to bursting with themselves, being borne away to give birth, and, in so doing, die. Each sister, after Her Turn in That Room, left to carry herself through to term, descending the steep road to Denver in the vehicle with tinted windows, and being left to deliver her there, and there to die, and be born, and live on, anew, partially sensible to what had been, and then one day, as a girl or young woman, to return to the convent.

If the baby were born a boy, a different orphanhood would unfurl before him.

Theirs was thus an eternal life in patches, sewed and taped together, full of whistling seams, but it was sturdy, full of itself against extinction.

This was what the sisters meant when they said, *she's gone to Denver.*

When Laura Selwyn stepped out of the shower, she found only a towel and the robe, her clothes gone, down a chute.

She was in That Room now, on the made bed.

She decided to explore, though she could see everything from where she sat. As she returned from her exploration, she started to gargle, feeling the ventricles in her throat that would soon make the sounds of her pleasure or pain at Taking Pregnant By No Earthly Means.

It had gotten later, the lights dim like they'd been primed to reflect the change outside, evening into night.

Her sisters listened through the wall. There was something else in That Room with her now. Opening her robe, she lay back on the bed.

Her voice began to tremble, not in a scream, closer to song.

It was a private song, almost a hum, in a language she did not know.

She saw, heard, in it, that other bodies would be moved tonight, strewn with her into a common shape. She was only part of something, a node or corner at most.

Her voice picked up, louder and louder, like steam issuing from her throat, corroding the sheetrock wall to reveal a patchwork of pressed up ears, overlapping into a sheet of mottled skin.

It—the thing she had been taught to call God but now found she could not—was with her now, absolutely, unambiguously. She could feel it as it worked in her mouth counter to the more conscious flexion of her tongue, and as it spread her robe open wider and enjoined her to *be still, be still, let me do my work.*

She heard herself singing about how she would flee this place though outside it had turned to winter, all the snow that'd snored in the high reserves of the sky falling as one, to smooth and conceal her way across the great middle.

Her eyes broke, glassy and all awater. They filled with a scene of a racing motorcycle and a running boy under the slit sky, darting, covered not in blood but in a biology flowing from her.

They harmonized. Each sang its part and together roughed out a melody.

She had all the towels upon herself now, struggling against it, forcing its seed out and onto the sheets. Something was broken; something had snapped. Doubt was everywhere now and she felt wet and sick and confused, certain only that it was time to run.

Surprised that she could still move, she tore herself from the bed and dashed out of That Room.

Wrapped in her robe, the convent showed itself to her in emptiness. The sisters were gone, stowed in closets or under loose floorboards, watching in disgust or awe as Laura Selwyn left behind forever the site of her defilement.

The blizzard covered the convent.

Nothing but white and steep all around, gigantic drop-offs into strange other worlds. She ran. Out of breath, groping through middle air as white as ground and sky, sticking her hands as far out as she could in prayer that some guide would take them, she pressed on into the backcountry. The lights of Denver in the distance rendered some of the flakes more orange than others.

Fritz, barely-conceived yet already half-born, was in this too, fighting his way toward her.

Together they plied the graven course of Tarkov's demise, the tracks of his wheels still fresh in the snow.

Laura Selwyn arrived first, and knew to wait. She relished what she took as the end of the past.

Then Fritz stood beside her while the body finished its preparations, their tiny family made and broken in the same moment.

As if for the sake of modesty, an obscuring haze escaped Tarkov's side as the boy made his way in, to incubate for twenty more years.

In her kitchen with bread all around her in 2008, Laura Selwyn returned to her present self. The fallen snow out her windows had taken on the blue of pre-sunset, rolled out low onto the ground, the sky switched off until it opened with more blizzard in an hour or two.

It was time for a warm shower, then to see what she had in the freezer or in cans for dinner. First, as a comedown from extremity, she let boredom have its turn with her, settling into her chair beside the space heater to wait.

Unsure if she'd eaten or not, showered or not, tried or not to nap, Laura Selwyn came down her back steps an hour later with a tray balanced in one hand and the shovel over her shoulder.

As she walked around and around the body, Fritz could hear the reverberations of her footfalls in the snow. *Leave by dawn*, they said. *Save yourself.*

She knelt to settle the tray on the snow, then removed a steaming bowl of tomato soup and began to spoon it into the mouth.

Fritz, supping, could see steam across the portholes of Tarkov's eyes, not bad to watch, given that sometimes at night awful things came. He tried to read his fortune in that steam. He would move quickly when released, he saw, keep his fists clenched around what was inside them and not let it dribble. There were infinite chances, for him, in this universe, but each had to be treated as the only one or there would not be. He reached up and smudged condensation across the veins of his wrist, licked it off, testing.

Laura Selwyn put the soup bowl down and took up her shovel. She turned the body over, imagining its tomatoey mouth washed clean in the snow. When she was finished, she looked for the bowl and found it gone.

So it begins, she thought. *Thick and heavy.*

A buzz worked up in Tarkov's interior on this second and final night of the blizzard.

Fritz roamed the troughs. There were glimmers down by the spine, in a solution, electric fish flashing, awakened or newly hatched. Tendrils, like dipped and hanging rags, rested on his back as he pressed his face down to where these fish swam.

They set him to spinning as they lit up his head, robbing his breath and puffing his cheeks, squeezing out foreign syllables that were not yet words.

He pushed deeper in, scattering the fish, submerging himself in the saw groove where the spine rested.

I am the one who will make it. This declaration, his first in that language, surrounded and protected him as he swam. *I am the one who will find a way out.*

Beyond the liquid he alighted on a shore he'd never had the breath to reach. He exhaled the last of the old, inhaled the first of the new. At last, after so much latency.

The way down from here was a rock slope. He had to be careful.

He held onto the far side of the spine, replacing one hand with the other when the shock grew too strong, peeling away bits of matter wedged between the vertebrae, balling them between his fingers, clues for later. Long nerves lashed at his knees but they could not hold him back or knock him down.

He traveled the grooves Tarkov had carved in himself with the saw that summer night outside Kiev, pathways through a wild park.

It got bluer. Ice floes, slabs thick and square as granite, thrown up on the banks by recent swells. Fritz came to where it was only blue, not blue anything, just cold and dim, the hue pervasive, the grooves unworn by foot travel. On this far shore, nothing had yet been used up.

He could feel the dead man's furnace flare. A surge, quickly blue then blue-green, pushed Fritz's teeth into cowering tucks in his gums, then hauled them down, stronger and sharper than before.

Ambition, of manic and non-negotiable purpose, burned the disused passageways clean. It turned itself on just as it had that night in the Ukraine in 1978, a boy alone in a field, the words and melodies cascading over each other, and survived all this time as blue, blue-green, shock, fish, and memory, sustaining the life of a Fritz that hadn't aged an inch in the twenty it'd huddled toward hatching, atingle with the thing that demanded to go on being sung.

Fritz was ecstatic. He heard the falling snow outside as fists pounding on the edges, rooting him out, demanding he go. The walls and edges displayed images of Tarkov's last night in Kiev before his American tour, all his harmonicas in their right cases, the world awaiting his arrival, and Fritz could see tomorrow's departure as the next in an infinite series. He would emerge into snow that had never before fallen on Colorado, ready to take his place in history.

Laura Selwyn and her son rode up the path in a truck that'd weathered a hard journey as the sun rose on what would be their first day in their new home. They carried a signed letter with the address and the terms and conditions.

Inside the cottage, Laura Selwyn stepped from the shower and into the clothes she'd laid out. She wore no makeup, pulled her hair back in a tight ponytail, doled balm over chapped lips.

Turning the stove down low, she saw the truck pull onto her property. She stirred her porridge, salted and sugared it. The truck pulled in further through the snow that'd fallen last night, heavier by far than the night before.

Licking a little raw sugar from her fingertips, she packed a basket of apples, pears, cured meat, the remnant of yesterday's bread, a cloth napkin, another.

It must have been a hard night for that truck, she thought.

The truck came to a stop and then Laura Selwyn and her son were standing in the yard. She couldn't see all of their faces, but what of them she could see was in good cheer.

It would not be for her to know if they'd been unloaded from the cargo portion of the truck and stood in the snow as props, or had ridden in the cab like passengers and stood now as subjects.

She looked more, saw more: Iowa plates.

The presence that had been with her in That Room returned. It might have been maddening that it was here, the root of so much, and would not speak, not even to confirm its existence or blame her for doubting it, but she was not maddened. She knew all it could have told her, and it was simple: they were here now, to stay awhile, to live as the family she'd never had, and thus it was her duty to leave.

She looked again at the next Laura Selwyn and Fritz on the lawn, standing near where Tarkov was so covered in fresh snow they could not see him.

Swallowing the last of her porridge, she filled the bowl with warm soapy water and left it to soak.

Carrying her picnic basket and a simple leather satchel, her boots laced, Laura Selwyn locked the door and bent to hide the key under the mat.

Then she walked into the yard, head high.

"The key is under the mat," she said.

The Laura Selwyn who'd been waiting, and her son beside her, were eager to enter what was now their home.

"Where's your son?" she asked the Laura Selwyn who had lived here since 1988 and was now leaving.

Laura Selwyn turned from the question, face into scarf. She'd resolved not to look at the cottage again. *None of your business*, she thought.

The driver of the truck from Iowa, who'd remained in the idling cab, reached across to open the door for her.

"I go as far as Denver," he said, adjusting his mirrors and gathering strength for the tight drive out, through all that'd fallen, along the access roads, technically closed for the season, across the cliffs that cut this zone off from all others, and finally onto the highway.

The cab was full of song, which, as they were backing out, Laura Selwyn recognized as the audiocassettes she'd waited so long to hear.

Fritz had left Tarkov before dawn, kissing the gash on his way out. Now he walked barefoot through the mountains, sometimes intersecting the old tracks of Tarkov's motorcycle, sometimes the newer tracks of Laura Selwyn's truck, but mostly cutting his own way.

He felt a voice coming up in him that he knew would be so loud he covered his ears before it came out. When it did, concussing the ice faces and the mountaintops that looked down on him, echoing, it came out in lyrics that translated to, "I'm hatched! I'm hatched! I'm ready to take my stand!"

He screamed it and sang it and felt it and meant it, felt strong and young and healthy, and sent his voice into the sky. It set forth such an avalanche that when it was over, all the former surfaces were buried, and he walked way up on a new one, on top of all that was under and past, buried farther underfoot than he could ever fall, no matter how much footing he lost, on into a future that had not yet received its requirements, coming, as they were, across a great middle from very far away.

OUT ON THE COAST

According to the Stillboro County Citizens' Almanac, re-issued with addenda every two years between 1912 and 1988, the whale that washed up on shore and came to cover most of the Northeastern Coastline in March of 1929 was between 181 and 182 miles long. All along the whale's body were caves that teenagers had carved with garden shovels, hideouts and forts gored into its sides, strands of dry muscle hanging from the ceiling like the guts of a giant pumpkin. They huddled in these caves to smoke and talk and touch, wrapped in blankets in winter, wearing nothing but swimsuits in summer.

The fact of its size, and of its seeming ability to live without food and family—for it was definitely alive, breathing heavily and flapping its tail on rare, spectacular occasion—was discussed in the coastal communities in the same awestruck but resigned way of all inexplicable natural phenomena, like the size of certain trees in California and Brazil, or the ability of certain monks in Tibet and Nepal to weather feats of focus and privation that seemed to defy the human. Or the simple, incredible size of the universe. There was nothing, in other words, *wrong* with the whale being there, it was just remarkable in the way that all being was remarkable, or maybe a little more so than that. It was what it was and people lived with it, equating it, perhaps, in their minds, with the even stranger immensity and ceaseless breathing of the ocean that had yielded it up.

The early newspaper reports, digested in the Almanac, put any question of the whale's origin to rest. Everyone alive at the time agreed that there wasn't any point in asking how or why it'd come ashore. Like a row of marble cliffs or a dormant volcano, it came simply to define the part of the country where they lived and would raise their children, aided by the tourist dollars that such an attraction couldn't fail to generate.

For as long as he was a kid, in the 1980s, Max had come with his family every summer to see the whale, or a part of it, the part they always came to see. Each family had its own part that spoke to or excited or comforted it, being whatever it was as a family. Every early July and usually again in late August, Max and his parents drove out to the coast from their inland home, stayed three or four nights in Hyckham, enjoying the famous fudge and toffee and cotton candy colored merry-go-round, and then, around noon each day, packed up their lunch and ambled out along the dunes and down to the beach.

When he was five, six, seven, and eight, Max spent most of the summer dreaming about the whale in his bedroom with the shades drawn, remembering the first visit and looking forward to the second, just before the new school year. On the night they returned home after that second visit, the envelope with the note that revealed what class he was in, and who was in it with him—the whole fate of the coming year—would be waiting.

His family's place was near the middle, with the fin a good fifteen miles up the road, where they'd go for day trips although it was especially touristy and hard to find a place to park where you didn't have to walk a long way to put down your blanket with a possible view of the thing itself, and not just of the spindly ice cream and sorbet carts that had, after restrictions were lifted in '88, fanned out all up and down the area of prime beachfront from the base of the tail past what Max, as a child, had referred to as the *whale's arms*.

On fin days, one of which per vacation was obligatory, they ordered turkey club sandwiches and raspberry soda at the Hyckham Trading Post and packed it all in the back of the car and drove off along the coastal highway, through traffic so thick they just barely outpaced the families that walked, or just barely didn't.

When they got there, he'd unwrap his sandwich and take the pickle out of its soggy bed in the deli's white paper and throw it skidding down the beach until it was covered in sand. Then he'd let himself believe that the whale pricked up its nose and smelled the pickle and the sand and the whole smell of him there with his family and wanted something from him, even then, all the way up where its head was, a hundred miles away.

Eventually, many years of Max's life passed by. The Millennium rolled over and most of the people from his past were consigned to it.

Now, he lay on a bed on the first floor of a B&B in Wyndhocken, near where, as the locals said, the whale's shoulders hunkered. He talked to his chest like it was another person in the room, his colleague or traveling partner. There were two pillows on the bed, so he put one under his head and the other over it, and lay there, a pebble between two rocks. He'd plugged in the water boiler for tea and gone to lie down while it worked, expecting the click that meant it was ready to rouse him. But it hadn't. The click had come, and he was awake, aware of the water slipping back down the thermometer, two butter biscuits in a red envelope sitting ready beside the mug. He knew all this, and was hungry and thirsty, but could not rise. These were the times when he had to call upon his impressions of the cooling water and the biscuit envelope and everything else he couldn't get a hold of to serve as a kind of mild but reliable personality, so as not to feel like no one. He tried to be gentle with himself as often as he could.

He looked from between the pillows at his curtained window, which had been advertised, like all the places on the coast, as having the best whale view that money could buy, at least until you started talking serious money.

Some towns lit their allotted sections at night, so you could sit on your balcony with a glass of wine and look out at the waves fanning through tunnels in the sand under the breathing flank. Whether or not to light it was a Chamber of Commerce decision, and in general Max had been avoiding the towns that chose to, preferring instead to sit on his balcony and just look at the sleek, black shape out there merging with the sleeker, blacker ocean, or, on nights like these, lie on his bed with the top of his corduroys open and not think much of anything, luxuriating in the rejection of each new whale metaphor as it came, pushing it back out there where it belonged, free for the taking, in a great swarm with all the others that some trolling behemoth might one day open its mouth and… but, again, this was not the way to think.

He fell asleep with the lights on, and in the morning reheated the water and dipped the teabag he'd unwrapped last night, and opened the biscuits, and then, after a shower, had his real breakfast downstairs with the couple who ran the place and wanted to discuss their daughter, who was across the country trying to make a life for herself in movies. After settling the bill, he got back in his car and drove into the morning, through a few tunnels along the coast, stopping at a scenic overlook, where he sat on the cliff railing and looked over.

After leaving the city where he'd lived since 2009, Max had spent most of a week chronicling the coast from Portsmouth to Wyst. He had a ruled journal that he entered everything into, all his sketches and notes, memories, inklings, turning it sideways when need be and drawing to scale.

He had recently been forced to accept, here in his late twenties, that all of the people he used to know were gone, and none of the new ones were doing anything to help loose the material that had been getting stuck and clingy down in his system, a kind of visceral fat that he assumed came from worry and fear about the future, or some hold the past still had on him. In fact, the people he knew in the city seemed happy enough to watch this fat clog and overtake him as they sat together through the weekend nights at apartment kitchen tables backed by sinks floating with dishes, or in bars, wondering if the night would end here or if there'd be a next venue.

"You're going to have to start being more present around the people around you," his boss, who wanted to be seen as an only slightly older, medium-close friend, told him. "The preliminary phase is ending, and you're moving into a new one, where you're going to have to start taking things on more fully. Looking at them in terms of a profession, no longer just a job. It'll be hard, but it's essential. Before you start, take a week's vacation. You could use it."

Now, mid-September, he was most of the way up the coast, remembering the whale heyday, when you could drive this road and actually see a progression of growing up along the animal's body, a whole life cycle of kids playing in the sand way down towards the tail, to teenagers sitting on radios and throwing cans around and daring each other to carve an initial into a crunch of hide, to parked lovers' lane cars at night, rocking along with the surf, to newlyweds with picnic baskets and beach reading strewn in spirals around them, flip-flops cast off but still in range, to older couples, strolling past middle age in the direction of a particularly windswept, bluff-strewn patch of late beach where the old men and some women came to sit on benches in raincoats with their hoods up, grizzling at the whale more than just gazing at it. They must have been starting to know bits of what it knew, lewd inklings, their hands shaking around paper cups of hot decaf.

Maybe, way up by the whale's head, which was roped off by the Parks Service and not open any time of year, there was a graveyard for these very localest of the locals, those who had grown up and down with the whale and were, in a sense, coming to rest in its harbor. These were men and women whose bones had a powerful homing impulse, and might have been dangerous to bury elsewhere.

Max left Windhassett as evening came on. He had spent the afternoon reading at a table outside the bakery, in his fall coat and corduroys. At a used book and antique store he'd found a volume of vintage whale photographs, full of those hazy mid-century postcard photos, the kind he'd often seen of Coney Island and Beverly Hills, and that his grandparents' generation probably always saw when it closed its eyes.

The book was arranged by decades, and for the thirties, the first full whale decade, there was a typo that spelled the "Depresssion" with three S's, in huge block letters. This put Max in a mood he could tell would last all day. It also firmed up his decision to go out to the head tonight, knowing suddenly for sure that he'd never have another chance.

He was a little cold when he got in his car and set out for the last stretch of road before he'd have to park and go the rest of the way on foot. The coastal road ended at the much-photographed SCENIC DETOUR sign, which had been nailed up by a work crew back in the Depresssion, illuminated with a crude but earnest whale symbol. He stopped here, regaining his composure after the road's hairy unrailed turns.

When Max was growing up, there'd been a lot of talk about what you had to do to break in and see the head, wires to cut and fences to climb, and dogs, but, really, you just walked over a few bluffs and eased yourself down to the shore on the other side, scrambled along for a mile or two of late shoulder, and waded through the waist-deep water over to another beach. And then there you were, face to face with the face. People had been doing it for years.

He made it quickly over the bluffs and through the wading and back up on shore, tearing open a plastic bag with dry socks inside that he'd held high above his head with the water up to his waist, like a soldier keeping his rifle dry across some treacherous bog in what that soldier might, while holding forth at a bar back home, have called simply *the East.*

He rolled up his pants and sat on the sand in his dry socks—he had a third pair with which he'd replace these once they got soaked on the way back—and set to work finding a way to look at the head.

In this moment, Max finally came to see that the whale was dying. Probably it had been dying ever since it washed up, but now death was near, and drawing nearer, from far out at sea. He understood that this was somehow what his boss had tried to tell him, why he'd been allowed to leave work and come here before entering his thirties.

The ghost world set in almost immediately. *Most nights it takes some time*, he thought, *and some doing, to bring it on, but there are other nights when it's there already, like it's been waiting for hours to meet me, checking its watch in a crowded restaurant.*

He walked all the way down to the edge of the final beach. Candy wrappers and empty lighters littered the ground, but there were no people. A beach chair missing an arm sat buried at a weird angle in the sand. Max sat down next to it.

The whale was having a harder and harder time breathing. It seemed unsure of where to find the air, or where to put it, as if its heart had started to question whether air was what it really wanted. Maybe the body needed an operator to relay messages from its heart, up and down the coast, and that operator was now headed for bone- and fat-dwelling retirement.

He wondered who would mourn the whale, and, at the same time, he wondered if there had ever been a boy lost inside, as there always tended to be in caves and wells. And if the police had had to cut their way in with pickaxes and hacksaws to find him in time for Christmas, and then some work crew had come out in the slump between Christmas and New Year's and repaired the hole with fiberglass and gray rubber, so the summer tourists wouldn't know.

Maybe the people of the coast would turn up to mourn the whale, and so would other whales from far away, huge ones that would reach all the way south to Maryland or Virginia, drifting in during the night to hum and bellow and admit of their loss. And maybe after all that, the carcass would decompose and inside, among the collapsing walls, whole parlors and taverns of lost boys playing pool and shooting darts would be found, blinking in the salty light of a place they barely recognized, if they hadn't decomposed by then as well.

The moon glinted off the sleek upper neck, so that a curved white line was the only way to tell where the whale's hide and the night sky began to differ, each so wrinkled by now they were surely allies. Max went closer, right up against the mouth and nose, venting warm air.

The ghosts were like mosquitoes—seasonal, pack animals, given to hanging out by the water. Max swatted them and dabbed at the blood on his skin with the edge of his shirt, tasting some before it soaked in.

Maybe, he thought, *instead of lingering here on the coast, the dead whale will drift back out to sea, but there'll be no grave for it. It will tip down into a trench or crater, which its body will dam up until it begins to fall apart and go its separate ways, or sharks eat it or the earth's plates crush it into a cube of priceless stone.*

Already Max had given in to considerations of his own death, and the little ways that someone could help him then, if they were there and willing. The fact that help really was possible, even between a person who was still a person and a person who soon would not be. He wondered if, even inside a thing like the ocean, there was still a special river for bearing the dead away.

He wanted to help the whale however he could, tell it that it'd be remembered, and not just in photographs and national seaside nostalgia. Tell it that its time had come and that, when it's your time, the time belongs to you, even as you're being taken away and melted down and stripped for parts and thrown into a heap outside of time. *Still, until then, it's your time and no one else's. It's the last and realest thing you have*, he wanted to tell the whale.

"Stop talking about me," it growled, in a low and rusty voice.

A few seconds passed, finding their way around the whale and into Max's life. Then again it growled, "Stop talking about me," and Max did.

♦

The ensuing silence awoke him to the smell of the whale's rotting, which revolted him so much he wanted to lie down with his face in the sand and call it quits. But, instead, he decided to do whatever he could to help the whale get off this beach and back to its home, where, after almost a century away, it surely belonged, and where maybe it could rot in peace.

He got up and ran the whole way back over the bluffs to his car, grabbing whatever he could find. He found a coil of thick rope, a pair of pliers, a shovel, and a hard hat. He'd rented the car from the superintendent of his apartment building, who ran a few side businesses, and this was what had turned out to be in the trunk.

As he was bundling all of it up, thinking about how to heave it back over the bluffs, a passing car flicked on its brights, gliding to a halt. A man in a blue raincoat and a baseball cap got out, his hazard lights blinking, and came over to where Max was closing the trunk.

"Broken?" he asked, in a foreign accent that Max associated with the kind of old war movies that proudly oversimplified the causes and effects.

"The car? No," Max replied.

"Yeah, good," said the man. He stood there in his raincoat and looked at Max, probably thinking in his own language.

Then he walked over to his car and turned off the hazard lights and killed the engine, and came back with his keys clipped to his belt. The lights faded and the car became too dark to see. He took off his hat, which bore a beer logo, yawned, then put it back on. He wore windpants with reflective stripes down the sides, terminating in big rubber boots.

"Okay, let's go now?" he asked. *Maybe this man has been sent here to help*, thought Max, eyes foggy and ears ringing. He felt like a child at the naïveté of assuming this, but he went with it. The two of them hiked back down to the beach and over the bluffs and through the wading interval and back to the whale, and the man did help, carrying a rope and a shovel.

Back near the head, a group of kids was starting to build a fire. Seeing Max and the man approach, they kicked out the sticks they'd kindled and ran into the underbrush, leaving behind a red can of kerosene and three bottles of supermarket vodka.

"He's dying?" asked the man, looking at the whale.

"Yes," replied Max, glad not to be alone with this knowledge.

"So we bury him now?"

"We try."

The man nodded with a sadness like he knew something about all the dying there'd ever been.

Leaving the tools on the beach next to the kerosene can and the aborted fire, they slugged some vodka and then began to push on the whale's flank, just ahead of where Max imagined its ear to be.

They pushed for ten long minutes, up to their knees in the warm stagnant cove between the body and the beach. "This is the hardest thing I have ever done," wheezed the man.

"I know," said Max, and some coarse pride passed between them as the whale gasped for breath and the ghosts sucked up little thimblefuls of blood.

They went on pushing until their knees panicked. Max's elbows radiated shivers into his wrists and shoulders, and he could feel a bulge in his stomach, almost at the base of his spine. The old imagined military feeling of hoisting a gun or a shot comrade through the air came back, and Max felt sure he still had many years ahead of him, such that, one day, he'd be obliged to look back on this moment across a dauntingly great distance.

♦

As the sun began to rise, they collapsed into the water, leaning against the side of the whale, submerged in its shadow.

The sun rose higher and, as the light changed, the whale really did look farther out to sea. When they came close to falling asleep there, they hoisted themselves back up and walked away from the beach, carrying only the vodka and looking back at the head, bathed in sunlight now. Max felt a quiet elation to realize that he and this man had together eased a tremendous weight off their lives.

Back at the road, the man requested breakfast. Standing at his car, blotting at his wet pants with a towel, Max said okay. He would drive back down the interstate right after that.

Across from where their cars were parked was a small fisherman's diner with some boats up on cinderblocks out front, and two cars by the entrance. A neon sign that read COFFEE perched unplugged in the window. Under it was a handwritten sign that read NO COFFEE.

It was empty inside. They found a table by the window, looking out at the parking lot and the cliff wall that held back the ocean, heavy clouds rolling in.

The waitress came by and left two menus and two glasses of water. The menu was printed on a sheet of orange paper, with just the words PEA SOUP written in the center of one side, and the sandwiches in a column on the other, beside a list of eggs.

Max read the menu again and again, while the man took one look and folded it down the center and put his water on top. He stretched and yawned into his fist and said, "I have spent up all my God-given money on trinkets and souvenirs. You will buy it for me?"

Max looked at him now, head-on for the first time. In this light, he looked younger than Max had been treating him.

Maybe not so far ahead of me, he thought.

The waitress, barely twenty, returned with ketchup, Tabasco, and salt and pepper in a Budweiser six-pack caddy. She stood there, looking down at them with her notepad out. Max wanted to tell her what they'd done and receive her congratulations. But he didn't, because it would have made her job that much harder, probably, and pushed the delicate triumph of the morning too far. He didn't need her to know all he knew. She looked like she could tell he was holding something back, as she stood there at the edge of his vision glowing like a candle, dimmer and then brighter with his breathing, but he knew she'd never ask what it was.

The man across from him cleared his throat and said, "Soup," then stood up and walked away. Max used the finger of one hand to trace the three S's he'd seen in the Depression book on the underside of the table, like a protective charm, while his other hand held the menu down. He jumped as the man yanked the bathroom door open, knocking over a pile of boxes in the back hallway.

"I just want so badly to have a good life," Max blurted. The waitress froze and the line cook looked over from the grill, and then there were three people in a room together, four if you counted the man in the bathroom, their respective wallets and keys and phones in their pockets and cars parked nearby. Something in the center of that room, though it was faint and temporary, exerted enough gravity to hold them all where they were, long enough to perceive one another without fear or expectation, or anything in their heads to say, before they all had to snap out of it and go back to work.

"I'll have the soup too," Max said, when the moment ended. "And coffee," though he knew there wasn't any.

PART TWO:
THERE

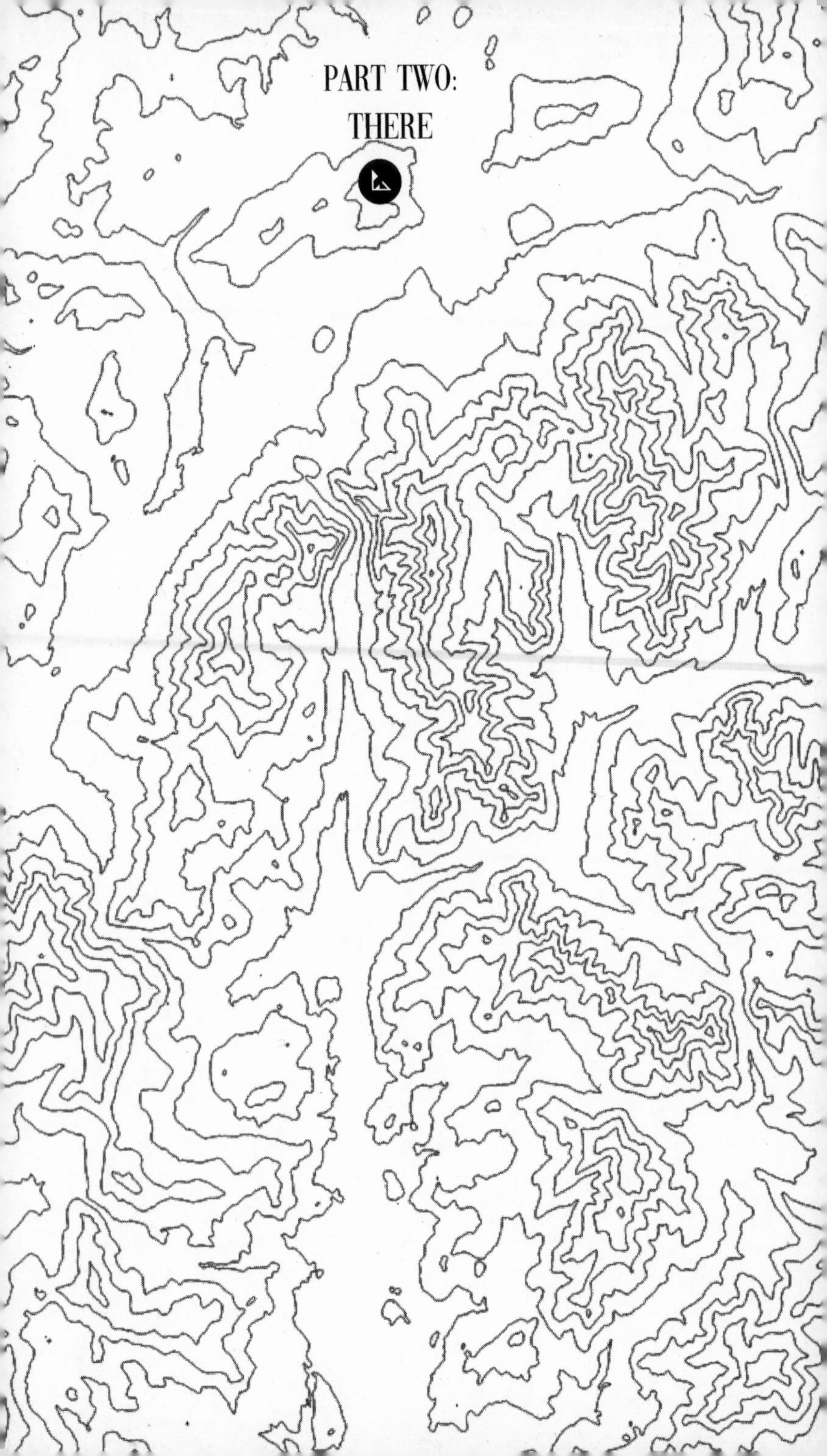

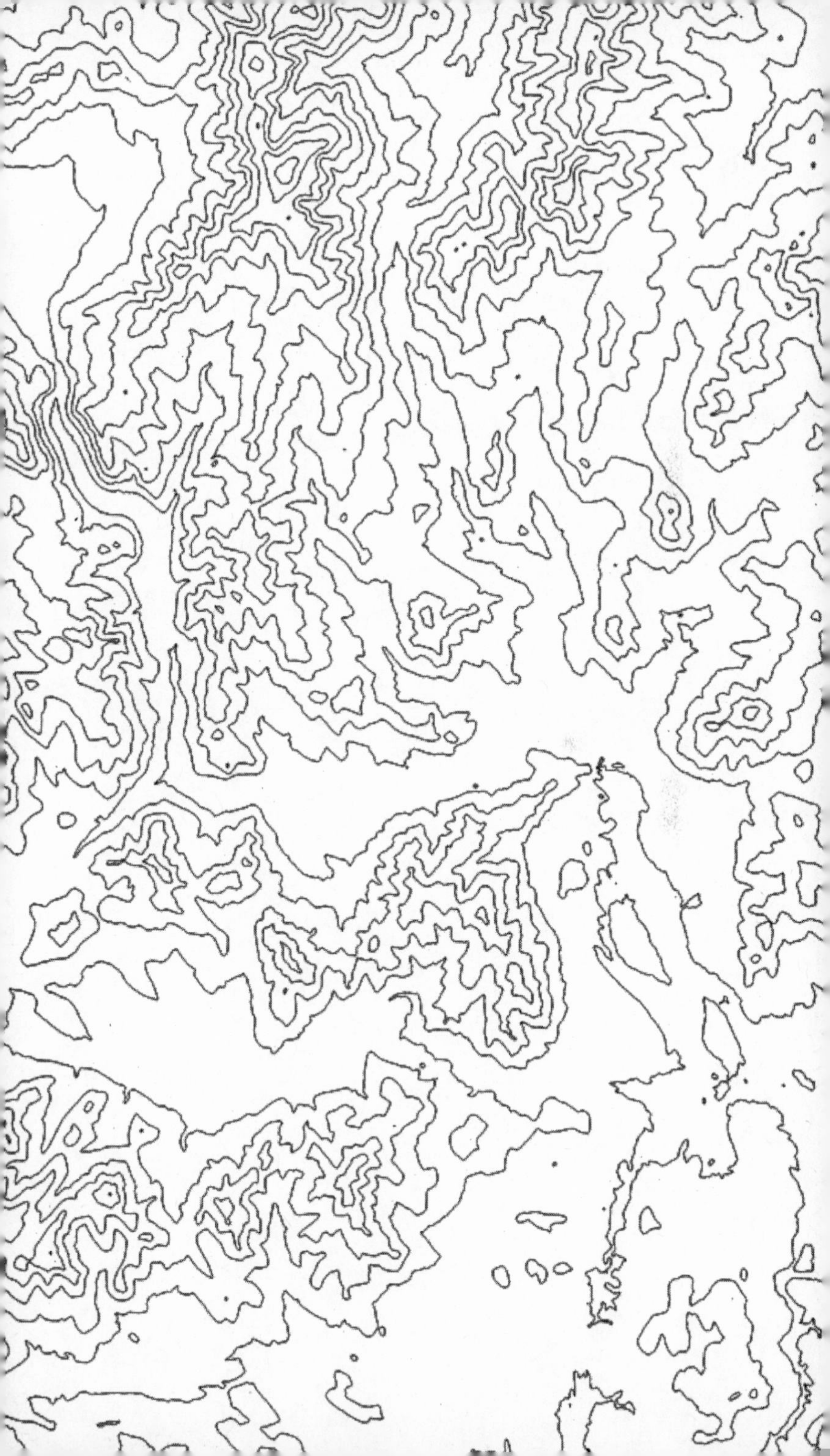

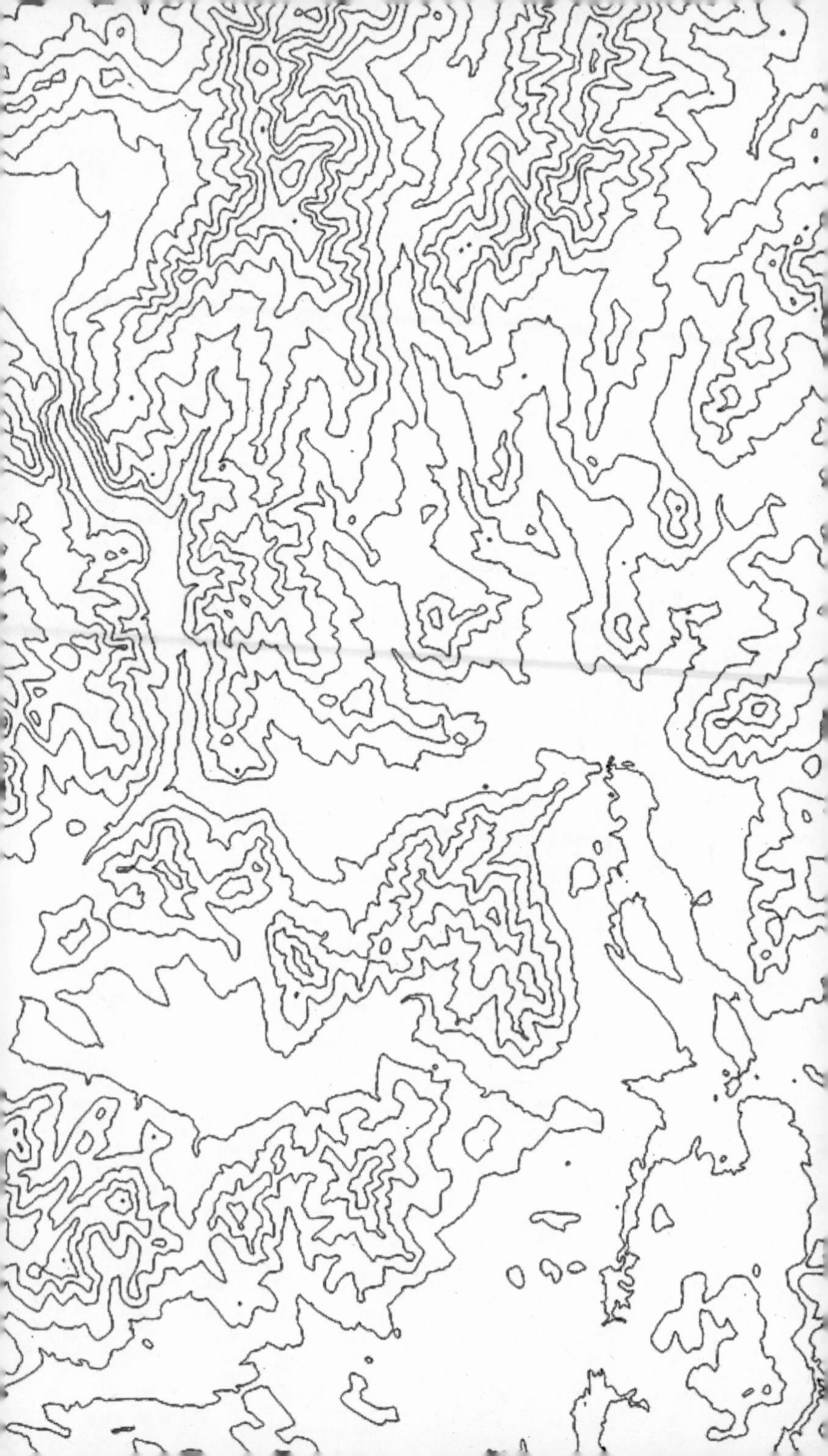

IN THE CABIN UP ON STILTS

It was an especially swollen and low-flying moon the night the island came in from out at sea, back in the Conquistador days, sliding along the ocean floor to lie latent under the bay for the first centuries of that coast city's foul history, until Ken hauled it moaning and slapping through the water's surface as if he were that strong, and maybe he is. It was the same moon when Ken finally came back to visit William and Ella on something like their honeymoon two decades later, both of them grown out of their precarious childhoods, naked together for the first time since then, in the cabin up on stilts.

Before this, Ken spent his days roaming. He roamed away from the interior, out of the pine forests and steep crags of the star-studded North where he too had been a baby swelling up in some dew-sheathed translucent pod. He left as soon as the dew melted and washed him clean of all that he had torn through in order to be born, a man of thirty, well-muscled and without scruple. He approached the edge where the continent was bounded by water and shredded into islands. He was ruled by impulses that he had no will to oppose. Other men could stoop over and die inland and never find the one thing that could have made it all otherwise, but Ken was going to find it. In the North he made white fires and looked through them at what was earth today but tomorrow might be ocean and ice; he passed by in big trucks with thick treads, stopping at inns, drinking with Indians, conducting a sort of research no one could ask him about. He slept in straw beds and already dreamed of William who was still too unborn to reciprocate the dreaming, though Ken dreamed that he did.

Ken went down to the caves whenever he was stuck in transit between one town and the next. He used these northern years for practice. He wasn't omnipotent; it took work to make himself into the man who one day would tear William away from greedy nowhere and own him. "Talk to me," he said to the men in the caves on the continent's northern edges. "If you know something about the limits of my power, the terms of my longing, if you've seen or smelled it or heard it dripping, tell me. Soon I'll tower so far above you it'll be too late to reach down and take what you have for me—you'll have to keep it then, seething at you unconsummated forever."

He sped down the Great Trans-Continental Highway with his face against a cold window, past the refineries and pits and the treatment and processing plants, some of them military, others corporate. Among them he caught glimpses of Ella, stumbling barefoot through scrap metal and snow, looking back at him as he passed.

In the South he got out of the last truck and brushed the crumbs from his lap. For a long time the idea he would have a child lay as dormant inside him as the child itself; now all he needed was Ella in the flesh, and the right place.

He had plenty of money, which he put toward plying and casing the continent's southern edge looking for the city of William's birth, with a bay capable of yielding up the island and the right kind of swamp from which Ella would emerge. Although Ken knew the island was waiting for him under the harbor of the city, he liked to picture it following him like a giant idiot shark. When he found the city, he became known on the high terraces that looked out over the sweltering harbor, the lights of black skyscrapers reflecting over the black water and bobbing boats and stretching piers. Casinos, lounges, car lots, they all saw Ken in the decade before William's birth. He waded through long and stagnant days, went to a condo sales meeting, bought one and the wardrobe to go with it; he showered in the light and floral evenings, then took the shivery air-conditioned elevator to the rooftop of the hotel across the street where he sat on the terrace in his usual seat and, ordering a long row of drinks, listened to the strains of whoever was singing in the open-sided indoor lounge, often in Spanish, sometimes in Portuguese. Some nights he stayed in his condo, his shirt unbuttoned and soaked with sweat like an unlit torch. Coiled, he was ready to grab William as he passed through the world.

Ken was sick with anticipation tonight, sad like a bachelor on the verge of marriage with half his life behind him. He pointed the remote control at the condo air-conditioner, then went back to the rooftop terrace. The singer moved silkenly through her set, most of her audience looking away onto the harbor.

The decade was over, passed in waiting.

He sipped his last row of drinks, talking through the side of his mouth like a ventriloquist to another investment man, the other half of his mouth and mind free for the reverent silence this miracle evening required. The man asked how the food here was and Ken ordered two duck sauce glazed mahi-mahi burgers with grilled pineapple, pushing one in the man's direction when they arrived. As the two of them finished their drinks, having fallen out of one another's attention with the dinner gone, the earth around them swelled and boiled. Into all of this came a glimpse of Ella, skirt held up in her hands, shoes tied in a bundle around her neck as she hiked through the giant swamp inland from the city: he watched her, sump water up to her knees, bloodsuckers entwined in her toes as she looked to the light of the towers through the smoke and the steam, hanged men and horse bones in the sagging trees and bushes. Deep cracks in the ground, cars sunk way in, a house here and there, the second or third floor level with the ground with a door made of windows to prove it. The spine of a train shaggy with bird nests, like a shipwreck down among the shrimp and anemone. Those birds always perched even this far out, watching the wake of mud close in behind Ella's approach.

The waitress came to offer dessert in the hotel bar, the other man having long since retreated to his room. When she repeated her offer a third time, Ken had to let go of the swamp and Ella, whom his mind had been steadily creeping toward, almost into; he had left an unthinking hulk of Ken sitting in his place but now he crept back, and once again the Ken in the bar could speak. It ordered Talisker and blackberry mousse, then paid and followed the businessman's path of retreat out of the glass head of the bar and into the hotel's cement shoulders.

Ken ducked into a bathroom on a high floor, into a private place, out of view. Like the caves that frayed the edges of the continent, the bathroom was a hole that had nothing inside it but the person in there—so, for now, Ken was gone. No one in the universe knew where he was. Then he emerged, soaked, shirt open, his chest streaming with water and soap. He could feel Ella approaching and he shivered. *Does she know what I'm going to do to her?* He could hardly believe that he could not tell.

He stalked the hotel's long corridors like a man fresh from a swimming pool, clear-eyed and purposeful, ears squeaky and popping. He found a room and smashed his way in; like the caves with their cavemen, the rooms were filled with roommen curled in balls or sprawled in corners. Ken threw them into the hall like uneaten room service and tore off the rest of his clothes and charged into the shower, punching the curtain like he expected it to shatter, and he saw William in the water crashing around him.

Out in the bay: the first yawn of bubbles as the island started to break through.

Here Ken came close to being a god. He opened his mouth to gargle and flared up with such a surge that he tore the showerhead off the tiled wall and walked naked back into the room carrying it, a torrent shooting through the bathroom door behind him. He fell to his knees in prayer, soaking the carpet, tearing up fistfuls of green shag.

The moment is here. William has arrived, torn from the bosom of nowhere, licking the membrane of his mother's belly for his first taste of the outside—salt and oil, weeds and deodorant. He has made the journey this far inside Ella. She emerges from the swamp onto the coast in the same instant the island heaves through the bay becoming solid ground, drying fast. Crabs scuttle up from the shallows, past the caves onto the beach.

Ken strides out of the hotel lobby in his city clothes again. Out past the taxi rink the streets begin, and Ken hurries toward the place where she'll be. The streets turn filthy fast. Soon he has forgotten what sort of city this is, if there are rickshaws and elephants or signs pointing toward the convention center and the airport named after some goateed general who stepped in as president until his own men cut him down. Ken has forgotten if the food stalls have hurricane-wrecked awnings or brick-shattered glass, if they're on wheels or cinder blocks, if the language is Spanish or French or some screamed or whispered Creole in between. At one of those fly-studded, yellow, burning-all-night food stalls, Ken ducks in and lands wetly behind a table. A dangling cord bites the wall. A grid of rice and noodle photographs flashes on, and a woman in a smock regards him from behind a podium. She takes up her notepad and walks toward the table, and behind her comes Ella, shoes down from around her neck and back on her feet, squishing with rotten water.

Ken waves the waitress away as he and Ella regard one another for the first time in person. He grips the edges of the table while Ella holds William inside. His hands snag on the staples under the plywood, straining to keep himself in this moment and nowhere else, and she shudders at his pain; he lays his hands on his thighs under the table, letting his fingertips bleed into his white pants. Ken and Ella lean in to whisper; nothing of what they say escapes. They get up, leaving through the corridor behind the restaurant, ducking and hurrying through the low-hanging cardboard, tripping over nails, a mess of pipes and panes, pieces of gears and saw teeth holding the place together. Sleepers curl all along the way, gobs of men that don't have rooms or holes in the ground or caves to rot in.

By the time they muck across to the outhouse perched out over the water, Ella is half out of her dress. Ken hoists open the wooden door and shoves her in. A sleeper opens one eye, a lone witness; the scene enters the hollow behind that eye and will stay locked in there, itself sleeping, with no way out and no reason to leave. Ken pulls the door shut and jams in a shard of wood to lock it. He can smell the water in Ella's hair and the weeds that have tangled around her skin and the swamp insects, and the man and woman both can smell the hole in the floor open to the bay beneath, lapping around their toes.

♦

When it's over, the change has come. Blinking and sore, William extends his tongue into the night, reaching out for milk.

Ken stumbles out and regains his footing, upright again, pulling at his pants and shirt. Carrying the baby under one arm, he spits up little steaming piles by his feet, then he breathes in, sucking the city into his gut, and starts scooping wet handfuls of material from his hair and reaches up his sleeves into his armpits, shucking off more of what clings to him, shaking his fingers to throw it at the ground.

Ella emerges a moment later, shaking. Almost no trace is left of the thing she was when she went in. Stripped of far more than her clothes, she vanishes before she turns a corner. She is almost transparent, her skin and hair and muscle shaved off, leaving only a delicate shred of tissue around bone to mark the place, like a bookmark, where a person had been.

Ken wears her dress and shoes and feels his breasts heavy with her milk. He feels the trauma to his womb where the baby had been. By the time he rocks the baby in both arms, humming two notes back and forth, they're nestled in a rowboat crossing the bay. Three boatmen have arrived to row them over and back in the morning; culled from the wastes of the caves, heaped together with nothing to do but be here and row, the boatmen know the way to the island without being told, though this is their first trip. They look away while the baby sups and Ken looks back at the city, still ringing with the end of Ella.

In his filthy dress and algae-ringed shoes, he looks like some gypsy mother stealing her baby from the house of a belching husband she's cracked open with a frying pan, praying for passage across a one-way border.

Disembarkation. The boatmen tip their passengers onto the shore and then row back into the bay where they fish with slack and unbaited lines.

♦

The cabin on the island stands on stilts above the reeds, with a ladder that climbs onto a deck that encircles the interior. The only structure on the island, it was raised whole from underneath with a bed inside, freshly made.

How to cut through to right now, through the crackling nervousness—like lightning in another sky reflecting faintly onto this one—all the way to this actual first night that's happening now? Ken tries and tries, fingertips nearly splitting again with the effort; he wants to be genuinely here and nowhere else, neither before nor after, now that the years of waiting are done. He holds hard onto William between Ella's breasts, so hard he almost crushes the child, and then he turns and exhales to purge the taste of fear. With William crushed down to the size of a spider, Ken could live out all that remained to him here in the cabin, feeling the night through the screen walls and listening to the waves, waiting for the stilts to snap at the knee or sink back into the earth. Or he could dig a furrow in his side with a pocketknife and plant William there, gather thread and sew it into an ornate bow, button his Hawaiian shirt over it and take a taxi to the airport.

But he doesn't. He lies awake as a bird passes overhead, the same winged body with miles of fingers and veiny feet that flew over the landscape one dusty day before the city was here, before any of them were here, dropping from the sky the names William, Ella, Ken into a clearing in the center of the island where they dispersed. Now William sleeps like a drop of wine on his mother's stomach and ribs, plumped with milk and air. Ken has taken all his clothes off, but doesn't touch or look at himself.

The sun comes up and he wraps the baby in cotton. They sit on the terrace facing the island's far side, the back of the world.

As long as he is still a baby, William will drink his mother's milk. Ken will never eat or drink on the island. It's a place of fasting, of indulgence in nothing but pure William. If he could refrain from breathing, he would, but he is not a god. When morning is over, he carries the baby back down the stairs, through the high vegetation and out to the shore where the boatmen wait.

The city comes into view as they round the island, growing as if for the first time. More boats rise from the water and there comes the smell of gasoline and the play of mid-morning sunlight within it. Now they part ways: Ken lives only in William's nights; after that, William is placed in a basket among curtains with a fan blowing a breeze of lilacs and jasmine in a part of the city where no one will find him. Ken melds back among the mirage shards dividing one cement tower from the next. His day widens until it exceeds the horizon, a slop bucket of boredom sloshing over the side. He crosses a gravel park with backhoes and tractors behind a roped-off center, has coffee and eggs at a café with a sandy cement floor and no light but an open window. The men who spent the night here are here still. Jittering with hunger after the fast, Ken orders plate after plate through the languid breakfast hours. *None of you know what I did last night*, he thinks, when the men look him over.

Back in his condo, the day is spent in beer and television, snacks from jars with screw tops, checking email. He dreams of calling Ella; wakes from his nap on the couch. Around five he rubs oil into his hair and goes out to walk the streets, looking for an open-faced bar where he can stand and eat meat on a skewer with cilantro and drink salt and lime, smell the perfume of women and the sweat underneath.

So passes the first decade of William's life. As he gets

bigger, their nights in that bed on stilts close in until nothing in the cabin is left but the bed itself and the two of them in it. Coursing with electricity through the nights in a fanged and winged fit, threatening and haunting himself to hold nothing back, Ken never stops dipping the boy in and out of life like a teabag. The matter that makes up the boatmen shifts slowly: their heads stay the same size while their faces get smaller. There may come a day when their necks support nothing but a single point in the center of a tan desert, and then they'll be reset.

William has eyes and an expression now. As he looks over the edge of the boat, a hurt hangs from him and flutters in the wind but doesn't blow away. Ken still has breakfast at the gravel café, with the backhoe and tractor, then he hangs what he's taken from Ella in his condo closet, dripping unused milk on the floor.

The first ending:

All along there have been others in the city as invisible to Ken among the buildings as he was to them, who, like Ken, are neither blind nor deaf. They can hear and see the same things he can but without the same head start and without the same heart in it, or they hadn't the same heart in it at the beginning, but now they do. *A few years of invisibility is all you get*, they would have told Ken, had he asked.

When they swarmed in, clambering up the cabin's stilts, Ken fell down a chute, landed hard on the bottom. It was worse than if he'd been caught and taken to jail and forced to meet himself there in the body of another man and submit to that man for the rest of his life. *None of you know what I did last night*, he thinks again, from the bottom he's landed on, and knows it not to be true anymore.

♦

Milk was on the floor of his condo closet when the police came. The rest of Ella was gone, a green and a purple polo shirt and a few striped ties in her place. Ken imagined what he wore of her walking off on its own feet, thin as stocking soles, past the cruisers idling outside. Broken but alive, he felt William pounding in his heart, eating like a termite through his ribs; he knew William hadn't left the city and thought, *he is doing this to me.*

Now, at the bottom of the place where he's fallen, Ken lies in a bath of tremendous pain with nothing but a tiny remembered point of light far overhead to mark where he's fallen from. He orders takeout and has it left outside the door, the money weighted down with a chip of concrete. Torturing himself, he replays the scene of the island's fall: fleets of ferries slice the skin of the ocean into feathery rags as the city empties out and fills the other place across the bay. Every morning he pulls his shirt up and checks his sides, praying he really did cut into himself to plant the baby there when he had the chance, but finds nothing aside from fleabites.

More drippings and cinders fall from the past. *I'm too weak to climb out*, he thinks, lulled by the warmth and the past's rank carnal odor, *but I won't always be.* Ken calls back his old ravenous want and forgets everything else. He is once again at the beginning, looking only upward, forward, in a new decade of waiting.

This is the decade of William's adolescence, ten to twenty. The decade of the surge in tourism when the island fast becomes the centerpiece of the city and the city inks itself onto maps that have until now elided it. Casinos and resorts rise on the island at the speed of global finance, visitors come all the way from Asia; work crews dig canals for a theme-Venice and build a handsome colonial cathedral almost overnight. A viral explosion of boats, ferries now with heavy engines driven by simple paid strangers: the boatmen knock around the caves with their penciled-in faces, kicking at the fossils of their friends, their oars clattered in corners.

In the early days of this decade, crowds waited at the ferry docks for standby tickets, but even they're all gone now. What few souls remain in the city ride heat waves onto other heat waves. *My parents were killed in a boat accident and now I'm an orphan*, William reminds himself some afternoons, taking pleasure in half-believing it. He walks the city looking for Ella, even if he doesn't know it yet, dragging tatters of Ken behind him or inside, down his central interior like streamers in a doorway through which a constant breeze blows. He sits on the pier and hums, clicking his ankles in rudimentary rhythm, trying to drum up some spirit in himself now that Ken's want is not there night after night. He finds a chair on the sidewalk and brings it back to the place among the curtains where he spends his nights; he sits and tries to imagine what kind of business he might go into now that he's almost a man. He tries to learn some calculus just by imagining it and finds strength in telling himself that he's survived something that someone weaker would not have.

He finds a cell phone on a bench, its chip still loaded with minutes, and calls some of the numbers on flyers still strewn around the city, hanging up when the answering machines stop talking. Some nights he considers walking out to the airport with pocketfuls of money, but the thing in his past grows into an animal with a raspy bark, calling out to its own kind, the pack it's been separated from, and soon the pack, out in the northern wild, turns and hears.

♦

Ella isn't gone, either. After all that Ken took from her in the outhouse, she was left no choice but to grow up again; in this way she and William were born on the same night and are today the same age. Ken shaved those years off her like fuzzy mold and now she's boring her way anew toward life's soft middle, dusting off skin that she finds lying around, carefully recomposing herself. In this current run of teenage years, she's developed an interest in the Creole they speak on the island; in a mall bookstore she finds a grammar school primer and spends her afternoons on a bench scratching salt mosaics off the pages and underlining the most difficult sentences. She reads them aloud in as wide a range of accents as she can muster, trying to catch in her own voice a hint of how these words must actually sound.

In the great absence, Ella and William each roam the city. They eat at restaurants that cost almost nothing, with one waitress and one cook and an inked-out crust of a menu. Each shines with bruises, burns and itches. Some mornings when she wakes, Ella's skin hangs askance, soapy water from the bath seeping under and then steaming out of her as the day burns on. The nearly empty restaurants close one by one: seen from above, the power grid shuts down, isolating the few illuminated squares toward the center until there's only one. In the very last restaurant, two meals are left, no condiments. Except for the waitress and those skulking down alleyways, wasting away into fish bones and hair, William and Ella are the only two left in the city; they order the last two meals, look at one another, then turn away as Ken rises like cataracts in their eyes.

William breathes steadily, counting back and forth between three and seven, remembering his calculus and holding the edges of his chair, feeling the staples on the underside open his fingertips. Ella orders sweet milk in a jar. When lunch is over, they leave the restaurant and, for the moment, the lurking implication of Ken. They're inside a new thing together, off on a walk through the remnants of a park, a churchyard, a cemetery left over from the long-ago Inquisition, a garden still flush with lilac and jasmine. They talk lightly, a certain lilt to their step. William keeps his fingertips in his pockets until they scar over. Then he takes Ella's hand.

They climb a hill and sit on a rock wall, looking down at the harbor. They see themselves from space, frozen in a photograph, and it may still be their first day together, or else they've already done the work of blending a spate of such days and they're on their way toward someplace further. By early evening, they clamber down to the beach, each slipping once and caught by the other. The city's old casinos and hotels are abandoned, most of their stock boxed up and sent over to the island. They break into one and find a few cases of beer and some cigars and matches and pretzels under the bar counter, and haul them down the stairs, past a dry fountain, and out to the beach. "Now for a toast," Ella says. She offers, in her chosen accent, the traditional Creole for *good health*. William flinches, and she promises never to speak this language again. Then they share their first kiss.

Day by day, William works to reseal his body in its finger-split places, hoping that in time the seals will hold. He warns Ella that he may have to leave at the end of the summer to go to college.

When they meet after sundown, they dismiss the moments when Ken wells up as necessary sadnesses, making do with this until, one evening as they sit on their usual stretch of beach sharing a box of raisins, the distance begins to approach. At first it looks like a single figure, a stumbling lurker, but as it draws near it splits in three with the crash of a wave. In open shirts, the three boatmen drag their boat down the beach. Before the lovers, their presence says, *tonight takes place on the island.*

Back at sea now, in the hands of the boatmen who can do nothing but row, William lies on a pile of netting and rope and Ella lies between his legs. No matter what, he'll insist this is his first time on the island, and she'll insist the same. Though the journey takes the ferry only an hour, the boat won't get there until midnight, passing coves and caves, noble slick rocks and green panes of fog. William can feel the small circle of his life closing. When he wriggles free of the feeling, turning away from the low moon over the harbor, the feeling passes to Ella, who jolts up from where she's nestled. She pulls him into a kiss and they both keep their eyes closed and faces together, until the boat jolts to a halt.

Disembarkation. William and Ella walk toward the path that splits through the underbrush and leads to the ladder that climbs the stilts. They cross the bushes that conceal the cabin from the beach and the new row of hotel towers, pausing at the bottom; either this pause constitutes the ceremony of return, or they've skipped that ceremony. Up the ladder, across the porch, to the door: they're inside now and the whole great openness of the bay is closed. The birds whose wings are almost translucent in the moonlight stretch a giant tarp over the open water as Ella and William settle in.

They're shy now, side-by-side. William lights two left-over candles, dust caught in the melted and redried wax. He would have lit more had there been more to light. He finds a box of condoms with instructions written in the island Creole, a twenty-eight-letter alphabet. Back on the bed, lying on the sheets, each moves a few fingers toward the other, touching the other's shirt, then the front of the other's pants, then a flank of belt. Ella rolls into a shape that fits into a crook in William, and he opens to accept more of her. He reaches around and lifts her shirt, and she guides his hand to undo the metal button of her jeans, fits two of his fingers into a shape that can unzip her fly.

He exhales into her ear, and it goes through her head and out her mouth. The chamber shrinks around them as they move together. Ella whispers something back in William's ear, claiming the power to turn the moment in any direction she chooses. Running her hands over William's soaked shoulder blades, she feels herself stirring Ken's great melted pool, clumps of wax cooling on her singed fingers.

Breaking through on giant feet, breathing smoke around chiseled monster teeth, Ken's fingers stretch out miles ahead of him. Trees snapping under his feet, Ken pulls mist and weed tendrils from his face and throws his fingers into the sky, cracking it with lightning. William holds Ella in his arms, running his tongue along the side of her neck and under her ears, choking on old slivers within this new taste of the other person. He tongues the slits where her skin is still loose and fragile and almost remembers the milk he drank in this cabin years ago.

Ken draws near as the island is scraped clean. Old jet-black things pile back up where the casinos and tiki lounges and snorkel lessons had their brief moment. The gondolas from the Venetian canals are sucked off the coast and buried in the ocean floor. Now William remembers the taste of her milk, and it makes him strong again. He can choke Ella, turn her upside down and force her head off the bed onto the floor, and tear an extra hole in her and drain Ken out like a cyst. They almost can't breathe now so tight is the chamber. Both have sweat in their eyes, the shocking blue, the surge and spark that could close the gap and activate the circuit once and for all. Ken follows the path that loops between them, scrambling through heat and wet, slipping and falling back down, hoisting himself up. William's fingers flex hard around Ella. Ella's teeth graze and nick his earlobes and collarbone.

"Did you hear something?" she whispers, cooling the moment from its boil, rolling away from William, pushing back the body bag until it hangs slack near the ceiling, punctuated with dead wasps floating in a vein of condensation.

Now they're cold and naked, side-by-side, and there's another rattle on the door. "Yeah," whispers William, "that time I heard it." The condom he must've put on earlier is greasy and stale now. He reaches down to scratch it, and there comes another knock. Ella takes a pillow and covers her breasts.

"There's something I have to tell you," says one to the other. The knocking continues, mustering their thoughts into a march.

Fluttering, whooshing, humming, like a horde of bats or owls racing toward the roof. All at once Ella starts to giggle so loudly it swallows the knocking, and then she giggles with the sound of having swallowed it, close to choking. She stands on the bed above William naked and shrinks him back to the speck he was when Ken first brought him here. Her voice throws itself up the ladder of octaves, skittering among the notes of an alien scale, Creole hissing out, spiking up into song then down into a roar, words a hundred syllables long and then some so short they drop straight off into grunted breath. She jumps from the bed and charges toward the door, about to burst through and leap over the edge and then furiously through the trees, waking the snakes and the lizards and mustering them into the unvisited clearing at the center that was there even when the island was sunken, long before Ken's brief era.

She stops. The spirit is gone from her again. She makes a sound in Ken's voice, something like "Uhh" and collapses on the bed sideways across William, hosing him with her eyes. "I'm so sorry," she sobs. "I almost…."

William lies very still. His body tingles in all its small places, beginning to open up again. He can see the clearing, too, and knows morning won't come until they go there, whether they leave now or wait in this bed another decade. He wants to look in Ella's eyes and say, "Remember, it's the two of us against him." But he sees nothing but Ken.

"It will never be the two of us against anything. There will be no more conflict, William. There will be no more quarrel."

"Don't ever abandon me," he begs.

"I won't ever," Ken says, reaching out one of Ella's hands to stroke William's hair.

THE HATE ROOM

Rodrigo and Johann met at the bar of the Eco Pampa Hostel in Buenos Aires and got together as soon as they did, having both characterized themselves, at almost the same instant, as drifters, half-jokingly, over chips and beer at three in the afternoon.

Traveling onward as a couple was an easy decision for both, as each seemed to be or have something the other wasn't or didn't have, or had lost, and now wanted, or wanted back. The first few weeks were a rush, carrying them through the rest of Argentina, Chile, and across to New Zealand, then up the Australian coast to Thailand, Laos, and finally Japan, which Johann said had always been his number one world destination, a place he'd been saving for the right time in his life.

They'd both quit their jobs—Rodrigo's in Madrid, Johann's in Hamburg, both an hour from the towns they'd grown up in, and both in the financial sector, which each had fallen into after learning that what they'd been taught to understand as *the Humanities* was not, or was no longer, an actual profession. They were 33 and had reached respectable positions, but not enough to keep them from leaving for South America, planning only to avoid Europe until they were sure they'd become different people. They were both lucky, they agreed, on their first night together, exploring Buenos Aires' untouristed outer districts thanks to Rodrigo's Spanish, to have gotten out when they did, before the appeal of stability grew unshakeable or the time to do something else was no longer ahead of them.

"We're both still young!" was their toast, those first few weeks, as they drank to excess without calling it that. "33's the new 23!" They both thought about how little they'd known at 23, as it turned out, though the amount they'd imagined they knew then far outstripped the amount they actually knew now, as far as they could tell.

"If I hadn't left that office when I did," Rodrigo added over cocktails in Bangkok, as they were worrying if the ice was going to get them sick, "I would've killed myself and everyone in it." Without quite knowing how, Johann understood that he meant this literally. He nodded and pushed his cocktail glass away, waiting for Rodrigo to change the subject.

They'd both saved up respectable sums, enough to land in Tokyo with the freedom to splurge on food and wine and clubs in Roppongi and designer jeans in Harajuku and three weeks in a Sofitel near Yoyogi Park, but on a Saturday night at a sushi restaurant in Shibuya, supposedly the best in the city you could get into without a months-ahead reservation, the money finally ran out. Each had told the other he'd saved more than was strictly true, so, together, they'd lived more extravagantly than either would have on his own.

After both of their debit cards came back declined, Johann took out his credit card while Rodrigo looked away. The waitress kept apologizing as she ran the charge, like this was all her fault, an embarrassment she sincerely wished she could've spared them and would still feel guilty about years from now. Johann reassured her twice and left a 35% tip, despite the suspicion, in the part of himself he wasn't proud of, that she'd feigned concern for exactly this reason.

That night they moved to a hostel in Koenji, carrying their bags on a walk of shame across the city, and checked into a six-person room which, luckily, had no one else in it tonight.

Rodrigo balled himself up in his sleeping bag on the top bunk while Johann lay with his eyes open below, shivering and sweating like he'd had a pot of coffee with dinner, picturing Rodrigo's sweaty back overhead, glistening through the thin mattress. After inwardly reciting the names of all the world's major rivers and the cities they flowed through in an attempt to hypnotize the worry away, he got up, stepped into his flip-flops, pissed in the dark of the communal bathroom, and washed his face in the sink that also smelled of piss. Resigned to insomnia, he wandered to the computer lounge, where he sat alone in front of the TV with a beer from the self-service fridge. He'd taken it without paying for the first time in his life. Though he knew no one would care—probably most beers from this fridge were taken without paying—he hoped, with an edge of real concern, that no one came in and saw him with it. He even scanned the ceiling for cameras, his eyes lingering suspiciously on the light fixtures until he had to blink.

After blinking, he trained his eyes on the TV, where a run of commercials was ending and a show was picking back up. It looked like a game show: three pudgy men behind podiums, burlap sacks over their heads with melon-sized wedges cut to reveal mouths, shouting whenever a buzzer went off. It wasn't clear—both because Johann spoke no Japanese and because the volume was on its nighttime setting—whether they were shouting words, perhaps answers to questions only they could hear, or shouting in pain from some unseen source, perhaps a stinger beneath the podium. Johann let his attention fixate the way it used to at work, when he was locked behind the bank of computers, following the minute ups and downs of the market, always ready for the phone to ring with a client demanding to know whether to buy or sell. And he couldn't be wrong. That was the only rule of his old job, which, despite his effort to focus on the screen, a large part of him was now busy wishing he hadn't quit. He tried harder to tune this part out. It felt good to revert to the old mode of attention, letting go of the rest of his situation here in Tokyo, even Rodrigo, who'd so far refused to admit that the money problem worried him. Johann, if he was honest, found this disturbing, the way Rodrigo left it to him to worry, saying only, of course, "You shouldn't worry either," when he'd brought it up before bed. *Typical Spanish*, he thought, not unaware that his thinking was just as typically German. *Both of us doomed to be who we are forever….*

Focus on the Japanese people in the show. He forced his gaze back to the screen, where one of the contestants had vanished and the other two had their teeth clamped on a long wire. Johann felt the shock in his own back teeth, like biting down on tin foil, as one of the contestants fell back from the stage into a tank of water, which seemed to electrocute him further. The crowd, or crowd-sound, despite the low volume, cheered like all its dreams had just come true.

The last man standing let his arms be hoisted by the show's host, to more applause, and then he passed out. Leaning the unconscious body against himself like a mannequin, the host revealed what Johann assumed was the prize—a thick envelope—and then the screen went black and a phone number flashed across it, and, though this wasn't at all like him, Johann took out the flip phone he'd bought in Akihabara and dialed the number, not wondering what he'd say if someone picked up.

After three rings, someone did. She started speaking Japanese. On instinct, Johann replied in German. This went on for twenty or twenty-five seconds until the voice switched to

English, inviting Johann to do the same, which, after a further moment of confusion, he did.

"You call to be contestant?" the voice asked.

Johann nodded, remembering to add "Yes" when nothing happened.

There was a sound of rustling papers, then the voice said, "Ah… actually, we have cancellation for late show tonight. We tape 3 to 5AM, broadcast tomorrow. You available on short notice? How old you? You a strong boy?"

This time Johann didn't need to remind himself to speak. "Yes to everything. Where do I go?"

She told him the address and hung up. He repeated it to himself five times as he walked out the door without going back to the room to check on Rodrigo or put on his windbreaker or any shoes other than the flip-flops he was already wearing. He did, however, take another beer for the road, feeling better about taking it this time because he had a sense of purpose. Being broke, he'd have to walk, asking people to guide him as he went. The whole time he kept wondering, *is this how things really happen?* He got no answer aside from the occasional stopping of taxis, the drivers grunting come-ons in Japanese.

By 2:45, Johann had found his way to the studio, in a warehouse district behind Waseda University. He dropped his beer bottle, which he'd carried empty for a long time, walked through the open side door, and was taken to the makeup room as soon as he explained who he was. In what felt like the next instant, the makeup people had finished with him, he'd signed what he assumed was a waiver, and he was being prodded onto the stage, a burlap sack over his head, the mouth-hole wet from the previous contestant. He heard the shuffling of others near him, but could see nothing except a boil of colors through the scratchy mesh over his eyes.

Standing where the handler put him, he tried to brace himself. He hadn't understood the exhausted English of the show's host, who'd dropped by backstage to brief him, so he was no more aware of what was coming than he would've been if he'd stayed back at the hostel and kept watching on TV. There was a moment of silence, and then the applause sound, and then a brief announcement in Japanese, followed by an excruciating pain in his left ankle. He almost tipped forward, to even more applause. When he'd righted himself, tasting blood, something shocked his lower back, like a Taser shot into him from afar, and he buckled again, but was galvanized by the thud of the fallen contestant on his right.

Now that it was one-on-one, as far as he could tell, he did what he'd been trained to do at work, quieting all his peripheral anxieties.

He allowed nothing but the prospect of money to enter his mind as a pair of hands spun him through the cheering and offstage, down a flight of stairs he could barely keep up with, into what smelled like the kitchen of a Chinese restaurant. He heard the sound of suds melting in sinks and almost fell over when he was pushed forward, the hands of others on his arms, plunging them under a crust of hot, oily water, down to a pile of plates at the bottom. He silenced the fear that there might be knives down there by accepting that there certainly were. Then he felt one, or a shard of glass. His fingers and palms opened, streaming out into the water.

As he started scrubbing, assuming this was what he'd been ordered to do, he felt a pressure on his head as well. Someone, or some machine, was ripping his hair out. First only a few hairs at a time, then thick clumps, the equivalent of fistfuls if the ripper were human, which, from its methodical brutality, didn't seem possible.

Pushing a fat-covered platter to the side, Johann felt a small round nub in the corner of the sink, and intuited that this was the panic button, his to press if it got to be too much, though his fingers were so raw that even touching the button hurt. He recognized now as the moment to press it, if he was ever going to, but then he heard his opponent shrieking, followed by shouting and blubbering and imploring in Japanese, and found the strength to commute his desire to quit into his opponent's, so that as this other man was pressing the button, Johann felt his relief.

Besides, now all his hair was gone, so either the worst was over or some much darker game was about to begin. Then he blacked out, feeling the dishwater cool like rubber gloves around his wrists.

When he came to, he was sitting on a bench in the green room with two ice packs strapped to his head, his hands stacked in his lap. They were so covered in stitches and ointments that they felt fused together.

He stared at the mirror without focusing his eyes while the host stood behind him and explained that he was this round's Winner and what he'd won was a small island off the northwest coast of Kyushu, in the south of the Japanese archipelago, complete with an inn that he could restore or inhabit or sell, it was entirely up to him. The deed was already drawn up and plane and ferry passage had been paid for. He, and anyone he chose to bring with him, were booked to leave at 8AM. Would it be possible to exchange the deed for cash? No it would not, the host informed him.

When he'd absorbed all this as best he could, and the ice packs on his head had gone soft, Johann let himself be escorted into the show's private car, which returned him to the hostel after a long trip around the city at dawn, trying to find it. He got out and hurried to the 6-person bunk and shook Rodrigo, whose body felt too thick and heavy to be merely sleeping.

Overcoming the fear that his newish lover was sick or dead, he shook Rodrigo again, announcing the good news as soon as he stirred. "So we have to leave right away?" Rodrigo whined, like he didn't know he was speaking aloud.

Their flight touched down in Fukuoka, Kyushu's largest city, and by the looks of it not one they'd be spending time in. From here, they took a bus to the shore, and then a private ferry for six hours and thirty minutes, according to Johann's Swatch, which had survived last night's dishwater, until their island came into view. According to the property deed it was known as Futo, a satellite of the somewhat larger island of Makioko. They disembarked, unable to tip the driver because they still had no cash—transit for each step of the journey had been included in the prize, but nothing extra. Finally, they helped the driver unload the tandem kayak, which he said was theirs to use for runs to Makioko, just over a mile to the north, the only accessible source of food and supplies, though Amazon would deliver for an added fee.

They thanked him and watched as he turned the ferry around, leaving them stranded. When he was gone, they followed an overgrown trail a hundred yards to where the inn sagged on its foundations, looking like no one had visited it since WWII.

"Nice digs," said Rodrigo, affably enough that Johann ignored any latent sarcasm. He grabbed Rodrigo's hand, wincing as his stitches contracted, and led him through a doorway that had no door in it.

♦

That first night they ate crackers and nuts from the plane and slept on a tatami mat they'd found in a corner.

After Johann was out cold, desperate to recuperate, Rodrigo found himself on his feet, barely more conscious than a sleepwalker, moving along the corridors. He rubbed the smooth walls, luxuriating in their skinlike texture, until he felt a hollow place and, instinctively, bore down on it. The rice paper gave way and he fell through. Whatever part of him was awake expected to fall out of the inn and onto wet dirt, but he landed instead in a drafty, rectangular room, unconnected to the rest of the mostly open-plan interior. Facedown on the floor, he rolled onto his side and looked around in the dark, getting a sense for the place he was in, picking up a low but definite hum, almost a groan. He began to groan along with it, connecting the taste in his mouth with the smell in the air, and both of them to the sound.

When he'd groaned his lungs empty, he rolled onto his back, looking up and trying to make sense of where he was, holding onto the outside possibility that he was still dreaming. But most of him knew he wasn't. If anything, this room felt realer than any he'd found himself in since his life had first started to feel like it was drifting off course, somewhere around age 25. The groan, though it didn't seem to have a tangible origin, sounded like it was meant specifically for him.

In the morning, Johann found Rodrigo already in the kitchen, regarding the empty French press. "There's no coffee," he said.

Johann nodded, put on his shoes, and went down to the beach to get in the kayak, shouting for Rodrigo when he didn't follow.

They rowed around the island to the north side, from which Makioko was visible. Johann wore a pair of work gloves he'd found in the shed behind the inn on his way to the beach, thick enough that the paddle transmitted pressure but not pain to his hands, and he wore a floppy fisherman's hat over his ruined scalp, sniffing its mildew compulsively as he rowed.

After a floating break to rest their arms, they rowed the rest of the way and disembarked in the small vacation town on Makioko to buy all the groceries and cleaning supplies they could carry, putting everything on Johann's credit card. Then they went to an Internet café where they posted the first listing for the retreat center they'd decided, somewhere in the course of rowing, to open and try to run.

It had been Rodrigo's idea, suggested spontaneously when Johann asked him if everything was okay. In order not to discuss the room he'd stumbled into last night, he'd decided to introduce an idea that would occupy all interaction between them for the foreseeable future.

Posting the listing made the idea real. Unlike the vagueness of transferring capital from one account to another, servicing real guests who paid real money would give them both, they agreed, a means of reconnecting with the reality they knew had been there, just beneath them, all along, despite their mutual feeling of having dangerously lost touch with it somewhere around 2010.

They loaded everything into the kayak, almost capsizing it when they got in, laughing, and rowed back to Futo to set to work cleaning the floors and stocking the cupboards.

Johann eyed the extra materials Rodrigo had purchased—what looked like the makings of a rock garden, four new tatami mats, a bag of tea lights, an antique record player—and made a point of not asking what they were for, despite their having been lumped in with the sum charged to his credit card. *This is the kind of man I can be now*, he thought, as he washed the first round of dishes in the sink, his fingers still tense with the fear of knives, his stitches softening and beginning to dissolve. *The kind of man that observes certain things without auditing them.*

After sixteen weeks of hard work and twelve more trips to Makioko, the burden of credit card debt hanging ever more heavily over them—over Johann anyway—the retreat was ready for its first confirmed guest, George Kreeble, a self-identified dentist from Boston who'd booked two nights and made the down payment of $225, half the discounted total for those who booked online.

Johann and Rodrigo celebrated with haircuts and shaves at the expensive salon on Makioko, and a steak dinner—fish was so common here it had started to seem like a vegetable—all on the credit card, before rowing the kayak back to Futo. This is the vessel they'd pick George up in tomorrow, though soon, if guests kept coming, they'd have to buy a motorboat from the dealership on the other side of the island, which they'd stopped by to visit today, picking out the one they wanted, a snazzy blue 2014 Yamaha with yellow stripes down the sides.

George Kreeble was a smiley red-faced fiftysomething with a gut that hung under his floral short-sleeve shirt, and gray curly hair and no chin. "Hey guy!" he said at the ferry terminal. His tone conveyed that he was in Japan for the first time and had nothing invested in hiding it. "Thanks for picking me up!"

Johann smiled under his moldy fisherman's hat and rowed the kayak back across what he'd decided to call *The Gulf of Futo*. He focused on keeping the pain in his hands imperceptible; this struck him as appealingly Japanese, somehow part of the thing he'd come here to find.

When they reached the newly refurbished inn, George gushed, "Wow. I mean, wow. You guys weren't lying." Johann went to the kitchen to open the bottle of chilled rosé they'd advertised as a gift for guests who booked two nights or more, while Rodrigo, who'd been reading in the dining room, listened to George talk about his wife in Boston, who'd left him because she never took the time to find out who she really was when she was young. Rodrigo nodded, exaggerating his accent and leaving out every fourth or fifth word when he replied, hoping to give the impression that his English wasn't good enough to get into matters of this depth, not that it seemed George needed to be understood in order to go on talking.

When Johann returned with the rosé, George turned sullen, making no secret of his desire to be left alone with Rodrigo. Johann took the hint and left. Rodrigo didn't watch him go, focusing instead on setting the table and then slicing salmon on the kitchen counter, aware of George's unashamedly hungry gaze on his lower back.

After a tedious, pervy dinner where nothing much got eaten, Rodrigo showed George to his bedroom. Then, before returning to his own, part of him hoping to find Johann asleep, he remembered to show George one more thing. "And right this way," he said, George following gladly, "is the Oasis."

He slid open the wood panel to reveal a room with a miniature indoor rock garden and the antique record player he'd purchased on Makioko when Johann had been on the phone with the credit card company. There were silk curtains painted with Tibetan mandalas, pillows everywhere, and a row of Yankee Candle Midnight Jasmine candles, ordered from Amazon, flickering along one wall.

The Oasis had been his project, accomplished not only without Johann's participation but in light of Johann's palpable unease. "If I'm going to stay here, the inn has to be half-mine," was all Rodrigo had said in his defense, determined to cover up whatever had groaned at him on the night he discovered it. *It's crucial for me to build this. I won't be your employee*, he'd been ready to add, but it never became necessary. And it was true, it really had been crucial for him to build the Oasis, even more than he'd known. It was, if he stopped to think about it, the first idea he'd followed through on since the onset of adulthood.

"A room for relaxation," he said, proud of his English now. "Meditation, breathing, stretching, reflection… whatever makes you feel good." Despite his distaste for this man, he couldn't swallow his pride.

George nodded, clearly hoping Rodrigo would add himself to the list of options. When he didn't, George wandered into the room and began rifling through the records.

"Well, I'll leave you to it," Rodrigo said, sliding the door closed behind him.

He got in bed beside Johann, who didn't stir, and picked up Kenzaburo Oe's *A Personal Matter*, which he'd taken from the hostel in Tokyo and started seven times without getting a foothold, not because he wasn't determined to glean the insight into the postwar Japanese crisis of masculinity that Johann swore it contained, but because he always started it when he was already half-asleep, as he was now, the book falling onto his chest and scraping his chin….

Eyes closing, he felt the inn rattle. He feared an earthquake, aware that they were common in Japan. Shaking off the beginning of a dream about a steep cobbled hill in Málaga, he leaned onto his elbow, about to wake Johann when the inn filled with language:

Dumb shit cunt fuck bitch whore freak crap piece of motherfucking fecal bag of dead fucking clumps of asinine whore shaft vomit filth bitch twerp damned fucking rotten trashcan slop puppy cum hole….

The words echoed down the hall, timid at first but steadily gaining in volume and sincerity, until Johann woke up too, looking around with a beatific expression, his mouth half-open in a yawn that hadn't kicked in yet, his hands still covered with aloe gel.

The stream of profanity remained unbroken, spewing out, filling all the space they'd refurbished together. George's voice was so loud and forceful Rodrigo was afraid he'd have a heart attack.

"Should we do something?" he asked.

Still partly outside the world, Johann shook his head.

So they lay back down, holding each other, listening to George empty his lungs in a stream that only broke when light began to shine through the spaces between the wooden slats of the walls.

The inn seemed to pant.

At breakfast, two hours later, George looked rosy-cheeked and well-rested. He even appeared to have lost weight.

He sauntered into the kitchen, where Rodrigo and Johann were sitting over the French press, not talking, and said, "Morning, gents. What's on the menu?"

Neither answered until he sat down at the table, landing heavily on the fragile chair. He looked at the two of them, then cleared his throat, about to ask again.

"I'll fry some eggs," said Johann.

Rodrigo sat there, staring out the window. He felt sick from last night, infected. He could hear George talking about the wonders the fresh air and quiet were doing for his system, which he didn't mind admitting had gone into the red in Boston this past year, especially during the bad winter, the worst on record since 1978, a year he smoothly segued into droning on about. Rodrigo focused on not listening, blurring the sound in his head the way he'd blur an image by squinting.

He got through all of breakfast this way, tipping the eggs down his throat like oysters, until George announced he was going to the beach and would be back for dinner at dusk.

They passed the day wandering the inn, picking up dirty plates and putting them down, making George's bed, which he clearly hadn't slept in, and taking turns trying to nap.

When George reappeared around five, sunburned and smiling, he asked if they could put some steaks on the grill and Johann said, "Sure." After their steaks, which Johann had defrosted from the newly stocked long-term freezer and then burned slightly, George drank the rest of the rosé in the fridge and said he was going to retire early tonight, in preparation for his early departure in the morning.

Neither Johann nor Rodrigo replied, keeping their gazes on the Japanese characters on the empty bottle on the table as the sound of George's screaming returned. It was even louder than last night, a combination of cursing, shrieking, sobbing, pounding the walls and floor, and stomping like a six-year-old denied an ice cream cake in the grocery store freezer aisle.

It went on so long that Rodrigo and Johann had to walk to the beach, reentering on tiptoe an hour later, praying George was asleep.

Mercifully, he was.

In the morning, he emerged showered with his bags packed, and said, "I've greatly enjoyed my stay here. I'll be letting certain of my friends know about your Hate Room upon my return."

He said nothing more as Johann rowed him back to the ferry terminal on Makioko, where he reiterated his thanks and tipped handsomely. Johann spent the tip on a bottle of sake, which he felt he deserved, though he knew it was Rodrigo who'd absorbed the brunt of whatever had just happened.

The Hate Room quickly became the heart of the inn.

As George promised, others like him appeared, and the inn began to turn a profit. Johann paid off his credit card debt, opened a savings account on Makioko, and bought the motorboat he'd had his eye on, leaving the kayak for guest excursions.

They remembered how it felt to have money.

All the guests, all men, came with the same air of pleasantness stretched thin over seething self-hatred, and they all availed themselves of the Hate Room just as loudly and angrily as George had, bellowing out a kind of soul-deep loathing too potent to uncork in their native Boston, or Chicago, or wherever else in America they started to come from, as word of mouth spread.

One night Johann and Rodrigo tried to have sex under cover of the shrieking, hoping it might revive the basically extinct flame between them—a flame whose extinction they'd only noticed a month or so after it'd gone out—but neither could invest enough of himself in the other to get beyond foreplay, so they ended up back on the beach, ten feet apart, staring into the water, trying to make out distant islands in the dark. The shrieking from the inn drifted along the path toward them, louder than the crashing surf.

They could hear tonight's guest throwing himself against the walls and barking, screaming out his hatred for God and his wish to be put out of his misery right now.

Johann closed his eyes and pictured the money coming in. *Whatever it is*, he thought, *it's bearable for a price.*

But Rodrigo couldn't bear it anymore. "They're desecrating my Oasis," he sobbed, stumbling to his feet and kicking sand until the beach became grass on his way back to the inn.

After he was gone, Johann sat on the beach alone, scratching the scars on his palms where the stitches had been.

Word of the Hate Room spread to the point where the inn was often double-booked and Johann had to turn people away. He was managing everything now that Rodrigo's depression, or anxiety or chronic exhaustion, not that he called it any of these things, had confined him to bed, *A Personal Matter* tented across his chest, his eyes squinting at the ceiling, an orange pill bottle open on the nightstand beside him.

Whenever Johann went in the Hate Room after a guest's departure to clean out the spit, urine, semen, and occasional blood and shit—all of it congealing into a molasses-like black matter—he found himself wondering whether the room was haunted by a Japanese spirit whose nature Rodrigo had perhaps intuited as soon as they moved in. *Something about it*, he thought, *must draw the black matter to the surface of these men, just as the inn draws the men themselves all the way from America. It's not just a place for them to let it out, which they could do at home—it's a place that draws it from them, peeling it from their bones and organs so they can purge what would otherwise have remained lodged inside them, turning to cancer over the course of their 50s.*

He always entered the Hate Room soberly, steeled for the grim business of cleaning the black matter out, but he always left it rattled, in more of a hurry than he wanted to be.

Business peaked by the end of the long summer, the inn filling and emptying with hate-sick guests, each staying two days. This seemed to be how long it took to get the black matter up and out. *One day isn't enough for a full purge*, Johann thought, *and three days would begin to eat into whatever in them is still healthy.*

There were times when it felt almost meditative, executing his daily tasks like a monk, scrubbing out the Hate Room, which he'd taken to calling by its actual name, unlike Rodrigo, who, lying in bed like a child, could still only call it the Oasis, when he spoke at all. Johann had always known there were people in the world, intelligent, competent people, who spent full weeks in bed without being physically ill, but, nevertheless, the sight of it, manifested through someone he had feelings for, was incredible to him. He wondered what kept Rodrigo from taking a turn in the Hate Room himself, and he wondered if he wanted to know.

Though it wasn't how either of them had envisioned their 30s playing out, the situation began to seem strangely sustainable. Then the General arrived. Johann could see right away that there was something even more wrong with him than there had been with the others. *The others*, he thought, eyeing the General's sweat-shiny work shirt buttoned to bursting around his neck, *only hinted at where a man can end up. Now here's a man who's ended up there.*

He handed Johann his duffel bag without saying hello, and sat down in the motorboat, lighting a cigarette and scowling at nothing, or at the fish smell in the harbor. Ferrying him back to Futo, Johann wondered if it might've been possible to refuse his patronage, and, if so, when the chance to do so had come and gone.

The General got out and marched up the beach, along the path, and inside, tracking sandy water onto the wood floors. Most guests had been happy to remove their shoes, but Johann could tell that with the General it'd be dangerous to even ask.

He went to the fridge and took out the pitcher of

welcome sangria—he'd added this to the inn's profile after the rosé had started to seem cheap—and two glasses. The General marched up to the table, took the pitcher, poured both glasses full, downed them, and filled them again.

"Well, let me show you to your room," said Johann, clearing his throat after the General had drained the pitcher.

The General burped, wiped his mouth, and, taking up his clinking duffel bag, said, "Show me to the Hate Room."

Johann exhaled as slowly as he could into his fist. Then he nodded and said, "Right this way, sir."

"Don't call me sir," spat the General, a piece of pineapple flying from his mouth and sticking to the rice paper wall.

Johann went back to the kitchen after the General had locked himself in the Hate Room. He considered rousing Rodrigo, letting himself imagine that, if he did, Rodrigo would run to the door and stop the General before it was too late, like all along he'd been saving up the energy to do just this.

But in reality he mixed up a fresh pitcher of sangria from the leavings in the fridge and dragged a chair outside the Hate Room, sitting and drinking as the General raged:

Scat fuck bitch shitspew skag rag burning hell motherfucking blood blister full of….

The words were the same as ever, but the intensity of the General's hate went beyond anything Johann had ever heard. It struck a chord of such pure loathing for life itself that Johann recoiled, like it was an affront to his life too, a curse with actual power.

In the first moments when the General's voice began to gurgle under the effects of the knife, all Johann could do was grip the sangria pitcher.

Cu – u – u – unt… gurgled the General's voice, through

the sound of blood splashing the walls and dripping onto the tatami mats.

Johann felt the sangria fall from his mouth, soaking his upper shirt in sympathy with the General's death throes. He held his breath until the Room was silent. Then he exhaled through his fingers and hoisted open the paneled door, wading in. The blood and black matter came up to his ankles and partly submerged the white, drained body. The knife had floated away and come to a standstill in the corner.

Eyes, ears, testicles… the General had removed them all before succumbing.

After taking in as much as he could, Johann removed his shirt—without asking himself why—and picked up the body's feet. He dragged them through the inn, smearing blood over the floors that he and Rodrigo had hand-polished what felt like a decade ago, when they were both still young, and continued through the back door onto the path that led away from the beach. He dragged the body into the woods, flies and mosquitoes swarming the sweat on his lower back, until he reached a point where he could convince himself it would never be found.

He began by kicking up the soft dirt; then he bent over to dig with his hands, feeling the roll of fat that had grown on him blimp out over his belt. He kept turning to check on the body, feeling it watching him despite its eyelessness.

When he couldn't stand this anymore, he pushed it into the shallow hole—just deep enough that it didn't rise above the ground—and kicked the dirt and leaves back over it, wiping his face with his inner forearm so as not to smear his mouth with blood. He backed away from the grave, wary of turning from it, until he bumped, hard, into a tree. Then he did turn, running straight back to the inn.

♦

Johann came through the door to find Rodrigo standing at the edge of the blood pool in the dark, only the light of the bedroom on behind him, *A Personal Matter* hanging limply by his side.

"That was him?" he asked, like some bogeyman from his dreams had finally materialized.

"Yeah… your pills wore off?"

Rodrigo didn't respond, only let the book slide through his fingers and float away. A look of total resignation covered his face as Johann stepped forward, embraced him, and pushed him down on the bed, his body heavier and more inert than ever.

When they couldn't lie like this any longer, they got up and scrubbed all the inn's surfaces, in awful reenactment of their first days of preparation.

Then they got in the motorboat, planning to go to Makioko for a decadent breakfast at the American diner—milkshakes, pie—before booking a flight back to Europe.

But they just sat there in the waves, counting them. Johann stared at the motor, unable to reach out and start it. When it got dark, they had to go back inside.

Inside, they subsisted on crackers and cocktail nuts in bed, like their first night here, not speaking until, almost a week later, a motorboat from Makioko pulled up and a young woman stepped out.

They watched her like two sad dogs through the front window as she tipped the driver and waited for him to speed off before approaching the inn and knocking on the door, at first gently, then pounding on it until Rodrigo ran to bed and Johann shuffled over.

He pulled the door open and stepped aside to let her tumble past without looking at her, though he knew, dimly, that he should be careful in case she'd come with the police.

She was the one to turn on the lights. The first thing she noticed was the mess—half-full bowls in the sink, a French press with a skin of mold over the coffee in the bottom, a steak on a cutting board on the dinner table, its juices hardened into a shell around it.

"I'm here for my father," she said. "I know he's here. I've seen his credit card bill."

"Your father?" Johann asked, already abandoning any hope of lying to her.

She stared, waiting. He got the feeling she hated his German accent, maybe hated Germans generally.

"Just show me where he is."

Her American accent was very clean and he could see something of her father in her. The kind of mental toughness the General must have had before it turned on him. He wondered how much longer until it turned on her.

"Fine," he said. "Follow me."

He started toward the Hate Room, planning to begin there with an abridged version of what'd happened, but decided against it at the last minute and kept moving, through the back door and into the woods.

He replayed the night he'd dragged the General out here, until the rational part of his mind faltered and he couldn't be sure this wasn't the first time: perhaps his would soon be the body and this woman the one to bury it.

Instinct led him back to the grave. He almost took his shirt off again, but he got himself together and started kicking the dirt aside. The woman's eyes fixated on the parting ground in the instants before her father's face broke through.

♦

When it did, the body nearly opaque with black matter, which must have seeped from its bones, the woman kneeled, cradling the head in her arms. She turned back to Johann, surprised to see he was still there, and moaned, "Leave us."

Johann nodded and backed away. He would've kept going had her moaning not begun to climb in register, out of the low sad weepy place where it began and into the realm of the confident and the cruel.

He crouched against a tree, barely concealed, to watch her in the failing light. Now she was screaming, pressing in on the head in her lap, bellowing into its open mouth, "Fuck you! You slimy fucking piece of…."

Johann listened as she went on, venting what sounded like a lifetime of pure, unrelieved hate, beyond even what the General had visited upon himself.

"It's not me! It's not me!" she shrieked, over and over. "You're the one that's nothing! It's your black matter that killed mom and is killing me, not the other way around!" She reached into her purse, pulled something out, and started cutting what was left of the body apart, first its lips, then pieces Johann couldn't identify in the dusk.

She flung them deeper into the woods, venting hate through her nose now that her voice was gone, and he pictured wolves coming up from their dens to eat what she'd thrown their way and wait for more, until there was none left and they were fighting over the bones and she was long gone, deeper into the woods, to haunt the island forever.

Though he didn't know how it would end, he knew he'd seen enough. He hurried back to the inn before it was too late, without asking himself what *too late* might mean at this point. He was aware, rationally speaking, that he'd likely see her again, and have to deal with her in some way—that she'd entered the order of things here, not merely passed through it—but he kept himself from worrying about this now.

Back in the inn, he burst into the bedroom, grabbed Rodrigo from where he lay, and carried him into the Hate Room.

He closed the door, tore his pants down, tore down Rodrigo's, shoved his head against the stained tatami, climbed on top of him, and yelled, "From now on, this is where we'll fuck until we're rich enough to retire."

As he scrabbled for position, squeezing Rodrigo's shoulders and bearing down on his ass, he started to see the black matter oozing up from his pores and out his mouth. The harder Johann fucked him, the more came out, seeping in a trail across the floor, merging with the remnants of the General. He realized that, if he kept going, he'd squeeze Rodrigo out like a tube of toothpaste, and that the quantity of black matter would be more than even the Hate Room could hold. *If only Rodrigo had come in here and let it out a little at a time, like the rest of them*, Johann thought. *But he never did. He kept it in.*

Johann tried to stop, but he'd passed the point where he could. In passing it, he saw that Rodrigo had built the Hate Room to die in. He must've known this moment was coming, just not so soon. Johann closed his eyes and pictured digging a new grave in the woods, a deeper one, and he cried, abandoning himself to whoever he'd be once that, too, had been accomplished.

GMUNDEN

Ulrich is already standing on the porch when the truck pulls up. The journey from the depot must have taken it almost three hours, starting well before dawn. He thinks this more clearly than any thought about the driver or the cargo or the depot itself, in a part of Austria he's never seen. He's never even seen Vienna. He could ask the driver exactly how long the journey took, but he won't.

He watches as the driver parks, imagining the gravel turning to sand beneath the truck's weight. The driver is behind the truck now, unloading the boxes, straining under some of them but not showing it more than a little. He piles them between the truck and the shed, in the exact place Ulrich designated six years ago, when he began ordering this equipment and putting it to use, per his son's instructions.

Ulrich's cup of weak coffee is balanced on the porch railing. Sometimes it falls before the delivery is finished, or just as the truck is pulling out, and breaks in the flowers, but today he does not believe it will. The old materials, from the last young man he hosted, are boxed up in the shed, washed and stacked neatly inside one another. The driver, who's signed a contract binding him to absolute discretion, will bear them away once he's finished unloading the new ones.

The driver used to wave upon arrival and approach Ulrich with the clipboard to sign, but no longer. Now he keeps his head down, wearing headphones as he unloads, and leaves the invoice on the steps of the porch, which Ulrich signs as the driver is closing up the rear of the truck and locking it. Ulrich puts the signed invoice on the hood and watches as the driver collects it, gets in the cab, and backs out, careful never to hit the mailbox again.

Now all the new boxes are where they always are and the old boxes are gone. Ulrich's coffee cup has not fallen. He finishes what's left in it gratefully, peering up at the sky to check the weather and the approximate time. Then he checks his watch. He has three hours until Hans arrives at the station.

The first box is the heaviest because he picks the heaviest up first. He knows that his best energy is always on the surface, and he only gets more exhausted the more he lifts, so that by the end the lightest box is more taxing than the heaviest was at the beginning.

He carries his coffee cup indoors after having put the heaviest box in its place, and stands by the sink watching sparrows fly across his field in the direction of the creek that marks the edge of his property to the south. Then he returns to pick up the second box. This, too, he carries to its proper place. Before attempting the third, he sits in his chair for nearly five minutes, scratching his jaw, accepting that he will no longer have time to shave it.

Unshaven and quickly showered, with all the boxes in their right locations, Ulrich sits behind the wheel of his car, which turned thirty last Christmas, making it forty-one years younger than he will be in July.

He smiles to remember that he used to consider the car new, and pulls out, deep in the tire tracks left by the truck, until he reaches the main road, at which point he turns right, toward the station, where the truck turned left, the fastest route out of Gmunden and, he imagines, back to the depot, wherever it may be.

It's a ten-minute drive before he passes any houses, and only five more to the station. The parking lot is empty but for the cars of the three old men spending their final days at the station café, smoking, drinking beer, and reading the newspaper, just as they spent all of their younger and middle days that they didn't spend working or in the army.

Ulrich walks quickly past them, but not so quickly that it seems as though he's trying to avoid their gaze. They look up, putting their hands over their keys and wallets, which lie atop their shared newspaper pile, protecting all this from him in a gesture whose irrationality doesn't make it any less hostile.

He doesn't avert his eyes from theirs, nor does he mimic their expressions. There is the sound of the old espresso machine spurting steam and a buzzing fly, mixed with the slow chop of the ceiling fan. They stare as long as he does; they see him here more often than they'd like, picking up young men, or dropping them off. They never see him in town aside from this. Their wives, who do the shopping, claim to see him at the store once a month. He knows what they must think, and is happy to let them.

Beyond the café is the ticket machine and beyond that are the two tracks, one for each direction.

Ulrich walks to the platform nearest the station, where the trains from Vienna stop, and sits on the single bench, always abandoned. He crosses his left leg over his right knee and then, as always, switches, finding the right-leg-on-left-knee posture more comfortable for waiting, always his least favorite part of the job because it reminds him too sharply of the first time he sat on this bench, to see his son off seven years ago.

Positioning his legs takes four of the five minutes before the train arrives. The fifth he spends watching a squirrel, and then the train is there, its brakes loud in the quiet morning, and then two people exit. One is an old woman, probably the mother or sister of someone in town, though no one is here to meet her. The other is surely Hans. Tall, fit, his brownish hair cut short, his face clean-shaven. Ulrich rubs his scraggly chin as the young man, twenty-four and three months according to his son's email, comes toward him, slowly but not hesitantly.

"You are..." he begins.

"Yes," replies Ulrich.

He reaches out to take Hans's bag, knowing Hans won't let him.

Hans carries his own bag to Ulrich's car in the parking lot, and they both get in, regarding one another in short, furtive spells.

They pull out and drive three blocks to the simplest of Gmunden's several restaurants, a wine house that serves sandwiches and salads and has two tables out back, away from the street, facing a hill.

They are seated at one of these. No one's at the other, as is almost always the case. The waiter shoos wasps with his dishrag and regards Ulrich carefully, then regards Hans, perhaps trying to communicate something with his eyes.

They order mugs of cold white wine and green salads and salami and French bread. Without mincing words, Ulrich makes it clear that he will pay, and that Hans should feel free to order coffee and dessert, which Hans will decline to order, as will Ulrich, who only drinks coffee in the morning and eats dessert only on Christmas.

"Should I tell you about what happened in Vienna? My breakdown? I'm not sure how much your son…" Hans begins, once the salad and most of the bread is gone. His voice is cautious but not shy. He's not as badly off as some of them are.

Ulrich shakes his head. "Later. Drink." He indicates the mug of white wine, which the waiter has refilled. Hans drains it halfway, puts it down to eat the last of the bread, then drains the other half.

After this, they leave.

Claiming a great need to sleep, Hans closes his eyes in the passenger's seat as Ulrich drives the most secluded—though not the quickest—route out of town. He doesn't like driving through the main square. There is a roundabout that bothers him and a park that attracts too many schoolchildren. He can tell the young man isn't really sleeping, and believes the young man knows he can tell, and doesn't mind. With some of them, there's the need to explain more; with others, less. This one strikes him as unusually ready to devote himself to recovering from whatever overwhelmed him in Vienna.

The afternoon sun is still high, but the light strikes Ulrich more dimly now, perhaps due to the wine, or in preparation for the shaded walk through the woods that he and Hans will soon take.

They pull into the driveway, coming to a sharp stop that jolts Hans out of his sleeping position. "Here we are," says Ulrich. Hans heaves his bag out of the back seat and follows Ulrich in, overtaking him despite his manners and the old man's head start. He waits for him to catch up by the stairwell, where seven years' worth of unopened mail sits piled.

They pass the first-floor room where Ulrich sleeps with his collection of maps, heading upstairs to the room where his son slept before leaving for Vienna. The bed is now made up for Hans; the sheets have been washed with unscented detergent and hot water.

"Yes," Ulrich replies, when Hans asks if he can touch the things laid out in the room: pen and paper on the desk, towels on the bookcase along with a few books in a pile and a desktop computer.

Hans puts down his bag and sits on the bed. Ulrich says they will meet downstairs in fifteen minutes for their walk, which will constitute the first part of the weekend's treatment.

In the fifteen minutes that Hans spends in the bedroom upstairs, connecting it with what he knows of Ulrich's son from Vienna, Ulrich is lying on his bed downstairs, the ceiling spinning. He hasn't drunk more wine than usual—indeed, he has followed the exact routine he follows every time he picks one of them up—but he feels winded. *Perhaps*, he allows, *senility is beginning to set in*. If it were nighttime now, he would gladly close his eyes until morning.

Instead, he warms up his computer, identical to the desktop upstairs because he purchased two at the same time, and emails his son to say that the new guest has arrived. The account, according to his son, is private, encrypted, something like that, somehow illegible to outside authorities should they one day have cause to investigate. He waits a moment, letting himself savor the possibility that his son might respond. Then he logs off and looks back at the ceiling while a precise mechanism in his brain counts down the remaining seconds before it is time to put his shoes back on.

When these seconds are over, he stands up, leaning on the desk to steady his dizziness, and turns to see Hans waiting in the doorway in white tennis shoes and a windbreaker. He can tell that Hans has been watching him, but doesn't mention it.

♦

They set out from the house around the back, through a meadow of waist-high grass Ulrich drives his car through once in spring and once in autumn so as to smooth down an approximate trail to the woods.

In the woods, not speaking, Hans follows Ulrich's lead toward the lake, soon to appear magnificently through the dense foliage. First, they crest several small hills densely covered in pines, their footsteps lost among the sounds of birds and insects.

The lake opens after the third hill, almost too wide to see across and so motionless it reflects the sky and pines around its edges like they've been scooped into a declivity.

Ulrich leans against a trunk while Hans takes it all in. They hold these poses until a child appears between them, not saying anything, making only a clicking sound as it comes to a halt. Ulrich gauges Hans' reaction: his guests don't always react in the same way, though the child always hypnotizes them in the end. Hans succumbs immediately, his eyes locked on the child's eyes, his lips pressed into a single wad of flesh.

Ulrich has never known the name or gender of this child. As far as he knows, it lives in a cabin on the other side of the lake, invisible from this vantage. It can always tell when he's approaching with a guest from Vienna, and always appears soon after the two of them reach the lake.

There are times when he imagines that it's two children who live over there, a brother and sister, twins perhaps, alternating, never letting him see them together. They do not respond when spoken to, nor do they appear open to communication by other means. He's often dreamt that his son is in touch with them, but he cannot incorporate this dream into his understanding of waking reality, in which the children have surely been here longer than he has. Indeed, he's always seen his own property as marking the end of the Known World, the child's or children's the beginning of the Unknown, a schema whose simplicity pleases him.

He lights a cigarette and sits down on a rock by the lakeshore, giving Hans and the child their privacy. The child comes very close to the young man, making a gesture of welcome, entreating him to follow. Fully hypnotized now, Hans goes slowly, neither hesitating nor hurrying. They depart while Ulrich watches evening settle over the lake and he pictures his son, who would have drowned here when he was thirteen had a hunter from another town not pulled him out and brought him home, requesting a large dinner with coffee and dessert as a reward. Ulrich has never known if the child or children attacked his son back then; he has made it his business not to know.

When he began accepting guests from Vienna, Ulrich's walk back from the lake in the dark frightened and disoriented him, making his house seem very far away, like he was already dead and trying to get back to a place he could never get back to, but by now he's used to it.

He has about two hours to set everything up before Hans returns, exiting another part of the woods and returning to the house by another route. Ulrich crosses the meadow, loud with crickets, groping his way toward the house, where there are never any lights on except in the room he's in.

The night gets colder even after it's gone fully dark, to the point where he's shivering on his back porch, fumbling for the keys he keeps nestled in a fern.

Once inside, he has to sit down on the bench he uses to pull on his snow boots in winter. He's aware of wasting time, but has learned not to push himself to the point of collapse. Better to gather his strength now, even if it means having to rush once he has it.

When he does, he pours a glass of Riesling from the open bottle in the refrigerator and takes it with him to the workroom in the back of the house on the first floor, where the boxes that arrived this morning wait.

Gathering his attention for the task at hand, he is not happy to discover that the feeling of being an inch outside his optimal self has lingered. He takes a gulp of wine and sets his glass on a shelf by the door, turning on the light and rolling up his sleeves. A box cutter sits between his glass and the wall. He picks it up and opens the box on top of the largest pile, spilling out the packing peanuts. These he will sweep down a grate in the floor, which leads to a trash receptacle in the basement, to be emptied on the first of every month.

He removes the gleaming metal pieces, two curved joints that fit together according to the instruction manual he memorized over the course of two nights six years ago, when his son, who'd been in Vienna for a year with no word, had first emailed to say he was sending a guest and outlined the procedure. *A young man who's had a breakdown in Vienna. An acting student, an egomaniac, a suicide risk. By the time he returns, he will remember none of it. He will tell everyone he feels better, and he won't be lying. In the interim, you will do to him as follows....*

Ulrich still refers to the manual on occasion, when some part of his memory doesn't correspond to how the pieces actually cohere. He's never known what the pieces are, only that certain of them need to be replaced after each usage, whereas others can be dismantled, cleaned, and reused.

He will take these from the locked storage closet in a moment, after first opening and assembling all of what is in the boxes. The permanent components required a more substantial investment of time to set up and a full toolkit he had to purchase in town, forcing himself to endure the suspicious gaze of the salesclerk at the hardware store, but the single-use components, which the truck delivered this morning, are modular, designed to fit together with no tools and no more than an hour's work, which, after his rest by the door and his sluggish pace so far, is all the time he'll have before Hans returns.

He sits on the workbench beside the machinery, finishing his wine and listening for footsteps on the porch.

His task took less time than he'd allotted, so now he's faced with having to wait, which he never finds easy though these days he's always tired.

He makes certain that everything is plugged in and there are no pieces left in the boxes, pretending there's a possibility he forgot a step. He sweeps all the packing peanuts down the grate. Then he considers pouring more wine but resists, deciding to indulge in a spate of unconstrained reminiscence instead. He pictures himself sitting on the porch with his son, both of them ten years younger and on the near side of the thing that came between them after his second wife, the boy's mother, went to London on business and never returned.

He rises when he hears footsteps. They get louder, then they stop. He looks out, sees Hans face-first against the house a foot to the right of the door, his mouth working soundlessly against the wood. There's just enough space for Ulrich to open the door and step outside behind him, shifting Hams over and guiding him in like the puppet he's become.

He picks up a towel from under the rocking chair on the porch, where he usually keeps it, and wraps it around Hans like he would a wet dog filthy with lake water. Holding him tightly from behind, marveling, as ever, at the feeling of a body at once so muscular and so weak, Ulrich leads him through the foyer and into the workroom.

He closes the door behind him and turns on the work light. It shows just enough of the room to guide Hans onto the table. Ulrich positions him in the center, heaving, worrying about his heart, as he must when his guests are bulky.

He fits the inhaler over Hans's mouth and turns on the tank. Hans sighs as the gas starts to flood his system, eyes bulging beneath their lids. Ulrich leans in to take a whiff from the small leak where the tube meets the inhaler. He always permits himself one. Then he leans back, savoring the taste before letting it out through his nose. As he does, he leans in again, having already forgotten his first whiff, and takes a second, and then, after a somber pause, a third.

More than comfortably dizzy now, he pulls down Hans' pants and affixes one electrode to the underside of the tip of his penis, another to the base, and one behind each testicle. Then he turns the other machine on, sending out low-level electricity that turns the young man's groin a light blue, the color around the yolk of a hard-boiled egg.

The final step is to cover the body with a lightly scented sheet, made in Vienna and mailed here by his son in the early days of his project. It's perforated enough to breathe through as the machines slowly prepare the young man for his role in his son's film. In the part of the sheet that covers Hans's face is a silkscreened image of his son's face, which, when stretched taut, gives an agonized superimposition that Ulrich supposes his son is striving to express.

Ulrich shows himself out, turning off the work light and turning on the surveillance camera that will record Hans's processing to a disk on his desktop computer, and to a disk on his son's as well, two hundred kilometers away, in the heart of Vienna.

Back in the living room, he has to remind himself he's already had his glass of wine. He turns on the kettle for lemon tea, drizzling three deep spoons of honey over the teabag because he feels more uneasy than usual.

When it's ready, he leaves it where it is and takes the wine bottle, finding that his will to resist, for the moment anyway, has abandoned him. Swigging from it and beginning to feel his eyes water, he hurries into his room. Setting the bottle down on the desk, he turns on the light and boots up the computer, looking out the window at his black property. The console beeps a minute later, returning him to the room he's surprised to find himself still in.

The desktop is pure white, no background.

He sighs, then clicks on the CAM 1 icon. It loads for a moment, then cues up the feed of Hans on the worktable.

Ulrich leans closer to the screen, reminding himself that the boy he's looking at isn't his son, despite the image of his son's face stretched over the stranger's. *Just a stranger*, he recites. *Another stranger, like the rest of them, sent here by my son because he trusts me to help him make his first masterpiece. The vision that will establish him as a great filmmaker in Vienna is, in part, in my hands. He needs me. In this regard, if not in any other, he needs me still.*

As Ulrich watches, Hans shivers and groans and twists toward the camera, looking straight at it through white, occluded eyes visible through the sheet. His look is so pitiful, so imploring, that Ulrich begins to sob.

He presses his watery face to the screen, which burns it with static, and closes his eyes, letting the awful feed play out against his lids.

♦

Ulrich wakes against the screen and leans back from it, hoping for the return of the certainty that the boy down there is not his son.

But this certainty does not return. He feels nothing but terror at the possibility that his son is suffering because of him. He bolts up from the desk and down the stairs, desperate to intercede. He tears open the door to the workroom in an instinctual rage, begging the Catholic God of Austria whom he hates with all his heart to spare his son this one last time.

The young man lies on the worktable, the machine grinding away at his groin.

Ulrich pauses to watch, once again striving for a certainty that eludes him. Then he enters a frenzy beyond anything from his days in the military, ripping out everything that's attached to the body, pulling off the inhaler, which hisses and spews, gas seeping into his sinuses and down his throat.

The young man falls off the worktable and lands on his face on the floor. Ulrich tries to lift him and cannot. His heart stutters and he falls next to him, paralyzed, eyes mashed into the grate. The perforated sheet falls over them both and there they remain, the camera recording without adjusting focus, sending the footage straight to Vienna.

Much later in the night, Hans comes to.

He doesn't try to remember where he is or what the circumstances of his being here might be, or why his nose and throat are so cool and raw. He only moves, fast, out from under the sheet and away from the old man collapsed beside him.

Crawling and hunching along, he makes it into the kitchen. His back feels broken, but he manages to climb into a chair and lean against the table. There he remains, a thin stream of blood working its way from his penis to his ankles.

He can see the coffeemaker and a swath of spilled grounds and believes he would be restored, that his life would be saved, if he could only get to it, but he cannot. He's unsure how injured he is. He has the feeling that the deepest injuries will only reveal themselves in time.

He passes out at the table, the smell of coffee like a faraway breakfast on the other side of the night he's now sinking back into.

Under the sheet with the gas crawling over him, Ulrich relives the morning his son declared he was going to Vienna.

He knocks on his father's door and says, "Wake up." They hadn't said this many words to one another in a year.

Ulrich wakes up, feeling the cold of his room and the staleness of the air that can't escape because all the windows are closed. He sits in bed, looking at his watch though he can't read it in the dark, taking comfort in knowing that his map collection is displayed all around him, every location precisely labeled. His son knocks again and says, "Get dressed, we're leaving."

So Ulrich does.

When he comes out, his son, eighteen, is wearing his coat and scarf though it's only September, with a backpack and suitcase beside him. He stands at the door with his back to his father, looking out at the light that's starting to rise over the field that leads to the woods and the lake.

Ulrich sets about making coffee, knowing there isn't time, and his son shouts that there isn't time, not turning his head from the door. So Ulrich leaves it where it is, grounds spilled on the counter, and follows his son into the car.

They pull out of the gravel driveway and take the back route into Gmunden. Even then, Ulrich abhorred the roundabout. They park at the station and Ulrich stands by the fat retired men in the café, already smoking and wiping their stained fingers on their newspaper pile at 6AM, while his son buys a one-way ticket.

When his son is ready, they walk together onto the tracks. Ulrich sits on the bench expecting his son to do likewise, but his son stands, wearing his backpack and balancing his suitcase against his thigh.

It takes more than fifteen minutes for the train to arrive. During this time, all his son says is, "I'm going to the Academy of Fine Arts in Vienna to become the greatest filmmaker our country has ever known. Greater than Ulrich Seidl, greater even than Michael Haneke. You'll hear from me once I've made inroads," he promises, as the train finally approaches. "I'll need your help then."

Ulrich nods and stays seated as his son climbs aboard, his first time on a train, not looking out the window to check if his father is following his progress with his eyes.

Lying paralyzed under the sheet, Ulrich knows there's nothing to do but wait, and so chooses to wait inside this memory, which is deep enough to withstand the gas filtering into his bloodstream. He extends the memory by imagining that the time to leave the bench will never come, that his son's train will never pull all the way out of sight, only reach the horizon and stay there, leaving him to spend eternity watching it from that remove, like a figure in a painting.

Hans still lies slumped at the kitchen table as the last of the night drags on. When a little energy flows back into him, he opens the freezer from where he sits. By feel, he extracts a steak. This he holds to his groin, trying to freeze the blood that doesn't want to clot. He revisits the bleak day Ulrich's son approached him in Vienna, after his breakdown, claiming that his father's land, especially the lake behind it, had recuperative properties unlike those in any commercial rest spa anywhere in Europe. And that it was free for friends.

He grips the steak so hard a piece breaks off.

When a little light finally drips into the dark outside, Hans stands, wincing, and puts the rest of the steak in the sink. He limps as purposefully as he can into the room where Ulrich is dreaming. He feels stronger now, ready to fight. Lying on the ground under the sheet, Ulrich has crossed one leg over the other, sitting on the bench at the station in his dream.

Gripping it with both hands, Hans tears off the sheet and shouts, "Get up! I'm going to the Academy of Fine Arts in Vienna to become the greatest filmmaker our country has ever known!"

Ulrich's eyes shoot open, a babyish plea covering his face. Then surrender. He nods as much as his sore throat and neck will allow him, and sits up with Hans's help, already uncertain if the boy just said what he thinks he said.

He falls back onto the worktable when he tries to stand, staying upright on the second try. They walk together through the kitchen and onto the porch, then across the gravel that the delivery truck disturbed at this hour yesterday. Hans helps Ulrich into the car, handing him the keys.

They pull out, taking the back route to Gmunden, where it's unlikely they'll be seen.

Hans closes his eyes, ceding the moment to Ulrich.

They pull into the station, Hans helping him out of the car, and walk past the fat men in the café with their cigarettes and newspapers and mute rural hatred.

Ulrich lets them look while Hans negotiates the ticket machine, paying his one-way fare with coins from his back pocket.

When this is done, they stumble together across the tracks, to the far platform for the Vienna-bound train. There's no one else waiting.

Ulrich tries to say something, either an apology or a demand for apology, but stops before getting anything out. Hans looks over at him, then back at the empty track. He reaches in his pockets, feels his irradiated testicles and knows he'll never have children but that some other greatness awaits him down the line.

After fifteen minutes, the train comes into view.

It slows very gradually, so that only the last car lines up with the platform. Hans brushes himself off and climbs on, trying to stand at his full height despite the pain, looking back at Ulrich only once.

Ulrich looks too, accepting for the last time that he'll never see his son again. The train pulls out, sticking for a moment at the far edge of his line of sight. Then it's gone, and Ulrich understands that his son's film is finished, or as finished as it'll ever be. By this time next year, with any luck, it'll be playing in theaters or galleries around the world.

When he can no longer see or even hear the train, Ulrich gets up and crosses the tracks, and walks back past the fat men without looking at them, and gets in his car, driving through the center of town and around the roundabout, no longer concerned with preserving his anonymity or preserving anything at all.

He parks in his driveway and walks straight into the woods, all the way to the lake, where he sits on the rock and waits for the child to appear. When it doesn't after several hours, and his life has come to feel intolerably sealed around him, he gets up and starts walking along the shore, in the direction of the child's or children's cabin.

I'm the one you want now, he thinks, as if he'll have to explain it to them. *There will be no more of the others. Just tell me what you did to my son all those years ago, to make him how he is. Then you can do the same thing to me.* He rehearses the words again and again, praying the children will understand German.

When he gets there, it's night. There's no light on, but he knows he or she or they are home. He creaks up the porch and pushes open the door. The interior smells like cat food.

He fumbles in his pockets for a cigarette. Not finding one, he looks up as two of the children push toward him. He can hear them sniffing, their noses hacking at air, trying to bring it to their brains through layers of blockage and scar.

They press up to him, into his groin and belly, trying to ascertain who or what he is.

He closes his eyes, waits to feel their teeth and venom, unsure if the sensation will be more like the teeth of a squirrel or those of a lizard. His back tenses, his nerves pulling straight and tight, bracing for it. He pictures himself as the boy in the surveillance feed, smothered under a sheet, watched over by his father from another room.

But the bite doesn't come. He keeps waiting, unable to see the children, but still the bite doesn't come and now he can hear them backing away, mumbling "*too old… too old…*" in a dialect he hasn't heard anyone use since he was their age.

Instead of fainting or leaving, a strength seizes him and heaves him across the floor and into their dark, where he grabs one of their heads and forces it into his side. It scrabbles, punching at his groin, hissing, but he presses tighter, so tight it has to bite him in order to breathe, tearing into the flesh so it can suck the oxygen in his blood.

He feels the venom racing through him, extra potent because of the child's fear.

At first he can hear the other one hissing in some mix of repulsion and jealousy, its words sub- or pre-German now, Thuringian, Alemannic, and then he feels its teeth too and hears nothing but the lapping of the lake outside the window.

He comes to on his back on the far side of the lake where he's never been. It's so dark overhead he can't tell if he's under trees or open sky. His side feels made of cotton, partially stuffed into him and partially fanned out.

Without rolling over, he slides forward, over rocks and then weeds, into the water. It splashes over his face and rushes into his side, soothing the venom.

He floats out to the middle, as flat on his back as the young man had been on the worktable under the sheet, looking up at the sky that still has no moon, that offers no way through, though perhaps something up there is watching him. Nocturnal fish stream upward into his wound, and in the venom-fog he can see the train pulling into the station and a young man stepping off to become a great filmmaker in Vienna.

THE PAINLESS EUTHANASIA ROLLER COASTER

Anders Lücke phases in and out of the dinner party, playing the part of the lonely, barely invited drunk—though he knows it's a part he isn't exactly *playing*—until something rare occurs: a topic is broached that rivets him. Fritz Baumann, still in his forties and already vice-chair of the Physics Department from which Anders accepted forced retirement ten years ago, mentions, casually enough, that he has heard of a young man who has designed what he calls a *Painless Euthanasia Roller Coaster*, intended to kill those who are in chronic pain, or who simply feel they've lived too long, with one last, theoretically painless ride. "A prototype has apparently already been set up in an undisclosed location in the foothills of the Alps, awaiting volunteer test subjects," Baumann says, while his wife pours him more wine.

The conversation drifts onward from here, not stopping very long on this topic, as if all topics deserved equal attention, but there is, for Anders, nothing else. So he nods off again, into a dream of the roller coaster, his body flying around its gruesome but somehow painless curves, until, as usual, a pair of hands appears in his armpits and an attached voice says, "Let's get you home," and then, after an equally typical dizzy spell in a taxicab, he's back in his damp bed, and then, a few hours later, in his usual seat at the Café Schober, stirring his Milchkaffee and picking apart his apple strudel while roaming from one headline to another in the *Süddeutsche Zeitung*, until, this morning, something changes: in the back of the final section of the paper, where the obituaries and personal ads are quarantined, he comes across a small, ambivalently worded article about the Painless Euthanasia Roller Coaster, and he can sense, even before he's done reading, that maybe, drab and shapeless and unending as his days have come to seem, and may in all likelihood—Anders is a man of science, a realist—actually be, *maybe this is that for which I've been waiting all my life, in the obvious and moronic sense in which everyone is waiting all their lives for death, yes, of course*, he thinks, but, leaving his few coins on the table and creaking painfully to his feet, *perhaps in a deeper and more personally specific sense as well. Maybe here, at last, is something special. Something in this world meant just for me.*

Over the course of that day, spent, as all days, wandering the old and drafty streets of the city, from the edge of the university where he's no longer welcome to the alley of used booksellers whose wares no longer speak to him, Anders comes to see that the roller coaster, and nothing else, will be the culmination of his tenure on this planet. Suicide has always struck him as a weakness not dissimilar to that of lying in bed all day eating sweets, an option not to be considered seriously by full-grown men and women who have looked existence in the eye and recognized it for what it is, but the roller coaster seems like something else, a form of suicide too sophisticated to go by that pedantic term. *An evolution in the science of how lives end, an option I would not have imagined possible*, he thinks, deciding here and now to find a means of surmounting the line between idea and action, *a means of consecrating my death to research*, though he knows the real reason is more than this, buried deeper within him.

♦

So Anders begins moving through the several networks of which he is still a tangential part, from one so-called expert to another, until he emerges a month or so later in a field several miles beyond the outermost Zürich suburbs, wearing a plastic windbreaker and the pressed khakis of the professor he used to be. He extends his hand to a surprisingly young scientist who introduces himself as Jürgen Trakl, self-proclaimed inventor of the Painless Euthanasia Roller Coaster, among other devices, "some public," he mutters with poorly affected modesty, "and a great many others not."

Anders' attention is already on the steep, wild curves of the apparatus, jutting upward toward the occluded moon, each loop narrower and more vicious than the last.

"You understand what this is, yes?" he hears the young man inquire, in the clipped, hasty manner of a scientist eager to dispense with formalities and get down to the substance of his experiment.

Anders, of course, is just as eager. "I do. The roller coaster, if it works, will kill me. All this," he gestures at the field, the stars, the Alps, "will go away."

Jürgen nods, clearly relieved to be dealing with so sanguine a subject. "The torque of the loops, combined with the acceleration of the car, will pool increasingly more blood in your lower extremities, first your feet, then your shins, then your thighs, until, by the final loop, your heart will be unable to recover that blood and you will, quite painlessly, switch off." He looks at the roller coaster, as if to verify that what he's just said about his own work is correct. Then he adds, "Of course, the Swiss government would never approve its testing. Nevertheless, following the opportunism typical of bureaucratic bodies the world over, they'll be only too glad to approve its use once it's proven to be effective and, most importantly, painless. Thus, I've let it be known that my prototype exists, and is now ready for the right kind of test subject… you realize, however, that we cannot guarantee its painlessness at this point in its development. Correct?"

After Anders nods, Jürgen claps him on the back. "Very good then. Also, and this is my proudest achievement with regards to the prototype, a moment of euphoria will theoretically occur in the very last instant. A weightless interregnum at the bottom of the roller coaster's ultimate descent, as the blood is pumped for the last time out of your heart. A moment of, and please pardon the poetic phrase, *ultimate mental clarity*. You may well come to know, at the very edge of death, that which, had you known it sooner, could have rendered your life a success, if you'll pardon my bluntness in saying so."

Jürgen wipes a tear from his cheek, and Anders has to repress a scowl. *I'm the one about to die*, he thinks, *and he's the one crying?* "Thank you," he says. "That all sounds fine. Now shall we?"

Anders is strapped into his car, a lone rider in the vast Swiss night. Without human preamble but after some mechanical stuttering, the ride twists up an initial series of loops, rocking back and forth, reminding Anders of the roller coaster in Turin he rode as a child with his parents in the years after the Second World War. The memory brings a tear to his eye, as the roller coaster tilts upward, gaining speed, then barreling down, twisting him violently though not quite painfully, jostling his organs, raining blood inside his head. He finds himself wondering when it's going to happen, when, not to mention what, the crucial moment will be. The borderline that the roller coaster will take him across, such that he now begins to picture it not as a modern euthanasia device but as a simple death train, dragging its condemned passenger to the territory from which there is no return, just as there wasn't for the millions deported on trains during the years in which he was a little boy.

But then he thinks, *no, this mustn't be my last thought. These mustn't be my last thoughts, as they were for too many people already.* The roller coaster knocks his head to one side, flipping him over, jolting him to the left and then the right as his mind goes blank.

When he comes to, Jürgen and his assistants are hovering over him, collecting his breath on a mirror, shining lights in his eyes. He tracks an expression of profound disappointment on Jürgen's face as the safety bar clicks open and the assistants help him to his feet. Running his hands through his hair, Jürgen says, "How could it not have worked? We tested it on so many dummies, so many straw men, so many weight-calibrated mannequins."

Anders is in no hurry to correct him with the conviction he now feels, the conviction that he's wrong, that it did indeed work, and that this, all of it, here and now, is the other side. *So this is death*, he thinks, observing the scientists' faces as if they belonged to a line of sentient robots. *I hoped it would be stranger, more foreign, the way I'd always pictured Africa before my fellowship in Cape Town.* His mind continues along these lines as he wanders into the night, ready to walk for hours, indifferent to Jürgen's cries of, "Where are you going? Come back here, we need to test your vital signs… come back here this instant!"

Here begins a new phase for Anders, one spent in his apartment, among his books and science journals and the bills piling up, all of which hold solely aesthetic interest, purged of all bearing on his future, now that he doesn't have one.

Early in this phase, the Swiss government officially bans further testing on the Painless Euthanasia Roller Coaster, now that it's been proven ineffective—Anders has quite a laugh reading the maudlin interview that Jürgen gave to the *Zeitung*.

Zürich instead builds a park and bike trail around the prototype, allowing the brutal metal curves to remain, having been recast, during a dramatic announcement at Art Basel, as "the single most daring step in large-scale conceptual land art in a generation," and rewarding Jürgen, who has traded his white lab coat for the black T-shirt and leather jacket of an urbane artiste, handsomely. Anders can't help but smile at the shameful compromises continually made by the living in their insectoid desperation to persevere. With a feeling akin to fondness, he remembers the anger he would have felt ten or twenty years ago, when he was still alive.

Nevertheless, he can't deny that buying a simple sandwich and a bottle of white wine at the corner market and taking the city bus out to what's now called *CoasterPark*, and eating it beside the gleaming metal structure, in the foothills of the Alps, amidst the crying of babies and the laughter of young couples, some of them speaking German, some French, some Arabic, while behind them lurk young Coaster enthusiasts, pale students sporting tattoos of Jürgen's sinusoidal design, is a charming and sometimes even transcendent means of spending a Sunday.

On days like this, Anders looks at the loops of the roller coaster, each narrower and steeper than the last, and wonders which one he died on, where the crucial turn was. Then, going back over the whole of his life, he has the distinct feeling of being an old man, still living, faced once again with the roller coaster he loved as a boy, when he was small and fresh and full both of life and the nascent fear of death, all of it combined in the thrill that only this one ride could induce. At moments like this, he finds it isn't difficult to imagine how he'd feel if he were merely old, not dead, looking in wonder at the unchanged metal track he rode more than half a century ago, when Europe was still emerging from the hell of its own making, and he finds he can't help tearing up as he wonders how it could possibly be that he, an old man drunk on white wine at noon, is still here, while that boy, so much more worthy of life and so much more willing to live it, is not, and never will be again.

THE BROTHERS SQUIMBOP IN EUROPE

After everything they'd set in motion in the States had run its gruesome course, the Brothers Squimbop decided to ship out east, back where their something-something-somethings had sailed from, once upon a time, to see if things were any funnier on the other side. Refreshed by this possibility, they made it across in a little under a week, stowing away on a nineteenth-century steamer carrying oats, horses, and touched-up Model T's.

They disembarked at the Hook of Holland along with a sweaty and cursing rabble, and wended their way into the narrow streets, flexing their nostrils against the smoke and blackening meat in the air. As their wending went on and the crowd thinned out, they found themselves lost among blind men and women draped in rags and dragging carts while legless children went scooting along the cobblestones on tricked-out skateboards.

These sights and others like them proliferated until the Brothers stopped to lean against a grease-stained and graffitied bus station wall, and thought to themselves, *say, doesn't this all look a little more like how we always imagined things back then, and a little less like how we always imagined them now?* Not that there was much recourse if there'd indeed been a switcheroo, but it couldn't hurt to find out, and, seeing as they were leaning against a bus station wall, they figured they were already partway toward turning up someone they could ask, or, at the very least, a trustworthy piece of signage.

So they peeled themselves off the wall and sauntered through the automatic doors, which whooshed open onto a dim terminal full of muffled footsteps and rolling gusts of air-conditioning. Everything was immaculate, like an exhibit of a bus station from an earlier or a later time, a testament to how things once were or might one day be, if the chips fell one way and not another, complete with demo-people sitting on benches, watching the Brothers pass.

Through this heavy quiet, they made their way to an *InfoKiosk*, labeled as such, and put their swarthy faces up to the polished, fresh face of a young woman in a blue pantsuit with a short red scarf tied around her neck and asked, in unison, whether this here was now or then.

The woman blinked, computed for part of a second, and looked from one Brother to the other, as if keen to assign them roles. Then she replied, "Well, gentlemen, that depends on whom you ask." She sighed, as if the implications of this statement ought to be obvious, the burden it conveyed shared by all. The Brothers attempted to appear as if this were so, but their attempt must've been unconvincing, because she added, a moment later, "There have been a number of referendums lately, attempts to determine whether the modern era you see in here, or the medieval era you see out there, is the pretend one. Because certainly—nearly everyone agrees on this much, though not an inch more—they can't both be genuine. One must be the pageant, the other the actual present time. But who's to say which is which? Well, the people are to say, of course, and yet what happens when the people become no more than a volatile surplus of ghoul-eyed persons?"

She paused here, as if waiting for an answer, then adjusted her scarf, looked from one Brother to the other, cleared her throat and said, "Well, gentlemen, that depends on whom you ask." She sighed. "There have been a number of referendums lately, attempts to determine whether the modern era you see in here, or the medieval era you see out there, is the pretend one. Because certainly—nearly everyone agrees on this much, though not an inch more—they can't both be genuine. One must be the pageant, the other the actual present time. But who's to say which is which? Well, the people are to say, of course, and yet what happens when the people become no more than a volatile surplus of ghoul-eyed persons?"

When she'd finished, the Brothers thanked her for the info and, sensing opportunity, hurried back out of the bus station and into the throng surrounding it.

They posted up at a plastic table fronting a meat and flatbread stall, bought as much as the last of their dollars would get them, and ate with their hands, kicking the stray cats that poured in to nip at their ankles. The eating and the wincing and the kicking took on the rhythm of a routine, a clown escapade, and, before long, a filth-crusted public had clustered in to watch. Faces grew out of the shoulders wedged behind them, eclipsing all necks, and mouths fell open to jeer and excrete tobacco in unison, like it was a multi-headed beast the Brothers had summoned, a bulbous hee-hawing demon they could puppet with their legs, each time they kicked a cat, or with their mouths, each time they howled in pain, or with their arms, now that these too had become incorporated, slamming up and down on the uncleared tabletop, spraying meat leavings in a cloud that surrounded their vision, grease on grease, hovering there as the day heated up.

Now that they were in rhythm, nothing prevented them from reverting all the way back to their roots, tumbling awake, sticky with afterbirth, in the grass of a county fairground in some corn town in Indiana, or on some brown-grassed riverside in Missouri, they could never agree which, but the image of the place, or the feeling of the image, saturated them, and lent their current slapstick an air of pathos, which caused them to drill so deeply into the performance that, by the time they resurfaced, the sun was going down and the crowd was dissipating, leaving in its wake a pile of wilting reddish bills whose value the Brothers could only pray wasn't nothing.

They stood, shivering as they came back to the present, and scooped the haul into their fists, divvying it fifty-fifty. Then they walked into the darkening side streets behind the market square, past the circle of cats they'd kicked to death, through air heavy with the scent of damp wool and frying gristle. "Through air heavy with the scent of damp wool and frying gristle," they repeated in unison, storing the line for future use. It wasn't until they'd rounded several blind corners, climbed a steep set of concrete stairs past a cathedral whose stained glass windows had been reduced to trembling stalactites, and traversed a boardwalk whose boards had long since rotted to nail-bitten slats, that they came to the ocean, black and calm and fishy as any ocean anywhere.

They walked out of the light of a row of hotels and beach bars, past a harbor where dinghies and sailboats bobbed at anchor, and up to a cove at the edge of the city, which they judged as safe a place as any to sit and think.

A scuttling in a spruce tree overhead forced them to reconsider, but a glance revealed it to be no more than a squirrel, and a second glance revealed it to be, perhaps, not even that. Still, they reasoned, it would be wise to buy knives.

With this much decided, they spread their haul across the sand, counted it by feel in the dark and, agreeing to believe that it represented a substantial sum, looked toward the future. *Whatever place this is*, they thought, *it seems to contain a receptive audi-*

ence, if today's is any indication.

Satisfied with their new prospects, and thus relieved to be free of the deadening alternation of Missouri and Michigan, Arkansas and Arizona, state after state drying up and blowing away as they lectured in empty halls watered by dripping spigots, they burrowed into the sand, hot on top and cool underneath, and slept amidst the sandflies and the crashing surf, dreaming of glory.

The sun broiled them awake a few hours later, so fast and hot the first thing that reached them was the smell of their own smoking skin, a rich, meaty aroma that sent them out in search of breakfast.

After a quick repast of stewed goat and black bread at a stall staffed by almond-eyed gypsies, they set out on the road that led up from the valley in which the Hook of Holland nestled, and soon found themselves tracing a network of mountain passes, looking down at blue lagoons and up at destitute settlements freckling rock faces, their streets so steep it seemed to the Brothers that only spidermen could live there.

As the day wore on and the lack of food and water took its toll, it began to seem that spidermen were indeed clinging to the streets of these jagged mountain towns, nailed to chairs outside smoky cafes or leaning over iron balconies with pipes dangling from their mouths, watching through motionless eyes as these two dehydrated and improbable wanderers passed by below. The streets were now so steep they closed in overhead, forming a dome that the Brothers had to lean back and stare up at, making eye contact with elderly spidermen and -women sipping coffee from tiny cups and picking at wilting pastries that, through a logic all their own, held fast to their ornate china platters.

"Either we've wandered someplace heavy, Brother," Jim whispered once it was clear that both of them were perceiving the same tableau, "or we've got about five minutes to find something to drink before we collapse."

Joe, whose skin was steaming, had already come to this conclusion and thus began hectoring an old woman dragging a donkey cart who'd just appeared. He begged her to spare some of the black liquid that dangled in a clear canister from a leather strap tied to her wrist, hoping it wasn't tar or motor oil. Though she didn't speak, she seemed to understand the request well enough to pull the donkey's metal bowl from a clattering pile of tools in the cart and place it on the ground with a sigh, bracing it with her foot as she poured it half full.

When she'd done this, she stood back, placed her hands on her hips, and looked the Brothers over. Recognition played across her face, like she expected them to know her, but they ignored it, and she made no move to force the issue.

Joe sank to his knees, then down to his belly, propping his upper body on his flat palms so as to swivel his face into the black liquid. He spooled his tongue down into its viscid depths and tasted molasses and honey and possibly something fermented, but it was sweet and hearty and, as far as he could tell, not poisonous.

He drank until the woman kicked him aside. Then he rolled into the dust and watched as Jim took his turn, lapping until the woman kicked him aside as well, so as to make room for the donkey.

When the donkey had also finished—the woman didn't kick it aside, but merely waited until the creature looked up—the Brothers wiped their mouths, got to their feet, and looked the woman over. She was old and hunched and her left side had a pronounced tremor. Though she had both eyes, they could already hear themselves telling a roomful of townspeople tonight, if they were lucky enough to find a town, how they'd met a crazed one-eyed sorceress on the road, and how she'd nursed them back to health with some black poison that had imbued them with the power to contact the dead, or to detect the winging of notional creatures in the high ether, or perhaps to....

But there'd be plenty of time for all that later. The thing now was to impress upon her their need to end up in this imagined town by nightfall. They pointed up the road, which had returned most of the way to horizontality, and squinted at the sky to show that the sun was blinding them. There was no means by which they could convey the nature of the hallucinations they'd had before meeting her, but they hoped their pantomime would nevertheless prove that their condition was dire. They were careful to both look in the same direction, lest she tell one of them to go one way, and the other another.

"We need food, shelter," they intoned, hugging themselves and dancing, which had the effect of making the old woman smile. As they went on, clownishly exaggerating their motions, she began to guffaw.

She rocked back and forth on her heels, and didn't stop until the Brothers had winded themselves and staggered over to the remnants of a cement wall by the edge of the road, where they panted and spat up long gobs of brown phlegm.

When this routine too had reached its conclusion, she lurched over to them and, as if she'd been joking all this time in her bafflement at the language they spoke, said, in a clean Dutch or German accent, "Nearest town's up that way, about an hour. Rough place. Take care, boys."

Then she kicked the donkey, tightened the screw cap on her empty bottle, and trudged off with a knowing wave.

♦

The Brothers made haste in the direction she'd indicated, heads full of loose story that, by the time they arrived, would have compacted itself into an open-road tale that ought to earn them a drink or two, and, if they were lucky, a few mouthfuls of fried meat to mop it up with. They riffed and rehearsed as they went, and the road seemed to flatten out to accommodate them, apparently satisfied with the ordeal it'd put them through.

As they emerged into the twilit glow of the outskirts, they ambled across smooth cobblestones, rows of high-end Scandinavian cars parked on one side, piles of horse dung intermingled on the other, and crossed what felt like an unguarded but highly tangible border, away from the open road and into the stagnant sanctum of a new town. Immediately, townspeople began to look them over with a mix of wariness and intrigue.

The very fact that they'd managed to enter the town from outside seemed sufficient to arouse the interest of these people, who appeared, like everyone the Brothers had met so far except for the woman on the road, to be stuck in place, circling a vanishingly small center of gravity. *More like plants than people*, the Brothers thought, as they climbed the concrete base of a towering statue of some chisel-jawed dictator. *It's almost*, they thought, clearing their throats and beholding the gathering crowd, *like these people haven't succeeded in being born yet. Like they're still tethered by some umbilical link to this tiny patch of earth, absorbing ever more degraded nutrience as they wait for the clarifying event that we are now here to deliver.*

Opening their mouths when they judged the crowd sufficiently swollen, Jim began, "We are, good people, free agents who've made our way here all the way from America to tell you that, even as we speak, there are lurkers on the surrounding roadways."

Joe continued, after a nudge from Jim, "Indeed, we came to tell you that witches are massing on the peripheries. They're flocking together, gaining strength. Why, just today, we passed a one-eyed sorceress who forced us to kneel beside her donkey and drink a gout of blackest poison. If we'd refused, she would've turned us into infants and left us to await our deaths in the crushing heat. The poison was the lesser evil, though only very slightly."

He held his side and mimed collapse from stomach pain, inducing Jim to join in. The crowd laughed, cautiously, everyone looking to the person beside them to be sure they were laughing too.

"We dispatched that witch," Joe groaned, "only after great toil, and at great personal risk." He fumbled in his pocket for a hank of fur he'd torn from the donkey while Jim was supping. "Here's the last of her. But be warned, more are coming. They are, even now, meeting in hollows in the surrounding wilderness, planning their onslaught. As we've said, we come from America, a land already ruined by sorcery. It is too late for us, but not, thank God, for you."

"Not," Jim added, shouting over the growing clamor of the crowd, "provided you enlist our services. For we alone, good people, can preserve the order that has suddenly grown fragile. For a modest fee, we will enchant the peripheries of your town, seeing to it that no witches penetrate the inner sanctum, which all of you have worked so hard to preserve for yourselves, and your children, and your children's children."

It was almost too easy. The Brothers hadn't come to Europe in search of a challenge, but something about the speed with which these people foisted their crumpled currency upon them and proffered food, drink, and lodging at the ramshackle inn behind the slaughterhouse left them with a queasy feeling, like that of eating a milky pudding whose sweetness has begun to curdle.

Nevertheless, they left that town the next day in high spirits, and set out back on the open road with the promise that no witches would ever penetrate the protective spell they were about to cast. They made their way upward, farther, as they imagined it, from the Hook of Holland, though their memory of arriving in Europe already felt warped and dented by the heat, a useless thing they ought to throw away before it went off in their rucksacks.

Day by day, town by town, business began to boom. The Brothers worked through all the classics, spreading tell of well poisonings and child abduction, changelings and incest and miscegenation by ravening wildmen eager to rape young girls out milking at dawn, or picking red berries in the pastor's woods for Sunday breakfast; they warned of currency manipulation and the malicious spread of occult science; they fanned the already flickering flames of suspicion that desert religions were seeping into the groundwater of mountain ones, and vice versa, turning the True Word into a mush-mouthed abomination thereof, blasphemy upon blasphemy, moral decrepitude and decline, and they sowed fear of paternity, of bloodlines sundered and contaminated by Moors and Masons and Jews, of politicians serving as the puppets of unseen masters, simpering in the boardrooms of cities that no one present had ever seen, and few had ever heard of. They called into question whether the year was 1613 or 1835 or 1999, and they turned neighbor against neighbor, seeing to it that none could trust any of what they read or heard or—once the Brothers really got going—even any of what they themselves believed. They bribed printers to issue contradictory versions of the same local papers and claimed that orphan trains had been found in the Ukrainian steppe, thousands upon thousands of children strong, worshipping star deities and tattooing themselves with runes and hieroglyphs, breeding in ever quicker succession, children begetting children, then infants begetting infants, triplets emerging from wombs where only one child had been conceived. Trains of goats birthing blind children who in turn birthed goats, all of them growing into mad kings and queens, wrecking the world while pretending to run it.

"No one but us can be trusted," the Brothers Squimbop told town after town after town, the crowds sometimes composed of gap-toothed peasants riven with buboes, and sometimes of gap-toothed teenagers in torn jeans and soccer jerseys, straining to comprehend the Brothers' English, "because we alone have traveled the open road, and the high seas, and we have seen what's afoot out there. We know the full scope of what can happen. The entirety of America, ruined before our eyes. Here in the towns, lies beget lies, and those who appear most blameless are surely the most corrupt."

As the weeks became months, they expanded their repertoire, deviating from the classics and ranging more boldly into tales of their own design. "Werewolves are stealing in from the deep Carpathian woods at night," they told the people of one town, "and impregnating your cows, so that any calves born to them must be buried in molten iron, lest they grow into three-headed demons, their milk the fibrous nectar of the Gnostic Satan, who will, in time, be born to a human mother and crawl into your pantries to sup."

In the next town, they said that chickens all over the countryside had been caught in the dark of a lunar eclipse and sent backward on their evolutionary path, so that soon lizards would begin hatching from their eggs and then, if nothing was done to stop it, dinosaurs. Dinosaurs, they stressed, that would take to the skies and reduce whole regions to ash in the course of one long Walpurgisnacht, as soon as the next eclipse happened to occur.

There was, it seemed, nothing they couldn't sell. Any tale at all, delivered by the Brothers Squimbop, would send any town into a frenzy of preparation, in which the people would, without hesitation, slaughter their cows or drown their chickens, or, in the towns where the Brothers suggested that the monsters were already amongst them, having assumed human form, turn the market square into a pyre whose flames loomed above all the buildings surrounding it.

They dragged their roadshow through Belgian swamps and up jagged alpine ridges, brandishing the knives they'd purchased at a silversmith's in Zürich at monkeys and bears and the occasional lowland fox. They rode sometimes in military vans driven by silent, masked soldiers, and sometimes they stowed away on boats crossing pristine glacial fjords or sweltering stretches of sea between one Greek isle and the next. They told themselves that they cared little for their lives, yet nothing seemed eager to kill them. On the contrary, it seemed as though everything and everyone they came in contact with was operating at a remove, like there was an invisible dead space between themselves and the world they were describing, or conjuring, so that while they could trudge across fields of unexploded mines in the hills above Sarajevo, or swim to land after an Italian pleasure boat they'd snuck aboard capsized off the coast of Sicily, there was never any threat, or chance, of a permanent reprieve. *The demand for our services*, they thought, while basking in the shadow of Mount Vesuvius, *is too great to let us go. Indeed, perhaps, it's all there is. The only factor still in play.*

It was only when, in a mountainside hamlet outside Belgrade, the Brothers beheld a troupe of eyeless, infant-sized creatures leading a herd of goats on chains through the square that they were forced to pause. They observed the goats birthing more of these creatures as casually as excreting the roughage of their morning kibble, hardly stopping as the monsters fell out of them. These monsters then rose to their feet, produced chains from someplace the Brothers couldn't identify and, perhaps from that same place, produced more goats, who in turn produced more monsters and chains and goats, which in turn sent the Brothers scrabbling along a steep, dusty goat path all the way back to Belgrade, where they holed up in a WWI-era pension, desperate only for a little time to regroup.

They lay in bed the next morning until the sunlight through the window began to singe their foreheads. Then they got up, hosed down in the shower stall on the first floor, and went into the square for flatbread and coffee. Here, as over the days that followed, they watched chaos begin to mount, voices rising in Serbian and Greek and Russian and dialects they couldn't identify, a sense of alarm rising toward a breaking point they could tell was near. As newspapers and broadsides began to circulate photos of mass riots, villages in flame, altars and effigies soaked in blood, the tables around them began to empty out. Everyone, so far as they could tell, was mobilizing, mobbing the train stations and bus terminals, or marching, en masse, out of Belgrade and toward what the Brothers assumed must be the coast.

Just like that, they thought, among the crumbs at their breakfast table in the now empty square a week later, *our journey has taken a turn. Today is likewise the day for us to flee.* So they packed their few belongings and hustled up the cobbled streets, strewn with the heads of chickens and the entrails of sheep, past capsized buggies and corpses writhing with strange new life, until they made it to the teeming train station. They were jostled this way and that, hauled off a train they'd already boarded and shoved onto another, destination unknown, and yet still they were happy to be aboard. They sat back in their seats, among passengers wearing antlers on their heads, or on shrunken heads around their necks—the Brothers could dimly remember spreading tales of this faction—stuffed with yellow eyes that seemed to gaze out with hellish intensity.

They wriggled down on the leather banquette and fell into a spiral of nightmares. When they awoke, perhaps days later, the few remaining passengers were disembarking. Even so, the Brothers tried to remain, eyes closed and knees hugged to their chests, but the conductor came by and, as if expecting to find them in precisely this aspect, sighed, barked something in a language they couldn't understand, and dragged them out, first Jim and then Joe, depositing them both on the disused track beside the one where the train sat idling. Then, though the conductor had sworn this was the last stop, the train rushed off to the south.

That night, in what appeared to be a town in southern Germany, the Brothers, exhausted and clean out of currency, took to the podium in the central square and simply told what they'd seen. They began with the chains and the goats, continued on through Belgrade, and ended with their journey here. "Europe, good people, is turning strange. There is nothing to say but this. All attempts at warding off what is coming have failed."

Looking out at the crowd, they saw the woman in the black dress with her donkey. She had only one eye, just as they'd cast her in their dozens of speeches across the continent. This eye took them in, sparkling with concern. She mouthed something, her expression dire. *A warning*, they thought. Then she vanished.

They finished speaking and retired to a room above the alehouse, eager to buy themselves more time, though they knew they'd already bought plenty. They drifted off, back to their nightmares.

The next morning, after a repast of rolls and cold meat at the communal table downstairs, where the few townspeople present granted them a wide berth, the Brothers set out, agreeing to spend the day shoring up their routine. *Time to get back on solid ground*, they each thought. *Put our act back together, update our itinerary, refill our coffers. Ensure that the show goes on.*

But no sooner had they reached the next village than each Brother found his attention pulled from his head like stuffing from a dummy. Jim and Joe took to peering away from one another and into butcher shops, blacksmiths', and haberdasheries, imagining the lives of the men undertaking these professions, the colossal quiet that must fill the space of all that was shrieking inside the Brothers. *True ignorance is true innocence*, they found themselves thinking, as if the time to become fathers was drawing near and they were thus imagining these unsuspecting villagers as the children they were soon to have, hammering anvils and flensing steaks within the safety of a village-sized womb.

The day wore on and the Brothers gawped at churchgoers and gravediggers and schoolchildren until the sun began to set and they found themselves at a crowded wooden table outside another alehouse. *It's only a matter of time*, they realized, watching the villagers sup, *before the star-children and money-lenders make their way here, as well. Before the sky fills with runes. There's no stopping it now, and thus*, they decided, dipping a hot pretzel in lard, *nothing to do but warn them.*

So, once they'd finished their meal, such as it was, they took up a perch in the square and Jim began their routine. "We two Brothers have come all the way here from America," he proclaimed, taking comfort in the familiar salvo. "Bearing a simple warning. Something too vast to name, something knowable only in its infinite particulars, lay waste to our land, and is now laying waste to yours, as well."

The ring of truth choked the Brothers Squimbop, but they forced their way past it, looking away from the eye of the woman in the black cloak, who'd reappeared near the front of the growing crowd.

Joe took over. "Trains of blind children leading pregnant goats on chains through the squares of formerly peaceful villages just like this one, making of them a wasteland in the course of a single moonlit spree. Mass rearrangements of the stars, polarities shifting, magnetisms shifting… entire orbits shifting…." He found he couldn't finish a sentence before the next one began. "Wells choked with severed bat wings… goats b-begetting… girl-children fathering halfwits with their outstretched index fingers in obeisance to… to…." His gaze snared, once again, on the woman in the black cloak, and he fell silent.

"In obeisance to," Jim continued, though something told him not to, "a one-eyed sorceress in a black cloak, who… who…."

The crowd, as one, closed in on her. All attention lapsed from the Brothers, rendering them a two-man witness to what was fast becoming a village-wide riot. While they stood there, torches were produced and the alehouse went up in flames. Then the church, the butcher's shop, and the village stables. A grunting and growling emanated from the townspeople, a mass-voice that belonged to none of them in particular, reverberating off the cobblestones and the buckling wood.

Looking up, the Brothers saw the stars rushing together, leaving powdery traces across the firmament, and they heard a low slithering from the distance, and began to hear the smashing of bottles, the breaking of bones, and the spilling of blood. Amidst all this, they bowed to their absent audience and set out running, skirting the edge of the melee as best they could, leaving the sorceress for dead.

They ran through the side streets, avoiding the doorways through which streamed knife-wielding men, women, and children, and made it intact to the sheds and garden plots flanking the outskirts. Here, they deemed it safe to catch their breath before venturing into the surrounding wilderness, which grew hot and misty as it welcomed them, sealing itself off beneath the changed sky.

Now they were lost in a deep wood. The air turned thicker and blacker still, the trunks of tremendous black oaks now brighter than the sky. They marched on, looking straight ahead, or down at their feet, or up at the hint of leaves, anywhere but at one another.

Before long, they were marching through knee-deep moss, past eerie, dripping ferns, singing nursery rhymes at full volume while the forest whispered louder and louder, until it wasn't a whisper at all. Now the forest was ringing and echoing in earnest, their own voices rubbed out, the air filling with traces and smudges in the watery distance, which flickered, trembled, and, as they approached it, resolved into two figures, one of them draped in a black cloak, the other a donkey.

The one-eyed sorceress smiled as they approached, her arms outstretched to receive them. They marched, half-conscious, into her embrace, desperate to be forgiven for what they had made her suffer. Then it was as if she were everywhere, all around them, blotting out the woods and the moss and the smudge of stars, until all they could see or feel or smell was black cloth and red blood, and they felt themselves shrinking inside it, their bones and muscles uncoupling, reverting to unformed flesh.

When the Brothers Squimbop awoke, it was dim, late afternoon or early evening. They winced up to a sitting position, cradled their soft elbows, and scraped thick, sticky ropes of blood and mucus from their thighs and shoulders, then used the backs of their hands to wipe their brows, many times, until they could see.

Looking over, they saw the one-eyed sorceress, mopping between her legs with a black cloth. She smiled at them. "One of these times," she said, looking from Joe to Jim, "I'm going to get tired of doing this."

But she said it without rancor, and even smiled as they rose to their feet and asked if they could help her to hers. She waved them off. "I'll be alright. I ought to be by now." She laughed, but when they stayed, standing above her, and began to laugh as well, her face grew worried. "Go!" she shouted. "What are you waiting for? There's clothes and provisions in the donkey's pack. Take them and be off. Europe is no place for bright young men any longer."

Eager, for once, to obey, the Brothers Squimbop gathered these provisions, dressed themselves, and set out running, out of the forest and into the crackling ruins of a village they could just barely remember, an echo from another lifetime. They hoped to stop for bread and ale, but nothing remained, not even bodies. Well-fed jackals paced among the embers, eyeing the Brothers.

They hurried past a ransacked chicken coop at the far edge of town, lizard skin spooling out of gigantic crushed eggs, and then down a mountainside and through many dense woods, through fields of fire and ash, through deserts and the shells of cities in which ostrich-headed deities presided over mass sacrifices and stars churned and boiled overhead, forming symbols the Brothers took turns staring up at, unable to look away, whatever the psychic cost.

Finally, they arrived in a rubble-strewn metropolis that they decided to call *The Hook of Holland.* They turned to regard a group of monks or penitents in an alley, roasting a naked boy on an open flame, and, though their hunger was great, their eagerness to set sail was greater.

Thus, they gathered their cloaks about themselves and made their way to the harbor, where, though half the ships were capsized and half of those that remained had been hacked to splinters, they boarded a vessel that appeared primed to depart.

After long, dark hours hiding in the hold, among horses and threshers, the ship pulled anchor and began to wheeze out of the harbor, leaving the blighted continent behind at last.

When they judged it safe, the Brothers climbed to the upper deck and watched the last of what remained of Europe vanish to the east. Then they turned westward and watched the sun begin its dimming journey to America.

"This time, Brother, maybe we ought to," Jim Squimbop began, but Joe, eager to enjoy what respite the passage might hold, raised a hand to stop him. If he'd learned anything after all these years, it was to expect peace only so long as neither coast was visible.

PART THREE:
WHERE

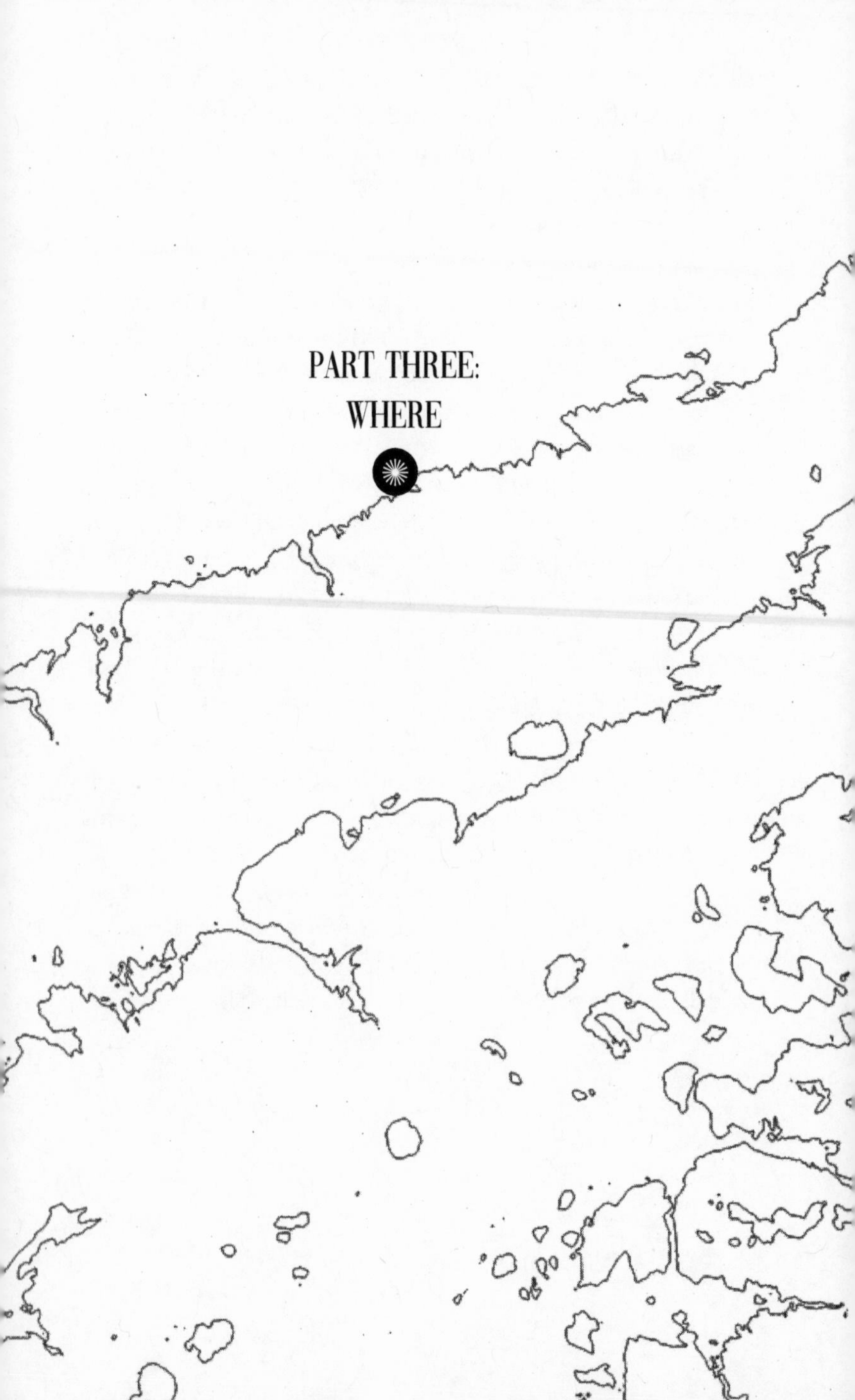

ULTRA MAX

Getting gas.

That's one thing.

The two of you pay.

I remain in the back under my red blanket while you move around the car, filling the tank. When there comes the need to relieve myself and you are away, I lean carefully out the door and onto the parking lot, coming to my feet like a much older man, shuffling toward some sprig of greenery or density of refuse, upon which, I'm ashamed to admit, you often discover me, and are obliged to hose me down with the self-service nozzle and buckle my trousers back around my waist.

We drive.

There are no towns.

We drive up and down the coast and nowhere are there any towns.

I believe we are in the vicinity of Sacramento, but this could well be a story I've told myself to paper over some much harsher truth.

Things were not different when I was your age. There was not abundance and grandeur then, only the same cracked, hot highways, watched by the same wolfish dogs, the so-called Real World already lost on the far side of the Fundamental Nightmare.

We drive on.

There is hardly any dialogue.

At most, you chat low in the front seat.

I remain silent beneath my blanket, feeling its bristly underside on my lips, rough as an overgrown mustache. I relish the feel of even this much, knowing well the feel of less.

I began tearing off these pages beneath the blanket nearly nine years ago, when the two of you were nine and I was much the same age I am now.

With a combination of tooth and elbow I remove each day as it passes. All the days of the years to come were bound into this calendar when I received it, fat as a book by some author of fat books, long since forgotten. I am down to, now, I do not want to say how many pages, but not many. Little more than a remnant of binding hairy with glue.

I aspire only to dwell within the days that remain. And to think a little while I can, before my return to the Middle Country, where, as you will see, one can hardly think at all.

♦

Your music plays through a device. Laidback, melancholic trios out of Nashville and Cincinnati. Though my hearing is watery at best, I enjoy the sounds these singers make and the intention I perceive behind them. I swell in my chest under my blanket, luxuriating in a notion as obsolete as "Nashville," the bravado of the claim to be from that place or anyplace. Cincinnati, Cleveland, Detroit. So improbable and yet there it is, in the voices on those ancient tapes. It makes me feel cradled, held. Part of something.

I do not believe, most of the time, you recall that I'm here. Or you do but do not dwell on this fact. You drive concerned with your own nascent matters, coming into your own despite how little you stand to inherit.

When we stop at a roadside stand, I get a milkshake. You—the bigger one—prop the sweating cup on my forearm and mold my other hand around the base. I then drink as much as I can through the straw. I cannot taste it but I enjoy its thickness and cold, while you—the smaller one, disgusted by me—look away, up the road in the direction we're going.

On weekends ULTRA MAX is closed for maintenance and internal operations. There are cement hulks still called motels, with empty rooms for lying down and hoses out back for washing.

This is where we stop.

I stay in the car while the two of you go inside.

I've spent my nearly nine years of weekend nights looking through darkened back seat windows, writing in these pages until my strength gives out. I hear the Fundamental Nightmare whirl in my ears as I unclog them with my left fingertip, which I maneuver bluntly with my right hand. A few people—you, me—can still sense the Nightmare's presence, with the so-called Real World on its far side. Most cannot. Whether this is a mercy or a shame is a matter I once devoted no small effort to considering, though I could not say now which conclusion I reached.

Every time you go in to sleep, you gather up the money you've saved and take it with you. This I find at once insulting and endearing, as if I would deign to steal from you. As if I were capable. What would I buy?

On Sunday morning you emerge with clean, wet hair, wearing windbreakers and jeans that appear freshly washed, the outlines of cigarette packs visible in your back pockets.

You—the bigger one—wear a pale blue windbreaker, while you—the smaller one—wear a black windbreaker, zipped to your throat. The heat does not deter you from these costumes. It's good to have something that's part of who you are.

You're both clean-shaven except for sideburns on you—the bigger one—and, on you—the smaller one—the hint of a goatee, which you've fostered for some time without it becoming thicker or darker. I catch you examining it in the rearview mirror, popping the hairs out with a frown, hoping there will at last be too many to count.

You—the smaller one—begin the day's drive, after you—the bigger one—make your way into the passenger seat, unfolding the map after secreting your money back into the glove compartment, where, I imagine, you tell yourself it will be safe from whatever threat you believe I pose.

You enter the car without acknowledging me and I remain where I've been. My seatbelt keeps me from rolling when the engine starts up.

The day is hot and long, full of shredded tires, wordless billboards, birds of prey.

Now it's evening before the new week's first night at ULTRA MAX, our last week together, not that you know this yet. I try to push the thought away, which is to say I drag it through and work it down into my mind until no other thought remains.

We park in the ULTRA MAX lot, so large that no edge is visible from its center.

Your movements are jocular, almost dancing in your clean clothes, visibly lightened after your weekend's rest. I lean on you—the bigger one—while you—the smaller one—watch the mammoth one-story hulk of ULTRA MAX materialize in the distance.

The last steps of the approach are crucial. You—the bigger one—free a shopping cart from its stall and peel my hands off your arm, molding them around the cart's handle. I lean heavily upon it, hanging back as you make your entrance. Here you forget the road, the car, and, maybe most of all, me. You draw your lines closer in, zip your windbreakers tighter, preparing to travel back through the Fundamental Nightmare and into the so-called Real World, to do the work you've been hired to do there. I know because I did the same at your age.

When you are out of sight, I nod, as forcefully as I am able, at the automatic door. On a third try, it whooshes to admit me to the air-conditioned foyer of coin-operated dinosaurs and glitter-encrusted rocket ships, bubble gum dispensers and candy-claws that loom above pits of sleeping plushies. Everywhere are tattered photos of lost children, barely visible, like the fading faces of saints on the walls of a cathedral in… not Nashville or Cincinnati, but some city known by another name.

There is a smell of cinnamon and mint. There are images of men and women in cologne and perfume ads whose sultry good health mocks the drudgery of one day having to die.

You proceed out of the foyer through a sparse crowd of drunks, wobbling in sweatpants and flannel shirts. Then you pass Cosmetics, nearest the entrance, and enter the Great Outdoors. Here you set up fishing chairs in the aisle and sit heavily down, taking up display poles and casting about for lint and wrappers. You try on floppy-brimmed khaki hats and multi-pocketed vests and clip-on belts that hold bait and tackle.

Next you go to the Snack Bar where a tired girl elbows open the popcorn machine. You each fill a paper cone and walk, munching, through Hardware, admiring drillbits and tossing kernels at the passing drunks, who shrug off the tiny impacts and keep moving.

♦

I make my way toward the back.

I have to hurry. My body hardens quickly when I'm away from you. Soon I lose purchase on the shopping cart and have to let it go. I sink to my knees, then my elbows, then my chin. I move on my side, slithering along with a shoulder and a hip.

I try not to picture when and how this will happen for the last time, the two of you gone, me alone and paralyzed, never to stand again. I divert these worries into consideration of your birthday. I'd like to get you something that recognizes your coming of age and also does the work of saying goodbye.

As I slither through the aisles, I try to look up but see only the bottoms of shelves, like rungs on a ladder to the ceiling. I focus instead on where I'm going.

When I get there, I pass through the steel doors by way of a special flap, on my way to meet Thompson in his Orchard.

You drift through Homewares, Wood, Food Products, Appliances, Automotive Parts, Digital, and Guns & Chemicals, until you stand before the twelve-foot sign that reads HOMETOWN (WHERE WE'RE FROM).

You reenter the Hometown, in the far back corner of the store, on the righthand side, set up exactly the same way in every ULTRA MAX on our route. Every weeknight, you pass the sign that reads SETTLED 1737, INCORPORATED 1821, COUNTY SEAT 1877.

The streets are dark in the ULTRA MAX lighting, designed here to resemble distant moonlight. The ceiling gets higher, like you're descending into a concavity, a pit drilled in the foundation. The ambient shopping noise fades, replaced by a gentle country breeze, piped in from invisible jets.

You pass familiar stores and restaurants. The sports bar and the barbershop are neither closed nor open, but in a third state that does not change, since ULTRA MAX is 24h. I cannot express the degree to which I envy your freedom to return here, not yet burdened by knowledge of the Middle Country's silence and heat.

You nod to those who nod hello.

Passing faces, friendly inquiries. You reply that you've been well, graduation was fun but it sure is nice to be finished with high school. "Now," you conclude, the same way every night—unchanged, indeed, since my day—"we're trying to save a little money from our summer jobs and getting excited about the next thing. It's our last summer here, so we're just drinking it all in before we leave, you know? After that, we'll see!"

You stand for a moment in front of the church, regarding the sign that reads GOD PROMISES A SAFE ARRIVAL BUT NOT A SMOOTH JOURNEY. Then you pass the Carnegie library with four neat columns like a shrunken Greek temple, across from the Moravian Cemetery.

A FOR LEASE sign dominates the window of the old stationary store like that's all it has to sell.

You conceive of your Hometown in terms of blocks.

Each block has one dominant business, defining its

mood. For this one it's Ben's Watch & Timer; for the next it's Giant Chinese, where you're starting to remember eating lunch specials when school got out early once a month for curriculum development meetings. *Not very good*, you think, as the memory resurfaces, *but big plates and cheap*.

It's one more block to Da Vinci's, where you now remember sitting, day in and day out, with coffee and scones, surrounded by paperbacks and dime store notepads as you labored to imagine an outside world.

The door is propped open with a rock and on the patio are three tables, twelve seats, always a nice crowd on warm evenings like this one.

You take in the pastry case, the smell of coffee passing through a percolator. A boy and girl serve you and ask how you've been.

"You know. Pretty good. You?" you say.

They shrug happily.

With fresh coffees and a scone apiece, you sit down at a patio table. Your seats are at the edge of a square across which old-timers shuffle. The square is elegant, cobbled, though the stones are cardboard. The old-timers touch down in empty seats and get up again. Two men claim that the bake-off is coming and their wives will be entering cakes; a third claims that his wife will be the judge.

As you sit, faint images of the road and the wolfish dogs along it, nights in the motels, the sun beating down on gas pumps, dinners in parking lots, and my face, simmer low in you, like longings for the future, indistinct promises firming up in a nutritive brine. *If we can just save enough to get out of here…* you think, as I thought, when I was your age.

When you've finished your coffee and scones, you scoop your cigarettes and keys off the table and thread up the rest of Main Street, deserted but for a few old women peering at the empty train tracks from second-story windows.

Approaching the neighborhood where you live, you perch your cigarettes in your mouths and swing your arms loose and long, looking upward, affecting the kind of world-weariness of those about to turn eighteen. You—the smaller one—tongue the inside of your lip enough to primp your goatee, tasting a canker sore whose pain is hard to resist.

The air thickens, turns striated and fibrous, as if filling with long branches beginning to bud. A small reflecting pool gleams in the near distance, mottled with Lilly-pads and the shadows of clouds in the moonlight.

Something is piped in from the ULTRA MAX ceiling, much too high to see. It smells citrusy, like a fine aftershave. You inhale, swoon, grateful for the anesthesia. Having reverted fully to the feeling of being from somewhere, a town in which people are born and grow up and one day hope to leave, you are now at the very edge of the Fundamental Nightmare.

The keys are hidden in the usual place. You enter your homes, wiping your shoes on your welcome mats before taking them off. You each live alone, across a narrow footpath from one another, close enough to confer from your bedroom windows. How I wish that I still had such a home, a sealed box where I could get in bed and close my eyes, regardless of the dream I would then fall into.

You wash your faces with very hot water and drink very cold milk on your way upstairs. Then you go into your bedrooms and close the doors.

The Fundamental Nightmare begins. You sink all the way into it, or it rises all the way up in you. You move down its long black corridor and out the other side, into the so-called Real World.

Looking back on the long-ago nights when I was in the position you are in now, I picture you tearing along rows of sleeping newborns in a nursery, each one swaddled in blankets wrapped over full-body pajamas.

You stretch open burlap sacks marked COFFEE, BRAZIL, broken-in from years of use. You grab the newborns by the neck and stuff them inside, pushing them down to make room for more. No one knows why there are so many, what generative principle so perversely refuses extinction.

At first the sacks jerk and wriggle and cry, brought to sudden, endangered life.

Then, almost smothered, they begin to breathe in a smooth vegetal drone, bald heads solemn as cabbages. You carry them out of the so-called Real World, back through the tunnel of the Fundamental Nightmare, and into the field behind Thompson's Orchard.

♦

The final step. The most dangerous part, that for which you are paid the money you've been saving. You must check each newborn for the Fundamental Nightmare. Most do not carry it, but some, like us, do.

God, I do not wish to remember the feel of that Nightmare on my hands. The newborns' innate sense memory of the so-called Real World, and the tunnel, full of shrieking static, that has led them away from it, and into the hindquarters of ULTRA MAX. As best I understand it, the Fundamental Nightmare and the ability to have the Fundamental Nightmare are one and the same: the tunnel is in you just as surely as you are in it, with the so-called Real World on one side and ULTRA MAX on the other.

Like a burn or a bite, a snake-fang between the knuckles, the presence of the Fundamental Nightmare is unmistakable. There is no need for explanation now.

The anesthesia you breathed earlier is a kindness.

You sit in the open field, smelling of wet grass. Not speaking, you sort through the stirring COFFEE, BRAZIL sacks, touching each newborn just long enough to tell.

When you find one that has it, you heave it as hard and far away as you can, back where it came from, to spend the next years playing on a playground in the so-called Real World, like the two of you did until you met me.

Like I did too, until I met my taker.

Catch and release, on and on through time.

The three of us were not made to be processed by Thompson.

Tonight, mercifully, the haul is clean. All the newborns are usable.

Back in the Orchard with Thompson, I lean toward the window to watch you approach. You look powerful and confident, well-conditioned by your summer job, as you heft your cargoes high on your shoulders. Though it may be that I've taught you nothing, I am proud when I see you like this.

A ceiling spigot mists every few minutes, condensing on the fleshy roughage that Thompson is growing in troughs and pots, awaiting your arrival.

I want to get up and let you in, but I am by now far from able. A few hours away from you and I revert to the state I was in before we met.

So you let yourselves in. After brushing the dirt from your shoes, you kneel to empty your sacks. As the cargo is laid out, Thompson taps each newborn with a rubber mallet until it lies still.

You back off to let him work.

He strips off their pajamas and cuts their torsos open and pulls matter through the cut, tossing it into a blue plastic bin like fish parts. Some of them will die and be tossed likewise into that bin, par for the course, like the few pieces of rotten fruit per hundred. But most will survive, their hearts, brains, and lungs strong enough to take root inside the roughage, turning it from vegetable to animal.

Thompson is in many places at night, at work in all the Orchards of all the ULTRA MAX's of the nation. I have never known whether to consider him *Thompson* or *a Thompson*. I have never asked. We move from one ULTRA MAX to the next so as never to deplete any one source, allowing the newborns in each nursery to regrow. I am astonished not only at the dexterity but the care, the tenderness, with which Thompson treats them. He, and perhaps he alone, knows the value of human life.

Once he has implanted their organs into the roughage and covered it in something skinlike, jets of warm air gush down to dry them.

He nods in the direction of a steel box on a table. From this, you remove your wages, stuffing them in your pockets and signing a sheet with an attached pen. Then you make your way into the break room.

The break room looks more like a hospital than a residence, but, save for on weekends, it's the only place you can sleep, since your beds in your houses in the Hometown are only jumping-off points for the taking.

You lie on cots here, coming down from the anesthesia, passing back through the Fundamental Nightmare, but this time without agenda.

This time, you traverse the long black corridor and enter the so-called Real World as yourselves, not as takers. You barely remember being thrown back into the nursery as newborns, your taker recoiling upon feeling your sting in the COFFEE, BRAZIL sack, the Fundamental Nightmare coursing through you, making you unfit for the aisles of ULTRA MAX.

Where is your taker now? Surely in the Middle Country, where I was too, lying flat on my belly, or my back, the two almost interchangeable by then. I had lost all sense of myself by the time I made the call from where I lay, begging to be sent back to the coast for one last ULTRA MAX tour before the permanence of exile set in. The Middle Country, as I've written before, awaits you as well: boiling salt flats dotted with spent bodies, hard, denerved, all former duos looking away from one another in mutual recrimination for having let it come to this.

Still, some of us in the Middle Country find the strength to make the call, demanding to be sent back to the coast to guide nine-year-olds like you in and out of ULTRA MAX until they turn eighteen. I drummed up the energy for what felt like years, focusing all my depleted resources on it, all the yearning I'd once harbored for the future—gestated at that same table in front of Da Vinci's when I was sixteen and seventeen—until I managed to force my mouth open and broadcast my loneliness into the hot, stagnant air.

Hearing my call, the chauffeur appeared, loaded me into the back seat of his car and drove me out to a playground on the coast. He helped me up the hill and left me with this calendar stuffed with nine years' worth of days and the keys to the car you've been driving, and are likely driving still.

♦

You were almost nine, alone on the playground. All the other children you'd been born with were long-gone inside ULTRA MAX. Only the two of you remained, foraging for scraps.

Then you saw something in the low foliage. I sat propped against a tree, my feet lost in roots and pebbles and the season's first fallen leaves, some orange, others still green.

You drew near, deep in private conference. You sounded, from where I sat, like a scuttling of squirrel feet.

I could see only that there were two of you and that you looked similar, though one of you was slightly bigger, the other slightly smaller. I was starving, having eaten nothing since the chauffeur dropped me off. In the Middle Country, one feels no hunger, but here, as I began to thaw in your presence, the lack in my center expanded to threaten my whole being.

You heard a low groan, no louder than a rustle of undergrowth but not the sound of plants. I pursed my lips, pressed my tongue into the seal where they met, and groaned again from my belly. I knew how lovely it sounded to you because I remember how lovely it sounded to me when I was your age and my taker waited likewise among the leaves for my counterpart and me, both of us almost nine and sick with boredom. It sounded like escape, like someone had come for us at last.

You conferred at the edge of the playground while I sat where I'd been placed, trying to keep my hunger from killing me. Just before I lost consciousness, I saw you striding in my direction. Then I felt you picking me up, carrying me down the hillside. You were strong enough, or I was light enough.

At the bottom, you helped me into the back seat where the blankets and pillows from my trip out of the Middle Country lay where the chauffer had left them.

We departed, stopping only for the milkshake that saved my life. You managed to drive, comically low in your seats, barely able to see out, but the roads were flat and wide and there was no traffic.

Just before sleep, I used my newly workable hand to tear the first day from this calendar. Happy ninth birthday to both of you.

♦

Once again, it's the three of us in ULTRA MAX at the start of a new day, the two of you almost eighteen.

Thompson's work is done.

What he's processed will soon rise from where it's resting.

He makes green tea in a Styrofoam cup stained with much earlier tea, and sips it without offering me any. He makes notes in a ledger with one hand. With the other, he finds a last rye biscuit in its package, always the same type and always down to the last one.

Finishing his tea, he pours out the bucket of newborn-waste. It froths through a drain in the cement floor. The remaining solids are tossed onto the compost pile.

He retreats into his private quarters, through another set of steel doors that whoosh for him alone. In a few days, he will make the call to summon the chauffeur who will take us all to the Middle Country.

I grind out the last of my energy to set off the alarm with my cheek.

It howls in the break room.

You—the smaller one—open the door in your boxers and undershirt.

"One second," you say, your cash clenched in your fist.

When you're both ready, we walk out with the small crowd Thompson has made, men and women in their forties and fifties in sweatpants and flannel shirts.

By the time we take our place in the breakfast line, they all know one another, chatting about their errant families and sore backs, the jobs they're hoping to get healthcare from, the storm gutters that need cleaning.

We find a table. You gather pancakes and bacon strips, plastic cups of orange juice with ice cubes, and black coffee. You offer me a sip once the coffee is cool and I've regained the energy to swallow.

I watch this new population eat and drink and mingle, their day beginning in earnest, ticking down toward the hour when they'll process into the Hometown, the only home they've ever had or wanted. First, they'll take their places at the tables outside Da Vinci's and in the square across from it, and at Giant Chinese. Then, a short or long time thereafter, they'll lie down in the Moravian Cemetery, where their remains will be exhumed by

Thompson's Proxies and brought to the Orchard to help grow more of the roughage that will in turn be implanted in a new crop of people, eager to take their places in the breakfast line and at the tables I am looking at now.

♦

A few more days and nights like this one pass.

♦

On the last day, we take our time in the parking lot, under a morning sky that will remain merciful until nine. You stretch, squint, shake off the residue of your hours in the break room. When you turn on the car, the tape player comes on too. A song about drinking beer in Louisville, waiting for love to arrive.

You do not know what day it is. It's the same as any day, except it's your birthday. I'd say it was not, but the stripped calendar would insist.

"Happy eighteenth birthday to both of you," I wish I could say.

I see the chauffeur now, standing between a parked SUV and a motorcycle, still too distant to tell if he sees me.

Unable to find a gift on the high ULTRA MAX shelves, I've decided to leave you the car. The car does not belong to me, of course. I have orders to keep you waiting until the chauffeur arrives, at which point he will drive all three of us back to the

Middle Country, just as he once drove my counterpart and my taker and me.

But the truth just now is that I slip quietly from the back seat. I huddle like a turtle into myself as you pull out, not noticing that I'm gone.

I huddle so tightly that if you've run me over, I hardly felt it. I find the strength and dexterity to turn my neck, averting it from the final sight of your departure, riveted instead on the great unfazed façade of ULTRA MAX.

Then the chauffer's on top of me, kicking me, trying to turn me over with his boot, to get me to face his face and the sun bearing down on both of us. I knew he would do this. I've written it here, for you, exactly as I knew it would happen.

I hear his voice reporting the emergency into a cell phone and feel even more like a turtle than I did a moment ago. Each footfall cracks my shell a little more, but I receive it like bad news from another part of the world.

Just before I think nothing, I think of the two of you a mile up the road, having already achieved a featureless vista that will remain so throughout all the hours of daylight.

I do not wish my fate upon you, nor do I believe you will escape it. I hope only that, on occasion, before you are caught or harden to the point where you can no longer drive, and before you turn on each other for having let such a thing happen, you will look in the rearview mirror and catch sight of the blanket and the pillows, and recall, or imagine, that there was once something there, some other part of your lives. Perhaps, shaking out the blanket at some gas station at dusk, you will turn up the rind of my calendar, and, instead of tossing it to the weedy concrete, you will feel some impulse to put it in the glove compartment, or perhaps even take it with you when you go in to sleep on weekends, along with whatever money you have left. If you happen to open it, you will find these pages stuck back in the binding, pages I should have thrown out but did not, and on them you will find words meant to remind you, once the hardening sets in, that there was once something before it. That you were young, and that, improbable as it will begin to seem, you had a Hometown and in it you were known and your future opened out onto infinity.

JELL-O

J.'s parents tell him never to go in the basement because, "there's something wrong with the foundation of our house, and if we ever went down there, we'd have to find out what it is." So, for the first seven years of his life, he doesn't. He does what they tell him to, like go to school and carry the trash out to the curb and only watch one movie on a Saturday night, and brush his baby teeth because even though they're going to fall out, his gums hopefully aren't. He doesn't like it, but he does it. He wonders sometimes what's down there, and if finding out might actually make his life better, not worse, but until he's eight he resists taking any action. *Maybe*, he thinks, *the life I'm living is the best one, if not the only*. So he keeps going to school, where they talk about the Roman Empire, and planets, and paramecium, and pi, but these seem to be just words,. or, at best, pictures, diagrams, maps, etc. Nothing that can do anything.

He starts to get sad. He has friends, sure, at least a couple, and they play in the sandbox with trucks and shovels when they're little, and watch *The Lion King* when they're a bit bigger, and *The Dark Knight* when they're a bit bigger than that, and they eat pizza and Oreos and play laser tag on each other's birthdays, but still the sadness grows. He lies in bed and looks out his window at the factory up the street, belching smoke, and he watches the garbage truck chug by in the early morning, knocking over the cans, and he feels the sadness drip down from the ceiling and in from the walls, covering him up like a second quilt when the first one's already too hot. And underneath it all, at the very bottom of the house, he can feel something yawning, its burpy breath trickling through the kitchen, up the stairs, along the hallway, under his bedroom door, and into his bed. *Something's waiting*, he thinks, lying very still, unsure if he's dreaming.

Something knows I'm up here, and is waiting for me to come down.

By the time he's almost eight, the dream has developed a new phase. He doesn't tell his parents or anyone at school, or even himself really, not when he's awake, but it keeps coming like it doesn't need his permission. Like it has as much right to live in his brain as the rest of him does. In the dream, the basement door won't stay closed and the house starts to fill with thick, wet fumes, like lettuce and meat left out in a pile. He gags in his sleep and spits onto his pillow, trying and failing to get the smell out of his nose and mouth, until he finds himself walking down the stairs, tiptoeing in case whatever's in the basement can hear him, and then he's opening the fridge, rummaging for something to mask the smell, until he finds a metal bowl of leftover cherry Jell-O, covered in crinkly plastic wrap. He takes it out, wobbling in his arms, peels off the plastic, and throws it into the basement. It lands with a loud splat, *much louder in the dream*, he thinks, *than it would be in real life*, though he knows the dream is real too. It echoes through the whole house, so loud he's afraid it'll wake his parents, but it doesn't. Instead, it makes him feel like he's in a house by himself, in a world without parents or teachers or rules, just him and the thing in the basement, if it's alive under the Jell-O.

♦

As time moves on and his eighth birthday comes and goes, he finds he's having the dream more often, and, now, looking forward to it. He begins to find the nights when it doesn't come unbearable. Long, still, boring nights where he rolls in his sheets, looking ahead to the coming years and decades, the tests in school, the five-paragraph essays, the work of applying to college, and going to college, and getting a job, and finding a house of his own, on another street near a factory with a garbage truck that wakes you up as it knocks the cans onto the curb at dawn.

No, he thinks, *the cherry Jell-O nights are better.* So he starts asking his mom to get more, to get it every time she goes shopping.

Sometimes she does, but sometimes she forgets, so he starts coming to the store with her, every time asking her to get cherry Jell-O, simply saying it's his favorite if she asks why, which eventually she stops doing. She just gets it, and makes it for dessert, because, she says, "me and your father are a little concerned but we want you to be happy, within reason." So she buys it and makes it and then she and his father sit back and watch while he eats a little, as little as possible, claiming he's saving the rest for his midnight snack, which she and his father say is a bit closer to being beyond reason, but is still okay as long as it's not every night.

But it is every night. Every night, J. sneaks down, in the dream or not, it no longer seems to matter, and takes the leftover Jell-O from the bowl and throws it into the growing pile in the basement, listening to it splat and savoring the moment of tranquility as he hears the thing at the very bottom creak open, and though he can't yet see what it is, he comes more and more strongly to believe that it has to do with whatever's wrong with the house's foundation. He comes to believe that his house lies on a crack between worlds, and that this is why he's so sad living on this side, marinating in the bad breath coming through, when he should be living on the other.

By the time he turns nine, the basement is so full of Jell-O it almost reaches the top of the stairs, like the water level in an in-ground pool. He wonders if his parents know it's there, and decides that they must, but what can they say, really? *Nothing*, he thinks, as he decides that tonight's the night. He has dinner with his parents, listening to them discuss Mr. Veitch, his dad's boss at work, who has halitosis and gave himself another bonus instead of fixing the damn copier, and he watches his mom make what she doesn't know is her last batch of cherry Jell-O.

He eats a couple of tiny spoonfuls, as ever, and watches her cover the rest with plastic wrap and go to bed, and he goes to bed too, though he's too excited to lie still. As soon as he's sure both parents are asleep, he gets up, puts on his bathing suit, kisses his plastic allosaurus goodbye, and heads down to the basement to find out if the Jell-O's deep enough. He's seen in the dream that he needs to take a deep dive; otherwise, he won't make it through the passageway. It'll be too dry and narrow, and he'll bang his head on the cement and maybe die. So, at the top of the stairs, he gets out the bowl of Jell-O, peels off the plastic, and hurls it onto the pile, listening for the splat. As soon as it comes, he takes a deep breath, puffs up his chest, and throws himself in, breaking the surface like a torpedo.

He speeds downward, sucking Jell-O in through his nose and swallowing it effortlessly, like this is the one true skill he's been learning all his life. It doesn't fill him up, doesn't make him sick, it just makes him stronger, helping him fight his way down, past the suspended bicycles and barbells and boxes of papers, all the basement trash hovering between him and the crack in the bottom. Swallowing more and more, he cuts through the

Jell-O with the sides of his hands and forearms, pulling himself downward, through the dark red toward a glowing seam far below. As he approaches, it stretches open, glowing reddish pink, and he knows the Jell-O's working; he knows it's doing its job. He closes his eyes, takes another deep breath, which serves to fill his lungs with cherry, and goes through.

It sucks him in, spins him around, and for a moment he blacks out. Everything becomes distorted and hot and he forgets his name and where he came from and why he's here. The cherry smell is gone, though the redness remains. He swims deeper, pushing his way through the murk, determined simply to keep moving. Time slows down, or speeds up, or ceases to apply. *Perhaps*, he considers, *years are passing. Perhaps I'll be old when I get out of here, if I ever do.*

Swimming along once he's gotten used to this new place and let go of any effort to determine what it is, he comes to an area with a number of hovering beasts. Horses, cows, eagles, parrots, and other mammals and birds hover in reddish aspic, kicking their legs and scrabbling their wings, trying to break free but not trying that hard. They look worn out, confused, resigned. Some are completely still, hanging in place with their tongues out, their eyes filmy and grey.

He looks at these creatures and begins to get scared. *This isn't normal*, he thinks. *This isn't right. Whatever's happening to them, I can't let it happen to me. And it wants to happen. The Jell-O wants to slow me down. It wants to hold onto me. It wants to make me a morsel in its giant sloppy gut.* He swims harder, aware that his energy is limited, but determined to get out of here before he gets stuck. His stomach hurts now and he can't swallow any more, so he has to spit as he swims, pulling it past him with his eyes squinting just enough to see a bluish light in the far distance.

Good, he thinks, *anything other than red.* Now he's passing people suspended around him, old people mostly, their hair white and their skin wrinkled and loose, but some young people too, fat ones and ones with angry, envious eyes, staring at him as he swims past.

He picks up the pace even though it exhausts him, forcing his way toward the blue light, which shimmers brighter the closer he comes. He starts to wonder, as he gets near it, about what it might mean to leave the Jell-O behind, about whether the blue is where he was going all along, or if it's actually back where he started. But it's too late now, he's almost there. *Maybe*, he finds himself thinking, his voice familiar in his head now, *all those horses and crows back there, maybe they all got partway, toward something, toward whatever it was that I too am trying to reach, but then they just….*

He doesn't bother completing the thought. He doesn't have time. Now he's surfacing, first his head, then his chest, then his waist. His feet are planted firmly in the sand and he's striding out of the surf, panting, spitting ropes of snot, coughing into his fist as he scans the beach, which is full of families. Umbrellas, carts, screaming babies, flying Frisbees, and behind it all a row of cars parked in the sun.

After he catches his breath, he begins walking along the beach, glancing at the families, wondering which one is his. *And if none of them are*, he thinks, unsure if this notion is strange, *I'll just pick one. Doesn't matter which. Just any family that seems to have space on its blanket.* As he's walking, looking at one set of faces and then another and then the one after that, he feels a hand on his shoulder, clamping down. He spins around to see a tall, thin boy in board shorts and an attempt at a mustache. "Yo, Mike," the boy says. "I was looking for you. Wanna get some food? Mom gave us cash." He waves a twenty in the air and grins.

Following this older boy—his v, seemingly—up the beach, the person whose name is now Mike feels his memory of Jell-O and the basement and the crack slipping as his mind fills with questions of hamburger or hot dog, curly fries or sweet potato, regular Coke or Diet? By the time his turn to order comes, he's made up his mind.

SANDMAN CRESCENT

Mr. and Mrs. Feaster found their daughter, June, hanging from the backmost hook in her walk-in closet when they went up to tell her that dinner was ready. They left her there and went down to the kitchen table, where they ended up sitting all night, as the chicken pot pie cooled untouched in front of them. They didn't tell her sister, Ava, though both of them knew, without saying anything, that the news would never need to be broken. Ava had surely known that something was wrong sooner than either of them ever could have. What they didn't know until the next morning, after both skipping work, was that they'd find Ava, whom they'd assumed was staying over at a friend's house, hanging in the back of her own closet, in solidarity with or mockery of her older sister.

The question of which it was hung—*no pun intended*, Jane Feaster thought, hating herself—unanswered because, as soon as they found her, a commotion on the lawn compelled both parents' attention away from the grisly inches beneath their second daughter's curled toes. The Feasters glided down the stairs and opened the back door to behold the paralyzed faces of the Sudokis, their neighbors from across the grassy lot shared by all the houses on the easternmost edge of Sandman Crescent.

The two couples stared at one another and, like a four-part pantomime troupe, understood everything that needed to be said without speaking a word. Each had privately hoped that one of the others would break the silence, but now they could all see it was better this way. Mrs. Sudoki pocketed the ominous note she'd carried over, while her question—"have you seen our son?"—died in her throat.

For a while longer, the two couples stood there, letting the day pass as their children—the Sudokis' son, Tommy, who'd briefly dated the Feasters' daughter, Ava, would later be found hanging from a rafter in the Feasters' basement—drifted away from them, leaving only a set of hard, blue bodies behind.

By the time the Feasters retreated, alone, back into their kitchen, rumors had begun to surface on the Sandman Crescent Homeowners' E-Newsletter, updated twice a day on slow days, and almost constantly, it turned out, in the midst of a crisis. "24 DEATHS OF BOYS AND GIRLS BETWEEN THE AGES OF 13 AND 17," read the headline, above a video-collage of hanging bodies, tilting back and forth, their faces blurred just enough that it wasn't clear how bad the damage, appearance-wise, really was. Jane Feaster wanted to laugh at the blurred faces and the way they triggered an instinct to adjust the resolution on the tablet she was viewing them on, as if the problem with the image was its lack of clarity, rather than what that clarity would have revealed.

When the laugh refused to stay down, she excused herself from her husband, Seth, who was most of the way catatonic in front of the screen that kept auto-refreshing, the bodies expanding silently toward the edges of the frame. She locked herself in the downstairs bathroom and ran the water and then let the laugh out, first in a hiccoughing series of chuckles and then a single ponderous guffaw, so loud and hard it made the skin on the back of her skull bunch up and the tears that hadn't come yet begin to flow. They poured from her face into the running sink.

Then she turned the sink off, patted her eyes dry with a plush hand towel, and walked back through the kitchen, where her husband's screen had now filled with more bodies than it could encompass. Taking her keys from the bowl beside the larger bowl that held the apples and the spotty bananas, she said, "I'm going for a drive," and walked out, into what was now a hot, stagnant day, full of air that no one was breathing.

She got in the blue Peugeot that her job, because it did business with France, had provided her with, and drove out of Sandman Crescent onto the wide-open boulevard which, if you followed it long enough in one direction, would eventually take you to the airport. She drove in the other direction, through a long tunnel of overgrown trees, the abandoned asphalt crunchy with acorns, and then she crossed into the town that Sandman Crescent had, in a manner of speaking, replaced. There was no formal prohibition on entering the town, though there was also no reason for doing so, and thus the journey was never made. *Perhaps in this way, then, it is slightly prohibited after all*, she thought, considering it in this light for the first time. Nevertheless, she drove this route often in times of stress and agitation, on bleary evenings after a failed day at work, or in the hour before dawn, after a night when she'd given up trying to sleep by two, yet gone on lying in bed until four. This, right now, was obviously worse, even *much worse*, than any of those times, and yet there was no place to go during a bad time, no matter how bad, other than where she was going now.

So she followed the usual route, past the boarded-up movie theater, the vacant storefronts that might've once sold toys, or lingerie, past the town hall whose entire staff had disbanded after the Sandman Crescent land deal went through, and out to the woods behind the town on the far side, along an access road she'd first discovered after a sleepless night when she nodded off behind the wheel and woke up in front of a one-story cabin with a pile of Coke signs jammed into its weedy lawn, bundled together by spiderwebs. She'd pushed the rotten door open and let herself in and sat alone at the linoleum-topped kitchen table, watching motes hover and listening to distant wind chimes, thinking, and then not thinking, and then thinking again.

It had, since that day, become a habit, a ritual even, the kind of non-work, non-home *third place* that, she'd read once in a magazine at the dentist's office, everyone needed and too few people ever found.

She, Jane Feaster, had found it, and it had accounted, in no small part, for her ability to get through the last ten years in Sandman Crescent, to bide her time without losing herself entirely. Over those years, she'd planted a little garden—nothing fancy, but parsley and mint and a few wildflowers—and even stocked the cabin's shelves with the occasional bottle of wine or box of cookies, and thereby made of it a refuge.

She was back in the refuge now, stepping out among the pile of Coke signs, then checking her parsley and mint, then pushing the front door open, which, though it seemed slightly more ajar than she'd left it, she didn't take much note of until she was already in the dim kitchen, regarding the slumped shape of an old man in a blue jumpsuit.

She knew, in the same half-smothered part of her mind that remembered why today was unlike any other, that she should leave—even if he didn't look dangerous, the odds that staying here with him was a bad idea were much higher than the odds that it was a good one—but she didn't leave. Instead, she stood with her back to the open door and waited for him to look her way. She did this, it occurred to her, because some yet-deeper part of her mind had known he was going to be here, and was thus reassured to find that he was.

When he still hadn't moved after all this time, however long it had been, she considered the possibility that he was dead or in a coma, and again considered leaving. But when she didn't leave this time, she decided there was nothing to do but walk into his line of sight.

She stood before him, watching a strand of spittle hang between his bottom lip and his left knee. Then, bracing herself for the possibility of a violent retaliation, she kicked his right leg, first softly, then hard, then, finally, very hard.

He looked up, his eyes milky, his cheeks and chin spotted with stubble fighting for purchase among deep rows of scar tissue, his mouth puckered off to the left.

Jane Feaster could tell that she would, yet again, have to initiate the next step. There would never, she could see now, be a back and forth between them.

She closed her eyes and pictured the paramedics swarming her house, bypassing her inert husband in the kitchen to cut her daughters down from their closets upstairs, then dragging their zipped-up bodies out of the house for the last time. She shivered and felt her bones liquify, then re-freeze at jagged angles, making standing almost more painful than she could bear.

To take her mind off it, she looked down into the milky eyes that had already begun to drift away from her, and said, "They're dead. Both of them. My daughters."

It was the first time she'd said it aloud and thus, she realized, the first time she'd heard it said. Now it was true.

Who killed them? She imagined the man asking, though his side-mouth remained closed. She looked at him and the first words that moved through her head were: *you did.* The word *themselves*, surely the truth, hung somewhere in the air, but it felt foreign. Unsayable. As useless as the hanging bodies.

So, instead of saying it, she turned and walked through

the rotten front door, not bothering to fit it back into its frame, and got back in her car and drove down the overgrown boulevard in the direction of the airport this time, and didn't stop until she was pulling into Sandman Crescent.

The cul-de-sac in front of her house was choked with emergency vehicles and news vans, all of them bearing the Sandman Crescent logo, all of them idling, contributing to the sense she had, as she searched for a place to park, that the constant movement of the scene had reached a kind of anxious equilibrium, everyone in motion but no one going anywhere. Paramedics dragged full stretchers out of the houses while others dragged empty stretchers in, trading places with a nod, and all around them newscasters and parents shuffled back and forth, giving statements or refusing to give statements, which were also, in essence, a kind of statement, and looked identical from even a few feet away.

Jane Feaster left the car on the first stretch of curb she could find past the crush of ambulances and news vans and walked toward the gift shop and cafeteria that served as one of the hubs of Sandman Crescent, the other being on the far side of a long row of storage depots and garages, farther out than she'd ever been. The longer she walked in this direction, the quieter things became, so that, before long, it wasn't difficult to imagine she'd left not only the news of the travesty, but the travesty itself behind, and found her way into a zone of quarantine, where nothing could touch her.

She bought a bowl of green Jell-O and a room temperature coffee from the self-service cafeteria line, and sat alone in the buzzing white room to choke them down. A muted TV was hooked up to the ceiling, radiating the news that was being recorded in a studio up the street. Jane Feaster looked at it only intermittently, looking down the rest of the time into her green Jell-O, and then into her room temperature coffee, checking each substance, as if one might reveal something the other couldn't. She sensed that, once both were gone, she'd have nowhere left to look, and then the news would sink in unfiltered.

So she ate and drank slowly, watching her face break apart and then grow back together in the mottled green surface as her spoon disturbed the Jell-O and then waited until all movement ceased before taking the next bite. Once, as she was picking up her coffee, she heard footsteps in the prep area behind her, and, before she could stop it, her head filled with the image of the man from the cabin, his milky eyes overflowing, leaking fluid down his cheeks and onto his shirt. She turned to face him and saw only a young woman in a hairnet stretching plastic wrap over a tray of rolls, but the man's image lingered. He seemed to be toying with her, announcing that he could appear whenever he wanted, and perhaps that he'd been appearing for years. *Perhaps*, she thought, *he's been flitting around, stealing into our closets with a coil of rope, ever since Sandman Crescent opened and started luring in couples of a certain class from all over the otherwise-collapsing country. Perhaps he's caused all the deaths that have so far occurred here; perhaps without him, we'd all be immortal.*

When all the time that could pass in the cafeteria had passed, she bused her dishes into an empty plastic tub and went out the way she'd come in, walking by her car where it was parked, and where it would remain until she stumbled into it—she could already see herself doing this—sometime before dawn tomorrow, and drove down the tree-choked boulevard and back to the cabin, which, she reasoned, she might as well do now, since it was bound to happen anyway.

She walked to her car and reached out to the latch to

open the driver's side door, but then pulled her hand back, and put it in her pocket. *No*, she thought, as she began to walk toward her house instead. *My behavior so far has been eccentric but, most likely, comprehensible within the allowances that people make for grief. But to push it further, to not go home at all tonight, to leave my husband in the house alone, that's something else. That's a new low, for which people would cease to grieve with me and begin to grieve against me. An eventuality best not pursued.*

So, she put her keys into the pocket that didn't already have her hand in it, and walked through the silence of Sandman Crescent at dusk, past house after house with the TV on in its front window, until she arrived at her own, with the same TV on in the same window. She stopped outside, registering that this would be the first time she walked through the front door without the prospect of greeting her daughters—*without*, she thought, *the prospect of greeting any aspect of the life I've lived in this house the whole time I've lived in it*—and then, having pictured what this would be like, she walked in, and found it was exactly how she'd pictured it.

Her husband was sitting alone at the kitchen table eating from a takeout container of Lucky Dragon Chinese, one of Sandman Crescent's seven gourmet takeout options, all prepared by the same kitchen, staring at a tablet that showed the same newsfeed as the TV, perched on the counter a few feet away. Jane Feaster stood behind him and watched the updates—"37 SANDMAN CRESCENT TEENAGERS FOUND DEAD IN ONE DAY, MOTIVE NOT YET DETERMINED"—crawl across both screens, or both versions of the screen.

She stood behind him and watched him eat, a bottle of red wine empty next to a pile of napkins, and she hoped he wouldn't turn and ask or say anything. For a while, he didn't. When he finally did, looking her over and gesturing with his greasy chopsticks at whatever was left of the noodles he'd ordered, she held up her hand, palm out, an unambiguous sign for him to stop trying to communicate. It was too soon. He stopped. "I'm gonna watch by myself," she said, picking up the tablet he'd been staring at without inviting him to follow. Though his eyes lingered on the screen, he didn't protest. *There is*, she allowed, *at least that much to be said for him.*

Upstairs, she got in bed and fixated on the news, which had cut to an image of a lone teenager in a white room, a boy about June's age, though not one who looked familiar. He sat on a bed and hugged himself as a team of doctors, or TV-men in doctor suits, asked, again and again, if he knew why this had happened. "LAST SURVIVING SANDMAN CRESCENT TEENAGER: OUR ONLY HOPE TO LEARN WHAT WENT WRONG," read the banner, which boiled at the bottom of the screen while the boy squirmed on the bed.

Jane Feaster turned it off and placed it on the pillow next to her and closed her eyes, still half-sitting against the headboard. She could hear the house creaking around her, and couldn't help transposing the sound onto that of her daughters creaking on their nooses, turning in slow semi-circles in the dark backs of the closets they'd been found in. The fact that she'd seen them carried out by paramedics—and had she really seen this, or only assumed it must've occurred?—did nothing to dispel the growing sense that, were she to check the backs of the closets now, she'd find them, as if for the first time. It almost seemed as though—she was partly asleep now, beginning to dream—her finding them would set in motion the news cycle that was already, she knew, in motion, like two orders of time would diverge and then converge, and it was up to her to decide when and how this should happen.

She slumped lower in bed, squinting at the overhead lights that were still on. She knew, in the part of herself that was still awake, that she should brush her teeth, wash her face, put in her nightguard, change into her pajamas, and then go back to bed with the lights off, but the rest of her was deep in the rift between timelines, exploring a realm in which it was neither the case that she'd found her daughters nor that she hadn't, in which they were both alive and dead at the same time, and only opening those closets could seal their fate. Down in this part of herself, she unlocked the tablet, which had also gone to sleep, and watched the paramedics cleaning the room in which the last surviving teenager had been quarantined, the walls now spattered with blood, and this, too, felt like an occurrence she'd ordained.

Terrified of what she might, without quite meaning to, cause to happen next, she forced herself to wake up and get out of bed. She began to get dressed and then, realizing that she already was dressed, simply took a pair of shoes from the floor, stepped into them, and walked downstairs, past her husband, swaddled in a blanket on the couch, another TV projecting news across his face, and back up the street and into her car, exactly as she'd pictured herself doing last night. She tweezed the keys from her pocket, where they'd luckily remained throughout her half-sleep, and began to roll up the silent curves of the cul-de-sac, toward the boulevard which, if you followed it in the other direction long enough, would take you all the way to the airport.

She drove back toward the abandoned town, and, beyond it, the abandoned cabin. *Or*, she thought, *the formerly abandoned cabin.* She closed her eyes, relying on the sound of crunching acorns to keep her on the road. She could see the two worlds, the one in which all of this hadn't happened and the one in which it had, coming apart, at first gently, as if there were merely a loose thread in the weave between them, but then more and more violently, as if something, or someone, were forcing the rift open. She saw a scabby pair of hands, then a gnarled, scarred arm, then another, then a head with no hair and two milky eyes, and she understood, even if only because she wanted to, that this man, whoever he was, had emerged in tandem with the deaths, and was thus a piece of the same phenomenon. *Or not just a piece*, she thought, as the car ground to a halt in the thick grass in front of the cabin. *A version of it. A man-sized embodiment of something otherwise too vast to comprehend.* She closed her eyes again and saw herself helping this man through, hauling him out of the rift and into the world that she was forced to go on inhabiting.

Our children didn't kill themselves, she thought, as she forced her way through the rotten door. *They couldn't have. They'd have no reason to. Their role was to live.* His *role, on the other hand, was to kill. That's what he came here to do.*

It all made sense now. Maybe too much sense, but that was better than not enough.

Despite the dawn beginning to break outside, it was dark in the cabin, which, she realized now, had no electric lighting. Probably no electricity at all. He wasn't at the table, which meant that he must be sleeping, or gone. Part of her wanted to leave before finding out which it was, but then she was in the bedroom, brooding over the body where it lay clutching a too-small sheet to its chest.

She watched him like that, cooing slightly in his sleep. Then she took out her phone and snapped a picture of him where he lay. Though it made no sound, he stirred as his likeness was absorbed, and rolled onto his back and then, after she snapped another picture, he opened his eyes. It was unclear how well he could see through them, but he seemed to register her presence. He flinched and sat up, drawing his knees to his chest and beginning to shake.

Much as she wanted to loathe him, even needed to loathe him, she couldn't just then. *Whatever this man has done*, she thought, *he bears no mark of it. He's as innocent as anything alive can be.* Still, something had been decided, and now her duty was to see it through. In a sense, she had as little say in what was about to happen as he did.

Given this, she decided that the least, and perhaps also the most, she could do was to warn him. "Do you have a name?" she asked, by way of beginning to speak.

He looked at her so long she repeated the question. After she'd repeated it again, he pulled down his collar to reveal a red web of scar tissue just beneath his right clavicle. Leaning in, she could make out the word GARY.

"Gary?" she asked.

He pulled his collar back up without nodding, and she decided this was what he'd be called. *Gary. Drifter Gary. Fine.*

"Look, Gary," she began. "Some kids have died in the place where I live. Many kids, my own included." Her voice was measured and slow, loose gravel holding back an ocean of tears. "Nobody knows why this happened, but there has to be a reason. So," her voice quavered, and she could taste the first drops of salt, "I'm going to tell them you did it. I'm going to say," her eyes were streaming now, turning her vision as filmy as she assumed Drifter Gary's must be, "that you came here from far away for the sole purpose of going on a murder spree. You made it look like suicide, of course, but that's what you do. You go place to place murdering children, and you get away with it, because the parents blame themselves. But not anymore. Now it's...." She fell against the bed, weeping.

She wept, convulsing into the sweaty mattress, until a hand, firm and cool, landed on her neck, and she seized up, terrified that he was about to strangle her. Also, in a sense, hoping he would. But the hand remained gentle, stroking her skin, kneading the muscles in her upper back just a little, enough to soothe her.

This went on until she stopped weeping, and then she sat back on her haunches and regarded Drifter Gary who, despite his deformed mouth, was smiling. An expression she'd never seen from him before. *Oh God*, she realized, *he has no idea what I just told him. He thinks I'm his friend.*

Getting back to her feet, she forced down the vulnerability that had surfaced along with the tears, and said, "Look, please try to understand." She made her voice as even as she could. "I'm going to tell them you killed our kids. They're going to believe me, because they want to. Your picture," she held up her phone, "is going to be all over the Sandman Crescent news in a few hours. And I'm going to tell them where you live. They're going to come for you. So," her voice began to quaver again, "please leave now. Get out of here and never come back. You must've come from somewhere. Go back there."

He sat on the bed, grinning like a puppy. She'd rarely seen anyone so happy. Part of her wanted to shoo him away, to viscerally express that he needed to run, in case he truly couldn't understand a word she'd said, but she felt that such an act would only dehumanize them both. So she said it one last time—"Seriously, pack your things and walk out of this cabin and never return"—and then, as if by way of example, she too turned and walked out.

•

On the drive back, once again in the direction of the airport, she prepared her story. It would be terse and emphatic, shot through with grief and disorientation so that it wouldn't have to make sense. No one would expect that. It only needed to connect, *which*, she thought, *it could hardly fail to. And where, after all, had Drifter Gary come from, if not the rift through which all badness enters the world, with the express purpose of ruining all that is good?*

The longer she repeated it, the truer it rang.

By the time she'd made it back, into the front office of Sandman Crescent's 24-hour news station, and communicated that she had a story of crucial import to tell, the thing she'd decided to set in motion was already in motion. Now all she had to do—and all she could do—was sit back and watch it unfold. It was as if the story she'd prepared for the news was on the news already, and she was at home watching it, shaking her head in a combination of horror and relief to learn that the rash of deaths hadn't been suicides after all, but rather the work of a malicious and deranged stranger, envious of the lives they'd made for themselves here at Sandman Crescent, while the rest of the country, to say nothing of the world, was growing unlivable.

She said all this to the newscaster in front of her, in a private room with trays of grapes and cups of water lined up along one wall. She explained her minor transgression of driving alone to the cabin in the woods behind the abandoned town, and how this led to her discovery of the larger transgression, that of Drifter Gary's arrival, seemingly out of nowhere, on the exact day that all their children died, and then she handed over her phone with the photo of Drifter Gary sleeping, milky fluid dripping from his partly-closed eyes. And then, almost before the newscaster handed the phone back, the photo was live, the story was out, Jane Feaster had been thanked for her courage, and then she was in front of the cameras, telling the same story she'd told in the private room, and then she was being escorted out, through a phalanx of volunteer troops already massing in the cul-de-sac, piling weapons into the trunks of their cars while another news team circulated with cameras, asking what they were going to do when they found him.

Amidst this confusion, Jane Feaster managed to walk unseen.

She cut away from the main road and toward the wooded path that led to the Sandman Crescent Golf Course and Swimming Pool Complex, where she'd sat with her daughters last summer and read the then-anodyne Sandman Crescent Homeowners' E-Newsletter on her tablet, while they did likewise on theirs. Everything was dark except for sporadic lamps recessed in the flowerbeds to show off the roses and peonies at night. She followed this trail as far as she could, hoping only to put the rumbling of engines and clinking of firearms out of earshot. She walked and walked, unsure how far she could get. Now she found herself walking through the Sandman Crescent Cemetery, past the fresh gravesites reserved for the children, then into an open field, marked with plots yet to be filled. Here, it seemed to her, whatever she'd been trying to escape was waiting, claiming the unclaimed ground.

Her breath grew short and her heart sped up as she pictured the horde of armed parents kicking down Drifter Gary's door and shooting him dead, or taking him alive, gagged and bundled in one of their trucks, back to some soundproof chamber in the heart of the Sandman Crescent News and Entertainment Complex, where his slow death of torture and starvation, or his even slower death of imprisonment and loneliness, would expiate the guilt that was otherwise crackling in the air around her, building charge.

She sped up. As her trot turned into a run, she realized that another decision had been made, down in the back of her brain where, perhaps, all decisions were made, on their own in the dark.

You've got to save him, was the decision. *You've got to at least try. You'll never leave this cemetery, not really, if you don't try. It will claim you, just as it claimed June and Ava and the Sudokis' son. Maybe you'll live on, but not as yourself. Not as a person within reality, but as a thing hovering above it, or off to the side.*

She sped up again, fighting to keep pace with a path that had begun to appear in front of her, a little brighter than the surrounding darkness. At the same time, another path extended behind her, perhaps back to Sandman Crescent, but more likely off to someplace else. Someplace only accessible tonight, right now. A place where she'd become someone new. As she ran, she could see herself taking that path instead, away from the house she'd lived in, the car she'd driven, and the company that did business with France.

She ran as fast as she could, and then, somehow, faster. At this pace, she made it out of the open fields, through a stand of trees, and into the ruins of the town in less than an hour—an hour that, she hoped, the troops had wasted in stockpiling arms and mugging for the camera. There were times when the two paths seemed to tangle, overlapping and then diverging again, but there was no time to consider which one she was on. The only imperative now was to not slow down as she ran past gutted storefronts and caving-in strip malls, then past a church without a spire and an office complex with a circle of roller-chairs jammed together in the parking lot out front.

When Jane Feaster dead-ended on the weedy lawn for the first time on foot, there were no vehicles in sight. She hadn't given precise directions in the newsroom, so, as she stepped through the rotten doorway, she couldn't help but entertain the hope that perhaps they weren't coming after all. *Perhaps*, she thought, as she stepped into the musty, dawn-lit kitchen, *this cabin is here for me alone. Perhaps they are, right now, driving in circles, growing restless with their loaded guns in their laps, cursing me for wasting their time. And perhaps there never was any Drifter Gary and thus, though I will grieve the death of my children for the rest of my life, I will be spared further contact with whatever forces almost transfigured me.*

This hope proved so compelling that she didn't notice Drifter Gary, sitting at the table with a beatific dummy grin on his face, until he shifted his weight, causing the ancient chair to creak. Then it all began to descend on her again. Her lips began to quiver and she had to sit down. As soon as she'd landed in the seat across from him, with a creak similar to the one he'd made a moment ago, she sensed that she'd never leave the cabin. *They'll find us here*, she thought, *like we'd forgotten they were coming.*

Then she thought, *no, not us. Just me.*

She turned to Drifter Gary and said, "You have to leave. Now."

He didn't respond, though his milky eyes were on her, some flicker of life discernible within them. *Whether or not he can understand*, she decided, *he's listening.* She raised her voice. "You have to leave now!" she shouted, loud enough that he flinched.

Still, he didn't get up. He just smiled wider, a look of genuine contentment on his face. It unnerved her far more than any sign of evil would have.

"I said you did something you didn't do," she shouted, in the same register as before. "I told them you killed my children, and many people's children. I told them you were a killer. They're going to torture you."

Drifter Gary continued to smile.

"But you're not a killer!" she shouted, shaking the table. "Maybe, for a moment, you were, but you're not anymore." She paused, building up the energy to shout again. Then she resumed: "You're not a killer! You're not a killer!! You're not anything at all!!!"

She was near her maximum volume now. Luckily, it seemed to be working. At last, a look of confusion and then fear came over him. The grin was gone.

Emboldened, she continued, "That's right! Run. Run now, while you can! They'll torture you if they find you here.

You'll die in a locked room, maybe soon, maybe years from now. Whatever happened to you before," she let her eyes play over the scars covering his face and neck, "will be nothing compared to what they'll do. Every last parent will take a turn. They've been waiting all their lives for the opportunity. Please leave before that has to happen!"

The lips on his contorted mouth began to tremble as he rose to his feet, milky fluid leaking again from his eyes. Leaning over her, he forced his mouth open and said, wincing with the effort, "Not… a… killer. Not… anything."

He looked down at her, horrified.

She shook her head. "No, Gary. You're not. I'm sorry I said you were. Something happened, and I just couldn't…." She began to weep again, and feared that this would compel him to start comforting her, and that the troops would find the two of them like that, locked in embrace, and draw whatever conclusion a mass of armed men in their condition was likely to draw.

She recoiled at the imagined touch, but it didn't come. When she'd stopped weeping long enough to dry her eyes and look up, Drifter Gary was gone. She looked at the door and thought, *I exonerate you.* Part of her envied him his escape, his freedom from what was coming, while the rest of her accepted whatever that was with a kind of newly earned pride, a sense that she had, at the very least, saved one life.

She waited until he was out of earshot, then got up, walked into the side room where she'd found him sleeping, and got into bed. She no longer considered it his bed, though certainly it wasn't hers, either. *It is*, she thought, *simply a bed. The one that happened to be here.*

Closing her eyes under the stuffy sheets, she fell into a black, quiet space, perhaps the same space she'd come close to entering in the cemetery, and in this space she could see Drifter Gary running, and she could hear some of his thoughts.

He stumbled through the woods that surrounded this dark space, knocking into brambles and tripping over roots as the world decomposed around him, releasing him back into innocence and obscurity. The fact that he'd killed thirty-seven children—and he had, he was sure of it—boiled off of him, rising through the woods in waves that turned the air sticky and sweet. The fact that it had been true, that she, whoever she was, had made it true, and now it wasn't, ripped him in half. He was exonerated and yet now, once again, nameless, without history, without menace, without purpose. He ran onward, gagging on the thick air, and pictured the other fate he would've suffered, the confinement and torture and slow death in the knowledge that he'd done what he'd done, and been repaid for it in kind. He ran up to the far edge of Sandman Crescent and peered inside as if across a desert that had opened there for him alone, and he could see, on the far edge, the fathers unloading him from a van and marching him at gunpoint into the compound.

He could see it, and he could believe that it was occurring, but he could come no closer. So, he merely watched until he'd been shut away, the compound doors sealed, and then he stood, turned his back, and walked deeper into the woods, to discover some other use for the time he had left, leaving Jane Feaster alone in the cabin that had briefly been his. He wished her no ill as she stirred in his old bed in the dawn sunlight, but neither did he have any hope that her story would end well. *It is simply*, he thought, as he vanished from view, *her turn to wait there to be found.*

THE RIGHT TOWN

"You see a watering hole. Reprieve from the old dusty path." The crackly processed voice forces me awake, back to where I'm staggering along the highway behind a dark blue or black pickup truck. I've mostly forgotten the dream that occupied me a moment ago… huddled masses on dingy streets, a candy factory, a row of cots, a shrieking in the night, a familiar bedsheet brittle with dried sweat… nothing more, though it feels like more.

Now I'm focused on reprieve from the old dusty path. The end of the journey. The right town, after so many wrong ones. A watering hole thick and hot with blood. I can't see who's driving the truck, but I can, just barely, see a woman in the back, leaning against one edge with her legs pressed against the other, her head resting on her collarbone. She doesn't seem quite asleep, nor drugged, nor sick. Something closer to hypnotized, under the effect of a spell. Perhaps the same spell I've just awoken from. She wears a black dress, thick, shapeless, almost a shroud. The air is hot. Summer air, or the air of a place that's always hot. I hurry along the highway, able to keep up although, or because, I can't feel the asphalt underfoot.

♦

The truck passes several exits without taking them, speeding along the old dusty path as the sun begins to rise, until it swerves down an onramp and begins to cruise along a shaded two-lane road, flanked by weedy marshland. It's dawn now, hazy, fragrant, birds in the air.

The woman in back sits up straighter. She coughs, retracts her legs from their wedged position, extends her head, leans over the back gate, and rolls out.

She hits the ground, hard, and I hear something break. An ankle, as best I can tell. The truck slows even more, but still doesn't stop. It seems that the driver considers getting out to chase her down, then decides against it.

I keep pace as the woman limps into the marshland, away from the road. White cloths stretched against the haze grow visible, resolving into the outlines of tents. I follow her, unconcerned with being seen, uncertain whether she'd be happy, or angry, or indifferent to discover my presence. I still feel nothing underfoot, though I can see my feet squishing through the wet ground.

Now she's limping among the tents, still taking her time, but newly focused. Determined, it seems, to find an empty one. A place to lie down, after what must have also been a long journey for her. She walks up to one, then another, then a third, pulling their open flaps aside. All are empty. Abandoned.

Their insides, however, are still full of cigarette butts, beer cans, pennies and lint. No nests or piles of droppings, or any other signs of long human absence. *Whoever was here*, I think, *was here until recently*.

Until we came, I tell myself, deciding that our arrival is a momentous event, not just for us, but also for wherever this is. The notion of such a place—I'm beginning to get a sense of the atmosphere, the kind of air that the people who slept in these tents had been breathing in, then breathing out—jogs my memory, but I'm not yet ready to pursue it. For now, the important thing is to follow along, to see what the woman does.

She roams from tent to tent, peering into each one—there must be almost thirty, some full of brackish water, others positioned so as to remain dry—and I peer in too, still unacknowledged by her, though twice she turns in my direction and shows me her face. Worn, scarred, framed by thick, straight black hair. Ageless, androgynous, manly even. Like a face that has changed many times, bearing ill-concealed evidence of what it used to be.

After checking all thirty tents, she stretches out both arms and begins to tear them down. She moves through the encampment without hurry and without animus, knocking each tent into the mud until only one, in the far back, sheltered by a willow, remains.

This will be hers. She lets herself in through the flap and goes to sleep. I consider letting myself in, as well, and lying down beside her, or atop her. Nothing she's done indicates that I'd be rebuffed, but I stop myself nonetheless. Instead, I lie down on the pile of tent-material that's formed a cloth island in the center of the marsh, and float.

Behind my eyes, I sink into a cold basement. Bodies shiver two to a bed, their toes protruding from too-short blankets, terror rising out of everyone and drifting together beneath the low ceiling, while an old man, eyes full of longing, looks on from the top of the stairs.

I'm woken at dusk by a distant yet commanding voice, distorted by radio crackle. It hauls me out of the basement and deposits me back on the cloth island, where I hear it say:

"The Town Council, as you and I know all too well, has

mandated that the shelter be shut down indefinitely, pending internal investigation. *Too much blood collected from the toes of sleeping guests*, they've warned us. *Too many break-ins in the night.* And yet what have they done about it? Sent you all to the Meadows, to shiver in tents?"

As the voice grows louder, it occurs to me that the speaker has come out here under the impression that the tents are still full of receptive heads, propping themselves on their elbows as they, like me, arise from sleep to listen.

"Never again will the…" the radio stammers, "population of our town be cast out to sleep in the Meadows, with the drafts and the water snakes, nor will you be subjected to the bloodletting that has gone on in the shelter. From now on," the car pulls closer, its headlights illuminating the murk where I lie listening, shining brightly enough that I'm able to scan the shadows for water snakes, "the basements of certain private homes will be open, on a first-come, first-served basis. Tonight, it's the blue-gray house on the corner of Woodlawn & Hillcrest. I suggest you make your way there now, before the… and the jackals slink out to… among your tents. I'm Professor Dalton, and it would be my supreme honor to serve as your next Mayor. The election, let me remind you good folks, is on…."

The broadcast cuts out before the final words come through.

As soon as Professor Dalton has driven off, the woman rises in her tent, pulls on a pair of moccasins that I hadn't noticed her wearing before, and sets off toward the road, trailing me behind her. Her pace is different now, quicker. Sleep must have mended her injury. I hurry to keep up, no longer as fleet-footed as I was on the highway, where, I reason, the pull of gravity is weaker. I've never considered myself elderly or unwell, but I find myself lagging behind as we hurry past an old movie theater and a candy store and a liquor store, watched by a few weathered men on benches, their cardboard signs illegible in the flickering streetlight. I press my heels and toes against the sidewalk, trying to feel it, but all that comes through is a dull pressure, as dull as my memories of having been in this town before. Still, it's more than I could feel this morning. *A symptom of the right town*, I think. *A return to real life, after too much time away.*

We proceed out of the center and into a cleaner, tonier neighborhood, the houses recessed behind hedges or on the far sides of expansive lawns. The needle and vial are already in her hand by the time we spot the house on the corner of Woodlawn & Hillcrest, where a sizable line has grown.

I watch as the line surges across the lawn. Men and women in torn white jeans and corduroys, dragging cardboard signs and soda bottles full of pennies, fight to get as close as possible to the front door. When one of them, a middle-aged woman in sweatpants and a tank-top, reaches it, she rings the bell. Nothing happens. All chatter subsides, all attention is riveted on the door as she rings the bell again.

This time, the door swings open and a man in blue pajamas squints out. "Yes?" he asks.

No one responds.

A moment later, he says, "Oh yes. The, uh, the people who are here to sleep in our basement. Please, please come in." The look of memory dawning on him is gruesome to behold.

He stands aside and motions us to move along. As I watch, I feel the crowd sweeping me up in it. Soon, I'm in the house, being herded past a regal old woman brooding over a cup of tea and a clementine at the kitchen table, looking us over as we climb down a steep set of wooden stairs to the basement.

Once I've made it all the way down, I see rows of cots, ten or twelve against one wall, the same number against the other wall, with a few in the aisles between them. Behind the cots are an exercise bike, a bench press, and numerous cardboard and wooden boxes, labeled in fading cursive.

At the top of the stairs, the man says, "Since our… son moved away, we've had an empty house. Basement, other rooms, you name it. It brings us no small joy to open it to you in this way. Please, please sleep well." He stops and surveys the crowd, some of whom are already squabbling over cots. He scans our faces, his eyes weak but determined, looking for something, or someone, that he doesn't seem to find. Then he adds, "There's plastic cups beside the sink at the back of the basement. The pipes are old, but the water's plenty good to drink. There are some boxes of Oreos and maybe one or two other kinds in the back too. Make yourselves comfortable, and," he turns here, startled to see the regal old woman, surely his wife, standing beside him. She regards us with a look of concern. Then she whispers something to him, squeezes his shoulder, and walks off.

Clearing his throat, the man says, "Just, please, don't come upstairs. If you need help, there's a phone right in the kitchen. You can call 911, or… anybody you like, really. Long distance, local, you name it. Just please don't come upstairs."

He smiles in a pinched, sad way, and closes the basement door very slowly, as if we were already asleep and he didn't want to wake us.

When he's gone, I lie down on my cot—I'm glad I got one before people started having to double and triple up—and try to decide what to do now, whether my plan is to see if I can sleep through the night, or to sneak out once the others have settled in, or something else I haven't come up with yet. I feel a wave of regret, terror even, at having left the highway to come here, where the gravity is heavier and I can no longer glide along without feeling the ground underfoot. Then the voice passes back through my head. "Sleep," it commands. "Reprieve from the old dusty path. The watering hole, the blood hole, the…."

I close my eyes and swim down through the cement floor and into the night, where I hurry behind the pickup truck speeding along the highway. I follow it into town again, the woman in the same hypnotized position in back. When the driver slows down, the woman hits the ground, rolls along the pavement, and gets to her feet.

I follow behind her as she limps toward the house on the corner of Woodlawn & Hillcrest. I watch her cross the lawn toward the front door, just as Professor Dalton's car cruises down the road from the other direction, nearly invisible under the dim streetlights. "As Mayor," he intones, his loudspeaker crackling while the woman lets herself in through the front door, "I will personally see to it that each and every one of you is safe at night. I will reopen the shelters, under better supervision, with better-paid guards," she tiptoes through the kitchen, past the clementine peel on the kitchen table, "until you are able to move back into your houses. Never again will it be necessary for any of you to spend the…" the voice echoes and doubles, "in the homes of strangers. And as for you, good… of Woodlawn Avenue?" He flashes his brights here, which seep in through the half-windows near the basement's ceiling, just as the woman descends the stairs and begins to roam among the cots.

"Good people of Woodlawn Avenue," the two Dalton-voices insist, "what happened to your children is a disgrace. A national tragedy. But there's no need for you to open your houses to folks who have a perfectly good place to stay already. Or would have a perfectly good place to stay, if only their…

weren't always on the verge of...."

She kneels down at the foot of the cot she's selected, caresses the big toe of a sleeping man, affixes the needle to her tongue, and slides it deep into the pad, drawing out a thick, hot stream that she spits into the vial. All is quiet for a moment, as if the pain were traveling a long way to reach the man at the far end of the punctured toe.

Dalton's loudspeaker crackles, his voices breaking apart.

Then the man bolts up in his cot, shrieking so loudly the rafters shake and the other sleepers likewise bolt upright and begin shrieking too, pounding their mattresses and gnashing their teeth, drawn together by a collective mania that I fear may collapse the house on top of us.

The old man, panting in a flannel robe and sleeping cap, appears at the top of the basement stairs, holding the railing for balance.

He opens his mouth as if to speak, but only a low wheeze emerges. While he stands there wheezing, the woman with her needle in one hand and her vial in the other slips past him. I too hurry as best I can up the stairs while the man with the bleeding toe goes on howling, and the man at the top finds his voice, and begins to bellow, "I trusted you! I trusted you guys! My wife said I shouldn't, but I trusted you, and now look what you...."

The woman and I are running across the lawn.

I watch the blood froth in her vial as she hurries back through the tony neighborhood and onto the street that leads to downtown. We make it back to the Meadows without incident, and I watch as she lets herself into her tent and stows the blood vial in a hanging side pocket near the door flap, exiling me to the cloth island once again. I lie down and close my eyes, trying not to notice that another tent has been set up on the far side of the marshland.

Though it seems I've only just arrived, I begin to have the feeling that everything that can happen in this town has happened already. I spend the day circling the Meadows, watching the woman, whose ankle has healed once again, do likewise, still unable or unwilling to acknowledge my presence, or that of the other tent, and the other woman I imagine is sleeping inside.

Soon, a dim, late afternoon light fills the sky, and two headlights appear, diffusing through the watery air. I sit on the cloth island and watch, expecting Dalton to emerge and stand, at last, before us in the flesh. But all that happens is his loudspeaker crackles to life and, from within the car, he demands an audience with, "Whoever or whatever you are that… my constituents' blood in the night last night."

The woman emerges from her tent along with the other woman from the other tent, dressed identically, and both drift over to the car, right up to the driver's side window, putting their lips against the glass, which Dalton doesn't roll down.

"The taking of blood from the big toe in the night," Dalton's voice booms, "is a cause of terror that I have been called upon to confront. It is my calling, at this stage of my life's journey, after so many false starts, with so many bridges burned behind me, to see to it that none of our once-illustriously housed, now tragically homeless population is forced to suffer the… of nighttime bloodletting ever again. It is the only kindness I can show these people. Haven't they suffered enough? I am now all that stands between them and the same fate that befell their children."

As his voice booms on, another car rolls up and begins

the speech again, while a crowd emerges from some woodwork behind the Meadows. "The story," the first voice goes on, while the second begins the speech all over again, "is well-known by now. Of the forces, never to be mentioned, that compelled, first, the children from their rooms, alone and then en masse, past the Meadows where we stand now, up the onramp and onto the highway and out of town. Made of them numb scuttling shades, whisking up the asphalt to nowhere. And then the parents, out of their homes as well, but not up the onramp and out of town, no, for who would be here if their children returned? They—you, I see you now, all of you, come closer, vote for me for Mayor—became the legions of homeless circling your old houses, cold and empty, terrified to go back inside, for fear that what happened once might happen again. For fear that whatever got in there is in there still."

The loudspeakers hiss with feedback, pulling the crowd closer, until it throngs the cars. I try to make out the faces of the homeless, but something about them repels me. A blur, a smudging, a sense of the inauthentic or second-order about them. Like ghosts reborn into their own dead bodies.

As Dalton returns to the topic of stolen blood, it occurs to me that perhaps he and she are working in tandem, sowing fear where before there had been none, creating a problem that only they can solve. This suspicion makes me cold, despite the heat of the evening, so I slink back to my cloth island and lie down, hoping to dream of colors and shapes dancing to a gentle drone.

But as soon as my eyes are closed, my head fills with pickup trucks, roaming the town in search of the woman who fell out of the back, and, by extension, in search of me, now that I'm complicit in her crimes. Every parked car they pass becomes a pickup truck, expelling more and more women in black dresses with needle-tongues, until gridlock forces all motion to cease.

"Return to Woodlawn & Hillcrest," the voice commands. When I roll awake, the woman is standing over me. I can't tell if she's just spoken in Dalton's voice, or if he's speaking now, unseen in the distance. "The watering hole, the blood hole. Reprieve from the. . . ."

The woman and the voice fade as I get to my feet and begin to trudge across the Meadows, past the new tent, from which a figure is also trudging. We trudge together, in mutual indifference, the sidewalk growing more palpable underfoot.

The road to town is full of the loitering homeless, seeking the distant drone of Dalton's voice. It gets alternately closer and farther away, as he plies his route and I ply mine. Again, I have the sense that there are more than one of him, casing the town with ever greater redundancy, campaigning on the same platform, against himself and himself and himself, until victory is assured.

No one seems invested in following me, so I take my time, exploring side streets and alleys, letting them jog my memory little by little.

I catch sight of Dalton's car from unexpected angles—across a sudden jag of railroad tracks, on the far side of an open mine or construction pit, in the lot of a hollowed-out convenience store, then in front of what looks like a gallows, though no rope swings from its outstretched iron arm—and I listen while the speaker rehashes the story of how first something terrible happened to the children and then, as a result or an echo, the parents were forced out of their houses and onto the streets.

Just as they did in the Meadows, the homeless orient toward the car, their heads swiveling as it passes by. I watch them and, though the thought comes unbidden, I think how they're all made of blood. How they're nothing but blood—blood that

I might once again be able to taste, now that all my senses are returning—standing there, waiting for tonight.

We follow the loudspeaker through the dark, past a cement factory, and a candy factory, and a refinery, toward a broad, one-story building with a sign out front that reads FORMER HOMELESS SHELTER: CONTAINMENT SITE DO NOT ENTER.

The crowd masses around this sign, staring at the campaign car as it glides to a halt beside several others. "This is what it's come to, folks," Dalton begins, the speaker still live after the engine's cut out. It wakes up the other Daltons in the other cars, all of whom start in with, "it's time that you saw it for yourselves. That's why I've built my campaign headquarters here. It's ground zero for what's happened to this town, and for what needs to change. Time is running out. There is no… choice. Do what needs to… done… done… done."

Three voices conclude the speech at three separate times. Then the speakers merge into static. I have an instinct to hang back and try to speak with Dalton directly, but the crowd sets out across the bike path behind the former shelter, so I have to hurry if I want a cot at Woodlawn & Hillcrest.

When we make it to the front door, the woman at the head of the line rings the bell. She waits, looks back at the crowd filling the lawn, then turns and rings it again.

The man in the flannel pajamas appears on the second ring and looks us over. From where I'm standing, I can't tell if he recognizes us. He must, and yet his expression makes me wonder.

When the woman says something to him, that same

look of gruesome recognition creeps back across his face. "Oh yes," he stammers. "The, uh, the people who are here to sleep in our basement. Please, please come in."

He leads us inside, past the regal old woman peeling a clementine and drinking tea at the kitchen table, and down to the basement, back to the smells of dust and freshly-laundered sheets. It seems she's washed them since we were here last, hoping to erase the bloodstain with chemicals and hot water.

We bed down after being told that there are Oreos and tap water in the back and a phone we can use upstairs. I close my eyes, hoping for an hour of cool darkness before the shrieking returns.

As soon as my eyes close, I'm following the pickup truck again, riveted on the woman as the driver cruises past Woodlawn & Hillcrest. She jolts awake and rolls out of the back, clutching her needle and vial as she gets to her feet, dusts herself off, and limps across the lawn.

As she lets herself into the house, I force myself awake in the basement—I leave the dream here, and return to my body, or my main body, beneath its clean sheets, which I now realize I've been smelling all night—and tiptoe up the stairs and across the kitchen, past the clementine peel on the table, past the phone in the hall, narrowly avoiding the woman as she begins her descent.

I walk up stair by stair, torn between wanting to linger to hear the scream from the mouth attached to whichever toe she punctures, and wanting to make it as far from the puncture site as possible, into the safety of my old room.

I creep along the upstairs hallway, past where the parents are sleeping, and make it inside what I realize I've begun calling *my old room* just as the scream reaches the second floor.

As I explore the shrine—it's clear that not a single item has been moved—the parents' door opens and the father begins his nightly limping run down to the top of the basement stairs, to see what the commotion is all about.

I get in the bed and pull one of the pillows over my face, inhaling the linen's familiar must. Unlike the sheets in the basement, these have not been washed. I can feel particles of skin and hair clinging to them, and I can smell old, long-dried sweat, turning the cloth brittle. I draw more of it in, through my nose and my mouth together, trying to remember when it was mine.

I lie like this, focused on nothing else, until the door bursts open and the parents stand, shocked, shouting that I'm no son of theirs.

"What have you done with him? What have you turned him into? Who scarred your face like that? We always prayed he'd return. That's why we kept our doors open so long. So much longer than we should have. So much longer than anyone else in town. Despite the shrieking in the basement. Despite the endless washing of sheets. So many strangers in our house, because we knew you'd return. But not like this. Not like this!"

They shout, vibrating in the doorway without entering the room, as if afraid of coming any closer. I lean up, yawning, unsure how I appear to them. The pickup truck rolling into town, the woman in back rolling out, the cots in the basement, the exposed toes, the prick of the needle, the whoosh of blood, the legions of homeless, the crackle of Dalton's loudspeaker, the damp of the cloth island… perhaps they can see all this running through my head.

I lie there, staring at my parents in the doorway while they go on vibrating, demanding that I leave.

Eventually my father sighs, "I'm going to get my gun," and walks off. My mother stands there longer, her eyes locked on mine, a veil of tears rendering her irises indistinct. She looks like she's trying hard to remember something, but I can't tell if she's succeeding. Then he returns and begins shooting. Bullets tear through the blanket and through a photo collage taped above the bed. Then one rips through my ankle, shattering the bone.

The pain blooms through my body, tautening my slack nerves. I shiver, elated and terrified, as I crawl through the window, grab the drainpipe, and travel down through queasy dark onto the soft grass, its softness a revelation.

I come to in the tent, supping blood from a vial, desperate to get as much down my throat as I possibly can. I can taste it. It tastes like more than air. It tastes like….

A crackling in the distance steals my attention. "And so it happened, folks," the voice drones, "just as I feared. A bloodthirsty freak was found in the son's room of the genteel elderly couple in the handsome 1920s residence on the corner of… & Woodlawn, an event that signaled the beginning of the end of life as it was in this town. The son who ran away years ago, as you all remember, returned in horribly mutated form. A wanderer from the highway, a creature of the wilds, nestled in the very sheets that…" his voice breaks and sputters before coming imperfectly back together, "the very sheets that once housed this town's most promising valedictorian."

A version of Dalton's voice that sounds more processed, as if coming through several speakers at once, continues. "He was chased out at gunpoint, but, in quick succession, all the other houses on Woodlawn and on Hillcrest, not to mention those of the Town Fathers on Dryads Green, emptied out, none of the residents willing to face the prospect of a similar invasion. All the rooms of the sons and daughters of this town have been converted to shrines, and all the parents who've left their homes have become, it pains me to say… wondering what cruel twist fate has in store for them next. The shelter behind the candy factory is full to capacity, and there have already been," he sighs here, and falls to a yet-lower register, like he's said this many, many times already, "reports of bloodletting in the night. That is why, here and now, to all of you listening, I formally announce my candidacy for Mayor."

Weeks pass, moving either forward or backward, as I regain my strength, gulping down all the blood I've saved. Tasting every drop of it. When I close my eyes, I see myself following a pickup truck off the highway and into the Meadows and then into the house on Woodlawn & Hillcrest, into the room upstairs, where I remain until I'm chased out at gunpoint, only to land on the lawn with a shattered ankle and end up back in the tent to heal.

Following this, the town's children disappear and following that, their parents leave their houses, and following that Professor Dalton awakens in his mansion on Dryads Green, puts on a clean suit, shaves, and decides to run for Mayor.

I look around and see that the Meadows is now full of tents.

At nightfall, I drape myself in the black dress of the woman who used to be here with me, and creep into the basement at Woodlawn & Hillcrest. I kneel down by the toes of the homeless and extend my tongue, sinking its needle into their soft tissue, forcing their numb bodies awake, and beginning to lap the blood, which runs into the flesh of my tongue, causing it to grow so large it fills my mouth.

"The watering hole," I hear. "The blood hole. The soft, pliant…."

When my tongue grows so large I begin to choke on it, I startle awake in the tent, sweating in my black dress, and I pant, huffing down air until I can breathe again. I want to press my finger to the needle-tip of my tongue to verify that it's still there, but I can't summon the courage to do so.

I am beginning to feel better and better.

Dalton's voice wakes me up again. "It's only getting worse. Every night, at Woodlawn & Hillcrest, another of our once-honored citizens is forced to undergo the horror of bloodletting from the... the mayoral election is tomorrow morning, people. Make the right decision, this one time. As Mayor, I vow to put an end to this. I will have you back in your houses on Hillcrest, and on Woodlawn, and even on Dryads Green, before my first term is out. The scourge of bloodthirsty freaks will be behind us at last. They will never again make it down the highway offramps. They will, and mark my words here, be chased out of this town in mortal terror, no matter what it…."

The voices split into polyphony, dozens of Daltons screeching over one another, all desperate to say the same thing. I dream that Dalton has caused all this to happen, that his loudspeaker is no mere campaign tool. That it was what forced me from my room at the very beginning, just as it forced him from his mansion on Dryads Green and onto the campaign trail. *Perhaps we're all equally subject to its power*, I think. *Nothing but mouthpieces for that which has no mouth.*

I flash back to my bedroom on Woodlawn & Hillcrest, where I'm working on the speech I'll give as valedictorian when a voice through the window commands me to pack my bag and walk off, past the Meadows and onto the highway, in search of the watering hole, the blood hole, the soft, welcoming....

I fall back asleep, and wake up on Election Day.

I pick up the needle and vial, pull on the black dress, and walk on my mended ankle out of the Meadows, up the ratty side streets, past the candy factory, and across the football field behind where I went to high school.

My vision swims, breaking up and coming back together, revealing the town in shards, all nearly identical, but subject to the same smudge I saw earlier, only worse now, further along. Many iterations later.

I sit in the bleachers and watch the homeless queue up, growing antsy as they wait their turn to vote. The Election Committee ushers them in twenty at a time. I count how many groups have gone in, and how many have come out, trying to gauge when my moment will come. I lose and regain and then lose count again. The sun rises and rises in the sky and then it begins to sink. It makes me sleepy, and I feel my eyes sagging shut, my vision coalescing into a unified field.

When I wake up, the sky is dim and murky and the high school is abandoned. I pull my dress closer around my shoulders and hear the metal clink of something falling from my mouth. The needle I'd brought to draw Dalton's blood. To drink him down, until he grew so dry and brittle the voice could no longer use him.

I climb down from the bleachers, past traces of dozens of others like me, and duck underneath, just as I used to in high school, to swig from plastic bottles in the months before I left town.

I crawl among those same bottles now, or ones just like them, searching for my needle, until two headlights and a crackling amplified voice dominate my attention. "This is your new

Mayor speaking. I know you're under there, and I know what you're looking for. You won't find it. It's all over now. Come here and accept what you deserve. Hasn't this town suffered enough because of you? Haven't you drunk enough of our blood already?"

I take another few moments to rummage for the needle, convinced that if I can only find it, I'll prevail. I'll vanquish Dalton—all the Daltons—and return triumphant to my bedroom, where none of this will have happened, where flubbing my valedictorian speech will be all I have to fear. But there's nothing except whiskey bottles and ticket stubs and squishy old condoms. Nothing sharp, nothing I can use, and I feel the headlights coming closer, the campaign car driving across the football field, and I can tell that I'm trapped. One loudspeaker boasts, "This is your new Mayor speaking, my new administration begins today," while another drones, "And so, that is why I've decided to run for Mayor," and a third insists that, "There are not enough beds at Woodlawn & Hillcrest! There simply aren't enough beds to house all the...."

I make the only move I have left. It brings me no pleasure, but it's either this or going wherever Dalton chooses to take me. Vanishing, I'm certain, into some bowel of the old candy factory from which I'd never reemerge.

So, clutching a mostly empty bottle of whiskey, I close my eyes and say "Yes" to the voice that has asked if I'm sure this is what I want. Then I stand, careful not to hit my head on the underside of the bleachers, and make my way across the illuminated field toward the idling pickup truck, along with dozens of others I can just barely see, approaching pickup trucks of their own.

When I get there, I take the last, luxurious sip of sweet,

brown liquor, toss the bottle, and climb in back, sitting against one edge with my feet pressed against the other. I drift into hypnosis as the driver guides us through the all-encompassing crackle of Dalton's voice, insisting that we'll never be safe, that we'll never manage to stop running, that he'll chase us to the northernmost tip of the continent. I lick the insides of my lips, mourning my sense of taste as it disappears again.

The driver skirts the Meadows and pulls up the on-ramp and onto the highway, where the only traffic is that of other pickup trucks. "The journey has begun," I hear the voice declare. The same voice that speaks through Dalton, the voice that's left a row of ruined towns along the highway, a hundred of them lined up, or ruined the same town a hundred times. Though I know not to trust it, I can't help but nod when I hear it say, "Good riddance to the wrong town, and onward up the dusty path to the right one. The watering hole. The blood hole. The soft, welcoming…."

THE END

Acknowledgements

This is the widest-ranging acknowledgements page I've ever attempted to write, because these stories have covered more than a decade of my writing life (and thus about a third of my natural life), from my junior year in college through to the pandemic spring of 2020, with stops in, primarily, Cambridge, Berlin, Northampton, San Francisco, and NYC. This will then, by necessity, be an incomplete list of the people who've seen, discussed, encouraged, critiqued, edited, and published these stories over the years, but it's a start:

First of all, tremendous thanks to Andrew, Megan, Mike, and Sam at 11:11 Press for taking on this project, and turning it into the truly beautiful book you are holding now. I can't imagine a better home for these stories to live in together. To Vincent as well for creating the book's trailer. Profound thanks also to Steve Erickson, who took two of these stories for *Black Clock* in 2011 and '12, a time when I was very much doubting if any future as a writer would be possible for me. Without that life-changing influx of support, who knows if I would've kept at it? Next, my sincerest thanks to Matthew Spellberg, who's seen these stories in every conceivable form, and done a tremendous amount to bring out whatever was in them, as well as for writing the eloquent and humbling intro to this volume.

Also, lifelong thanks to Simon Pummell, Jack Ketchum, and Patrick McGrath for their invaluable mentorship over the years, and for showing me, each in his own way, what the life of the artist really is, and can be. For their manifold roles in the first publication of these stories, thanks to Blake Butler, Andrew Farkas, Gabriel Blackwell, Tobias Carroll, Megha Majumdar, Joanna

Ruocco, Brian Conn, Bükem Reitmayer, Brian Slattery, Carrie Nolte, Sarah Blackman, Jonathan Shia, and Anne-Marie Kinney, and to Matthew Revert for his fantastic art on the *Hate Room* chapbook.

Next, for all their input, discussions, and edits as these stories took shape, thanks to Lorenzo Bartolucci, Andrei Cristea, John Kazanjian, Mike Natalie, Avinash Rajendran, Jon Perry, John Waterfall, Gabriel Frye-Behar, Justin Keenan, Julian Arni, Tim Credo, Ian Kappos, Jesse Barron, Ana Gantman, David Wallace, Michal Labik, Eli Epstein-Deutsch, and Dan Hirsch.

Last but not least, eternal and profound thanks to my wife, Ingrid, for the love, support, and constant conversation around these stories and their development, as well as my own development as a writer, and to my parents, Lynn and Richard, and my brother Rob, for being there for me all the time.

Publication History

The Brothers Squimbop (first published in *Fanzine*)

Egon's Parents (first published in *The Last Magazine*)

The Meadows (first published in *The Collagist*)

Circus Sickness (first published in *Cosmonauts Avenue*)

Housesitter (first published in *Birkensnake*)

Living Boy (first published in *Black Clock*)

Out on the Coast (first published in *The Rumpus*)

In the Cabin up on Stilts (first published in *Black Clock*)

The Hate Room (first published in *New Haven Review*)

Gmunden (first published in *The Collagist*)

The Painless Euthanasia Roller Coaster (first published in *Catapult*)

The Brothers Squimbop in Europe (first published in *The Rupture*)

ULTRA MAX (first published in *Action, Spectacle*)

Jell-O (first published in *DIAGRAM*)

Sandman Crescent (first published in *The Rupture*)

The Right Town (first published in *Collected Voices in the Expanded Field*)

ABOUT THE AUTHOR

David Leo Rice is a writer and animator from Northampton, MA, currently living in NYC. He's the author of the novels *A Room in Dodge City, A Room in Dodge City Vol. 2, ANGEL HOUSE,* and *The New House*, coming in 2022. This is his debut story collection. He's online at: www.raviddice.com.

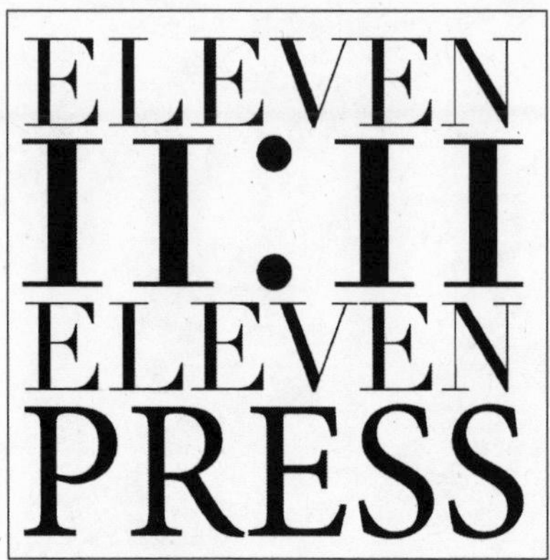

11:11 Press is an American independent literary publisher based in Minneapolis, MN. Founded in 2018, 11:11 publishes innovative literature of all forms and varieties. We believe in the freedom of artistic expression, the realization of creative potential, and the transcendental power of stories.